deceived

A STEAMY AND SUSPENSEFUL ROMANCE

HEROES FOR HIRE
BOOK 4

K.W. COLESON

isaiah

"Tell me about it, Isaiah," my therapist said. I felt her interested eyes roam my face as if she were actually touching it, trying to seduce me for my secrets—as if she'd cross that professional boundary. I was sure she had seen hundreds of hunky injured soldiers sit on this couch, but she'd never met one quite like me. This was only our fourth session, and the only progress I'd made was the number of slutty therapist dreams I'd had. She'd been front and center in every single one. Except instead of sitting in her chair with her legs wide open, so I could see up her skirt, and her silk blouse unbuttoned so I could see her tits, she leaned forward and jotted down something into her notepad. In my dreams, she'd asked me to bend her over the couch and take her from behind, fast and rough. In reality, she asked, "How have you been sleeping lately?"

The dark circles under my eyes answered for me before I could ever open my mouth. "Shitty." My snarky tone didn't seem to impress her, because she scribbled something else in that leatherbound notebook.

"The recurring dream again? Maybe I could help you dissect what your subconscious is trying to tell you." Her eyes met mine, imploring me to let her in. The only thing I wanted at this moment was for her to let me into her panties. I wanted to run my fingers through her long blond hair and smudge the fuck out of her ruby-red lipstick.

I shifted to try to hide my growing erection. "I really don't feel comfortable talking about it." And that was putting it nicely. I wanted to say, *Mind your own fucking business.* But that wasn't appropriate, nor would the VA appreciate verbal abuse of their physicians. Not to mention, I was the funny guy—I got by on making people laugh, not by making them cry. The only serious bone in my body was the one I lost on my mission. On the worst day of my life.

I relived that same day over and over in my head during my waking hours and in my sleep. It was the same dream she wanted me to talk about, but I wasn't comfortable speaking about it to anyone. I barely even spoke about it with my friends in a serious capacity, and they were there with me when it happened. The accident only came up when I made jokes about my missing leg. That was the extent of it, moot point. Conversation finished. I didn't *do* serious or uncomfortable. I'd had enough of that for a lifetime.

"Then let's try a different approach. Take a couple of minutes to think about the dream, then tell me how you feel," she pushed. I rolled my eyes in response. She'd spend the rest of my appointment gently poking and prodding, as if I were cattle. She'd pushed relentlessly since my first visit when I mistakenly let slip that I had a recurring nightmare. The number of times she regrouped and tried again was astounding. I'd like to see her do that after a couple of rounds in the sack instead.

I had a decision to make. I really did want the dream to go away, and I wanted to have better mental health. To do that, I was going to have to put in the effort, even if it wasn't something I wanted to do, even if I felt stupid talking about it. I'd been told that self-healing was work, and I couldn't do it all on my own. Damn Christine and her uncanny ability to meddle in the lives of her husband's friends.

I might be able to do what the doctor asked. She wasn't asking me to move heaven and earth. She was just asking for words. Fuck, I didn't even have to give her the play by play. But I could give her something to work with, and maybe that would help me in the process.

I could always lie, too, not that lying would really help me. I shouldn't care what my therapist thought, yet I did. I cared about what she wrote down about me on that clipboard of hersand if that hindered her from fucking me when I was no longer her patient.

I closed my eyes to do what she said, trying to trust the process. The horrible day flooded my thoughts, locked up my muscles, and sent my head straight to hell.

Our interpreter led us through the village. He was short and stout, seeming friendly enough. I always had a healthy skepticism of the national forces we partnered with. Sometimes it was hard to figure out who they really served: their newly formed governments or the terror organizations rooted deep in the communities using fear to manipulate the masses.

He was getting directions from a local who supposedly knew where our target was hiding out. Our intel from the skies only got us to this village, and the rest would be up to us. It was far from ideal. I'd prefer to know what building to breach as if there was an "X" painted on a map. In this part of the sandbox, with this terror network, it was becoming more difficult to get accurate intelligence. They were tightening up their loose lips.

We bribed the locals with several cases of clean drinking water and several boxes of medicines. In a poor area like this, deep in territory controlled by extremists, this was the jackpot to them. They'd take the goods and run but look over their shoulder for months on end, scared that their decision to answer our questions would cost them dearly.

The interpreter and the local were talking fast, and I only caught hints of the conversation. My focus was on my surroundings, looking for threats. While we somewhat trusted the interpreter, we didn't trust the villagers or all of their information, but sometimes it was all we had to operate on. It wasn't unheard of for teams like ours to be led into traps. In fact, the team we replaced on this mission was led into one, killing two men and wounding three more. They'd been shipped off to Germany, and we were here twelve hours later.

Our target was a rising extremist; he went further than any of his competition to recruit and suppress those around him. He had a metaphorical and literal trail of dead bodies left in his wake. Some of them were recruited Americans, used solely for the purpose of scaring the west. Our president wanted him dead and gave the green light for his execution. Of course, this was all highly classified. We didn't need their leader going so far underground that only the devil could find him.

"Something's wrong," the interpreter said. His transition to English jarred me from my threat assessment. We'd been slowly following the local as he walked through the village.

"What?" I asked at the same time as Garcia.

I heard a heart-stopping click, and the IED the interpreter stepped on detonated before I had time to react. It killed him instantly and sent debris flying. I was following behind him with only a yard or two of distance between us. I took the majority of the blast from the small IED. My body went flying backward, and my helmet bounced off Garcia's chest plates, snapping my neck forward. A sharp pain seared across my leg, as if I stuck it in a large bonfire, and then everything went black.

I woke up still in the street where the IED detonated. I flinched at the sound of gunfire all around me. Directly next to me was Strong. He was providing supporting fire as Mendez and Garcia moved my leg around. I felt a sharp pain, and I recognized it immediately: a tourniquet. They were placing one on my leg, and I knew what that meant; it was badly wounded.

"Don't look," Strong warned me as I went to turn my head to look at my injury.

"Fuck that," I grunted. The first thing I noticed was all the blood. My leg was lying in a large puddle of my blood. The next thing I noticed was that my blood covered Garcia and Mendez's hands. There was blood on their faces, but I had no idea if it was theirs or mine. I knew I had hit Garcia pretty good from the force of the blast; it was a wonder he wasn't badly injured, either.

"How are you feeling, Yates?" Garcia asked when he realized I was conscious.

I took a moment to assess my own condition. I was woozy from the blood loss, and I was in a world of pain and agony. My head hurt, but I had no doubt that my helmet saved me from a likely fatal brain injury.

"Pretty shitty," I said with a cough. Dirt coated the inside of my mouth and my throat, making it difficult to speak.

"I know, bud. You've lost a lot of blood. I need you to hold on, okay? We've got a halo coming in to get you," Mendez said.

I nodded, I would do that. I wasn't ready for the other side, I still had plenty of hell to raise.

Several guns were firing in the distance, then suddenly stopped. Likely the other squads half a click behind us. They probably moved into position to provide backup for my extraction.

"Is he stable enough to move? We need to get to cover now. We are too exposed even with the 82nd providing support," Strong asked.

"Yes, let's move him," Mendez answered as he tightened the tourniquet again. Son of a bitch, it hurt.

Strong picked me up like I was a sack of potatoes, while Garcia and Mendez grabbed their guns. In the blink of an eye they were running as gunfire started again, creating a cloud of dust.

I closed my eyes to stop the world from spinning as Strong's footsteps jarred me. I did my best to hold down the scream fighting for release. I couldn't give away our position now that we'd fallen into the cover of darkness. I couldn't put my team more at risk.

My vision turned dark at the edges, and I knew that sleep was about to find me again. I prayed that it wasn't my time and I'd wake up in Germany as good as new, although that seemed unlikely. I knew my leg was fucked. The loud whooshing sound of the helicopter blades spinning as it approached our position jarred me out of the almost sleep I was drifting to.

"The mission..." I mumbled. The halo would be a big red flag that we were closing in on him, and he'd slip away into the night. All because of my fucking leg. Where the fuck was the local?

"Was already blown the moment the interpreter stepped on that

IED. We'll get 'em, but you need to keep your eyes open. You need to stay awake," Strong ordered. Technically I was his senior, he didn't get to bark orders at me, but I'd let it slide. He was a large motherfucker, and I was clearly in no shape to do anything about it.

The weight on my eyelids was too much. "Give 'em hell." I closed my eyes.

"Isaiah, are you okay?" the doctor asked. Her voice was soft, like calm waves brushing up against the shore. It was startling how soft her tone was versus the harsh darkness of my thoughts. Her eyebrows were pinched together in concern, and her pen was temporarily abandoned on the coffee table between us. I shook my head to pull myself out of the depths of hell.

"Uh…yeah. I'm okay," I lied. It was a basic instinct: don't admit your feelings, others have it worse. It was the unspoken but widely known motto of all combat-related jobs.

"You don't need to lie to me, Isaiah. What you went through, it was tough." I almost forgot she would have access to my file and would know exactly how I was injured. Why'd she need to drag any words out of me? Wouldn't the nightmare be obvious? Her ruby-red lips kept moving. "Many guys don't make it out of something like that, but you did. It's bound to leave scars physically and mentally," she said, trying to make me feel better.

"Yeah…" I mumbled. *Tell me something I don't know.*

"Look, I'm going to lay my honest opinion on you, because I think you can handle it. Are you ready?" she asked. I liked honesty from others, as long as it wasn't in exchange for me trading mine.

"Hit me, Doc." I curled the toes on my remaining foot in nervousness and anticipation. I found myself doing that in anxious situations, to remind myself that I still could.

"I think that you've been putting yourself in too many stressful situations. Most special ops guys come home and look for a nice, quiet life, especially those with PTSD and physical disabilities—but not you, nor your friends. I think that the past year and a half have had more of an effect on you than you realize or care to admit," she said.

I might be locally famous for the part I played in bringing down two separate human trafficking rings. Our adventures and good deeds had been splashed across the papers all over the country, especially in the states where my buddies resided. The fact that Christine, Wells' wife, was an oil tycoon heiress and VP of her company certainly brought this into the national spotlight. It was certainly a hindrance in trying to find the loose ends we'd left behind. We hoped that laying low and time would help us fly back under the radar, and eventually we'd catch our guy. So far, no luck. I was still turning down requests for interviews, and the last time I checked with my crew, so were they. The media outlets were all determined to snag at least one interview from a participant in some of the biggest trafficking takedowns of the decade. I deleted hundreds of thirsty women's direct messages every day. Hook-ups were only fun when I had to engage in the chase, not when I was the prey.

"So what are you saying?" I could read between the lines. I knew where she was going with this, but I wanted to hear the words straight from the hot horse's mouth.

"You need to either tell your friends about what you are going through so you can lean on them for support, or you need to take a step back, out of the action," she said, slapping me with a truth bomb almost as big as the one that caused this issue in the first place.

I sat straight in my chair immediately, no longer keeping up the pretense of comfort. "Absolutely not. My friends are everything, our work, it keeps some of us going. It keeps me going. I'm not going to jeopardize what we do by dragging them down with me. If I told them about this, they'd worry about me instead of the mission. They'd tell me to take a step back, a break. You don't understand, I won't be left behind, not again!" My outburst left me breathless. My chest rose and fell as I struggled to gain my composure. The doctor, on the other hand, looked pleased with herself. The sexy siren pushed me into feeling something, sharing something I otherwise wouldn't.

Her pleased expression turned to one of calculated empathy. "Isaiah, you misunderstand me. I'm not saying to stop, but maybe take a small break, do something to help you recover. Go on a trip where you don't need to rescue someone. Even people in a normal nine-to-five take vacations for their mental health." She leaned forward so that I had to look her in the eyes. "If you can't talk to me about it, then you should talk to them. You told me that your friend Wells went to a therapist a couple times, and it helped him. He won't judge you, and I'm willing to bet neither will the rest. You went into battle together; they carried you out of war. If anyone can understand your demons and help you, it's them. You have a choice: let me in or your friends," she said, laying out my only options. She sat back, her posture showing how firm her ultimatum was, and also how firm and perky her chest was.

"Fuck…" I mumbled.

What the hell was I going to do? Definitely not quit, that was never an option. My nightmares had increased in frequency, and I was getting less sleep. Logically, I knew I needed to do something. I didn't like what the doc was saying, but she was the expert and probably knew better than I did.

I was going to have to figure out something, but it sure as shit wouldn't be her.

CHAPTER TWO

natalia

"Ambassador Ali, there is another suspicious vehicle outside," Kareem, my assistant, said. I could hear the urgency in his voice. It felt like we had been in the same scenario a million times since I became ambassador. In reality, it'd probably been at least thirty. Either way, enough was enough. The danger never became less, no matter how many times we faced a security threat, whether it was suspicious packages, drive-by shots fired at the embassy walls, or the occasional man trying to blow up the front gate or scale the wall. The embassy was a fortress, but even stone walls could crumble.

I huffed out an annoyed sigh. "Shit, we don't have the time or the manpower to deal with that right now," I said harshly. It went without saying Kareem knew how busy I was or that I was stressed up to my eyeballs. At the moment, we were in the middle of an open house—while the term was typically reserved for schools or selling houses, it was what I named our aid distribution events. We opened our gates to those in surrounding communities who needed aid. Most often it was women and children from poorer families or those who had abusive husbands or fathers. It was meant to be a safe haven for these families to seek food, temporary shelter, medical treatment, and resources. It was also a safe place to sell information for the possibility of asylum in the United States.

I lifted my head, which was bent over the leg of a little girl who had large cuts on her legs—cuts she sustained when her father pushed her down the stairs. The girl, who was no more than six years old, whimpered as the alcohol wipe I was using touched her lacerations. She was lucky that they wouldn't need stitches. Her father would never need to know that anyone had patched her up. Sometimes our interference could make matters at home worse.

"I'm sorry, honey. I know that it hurts. This will help make it better. It will clean the cut and you will be as good as new soon," I told her in the sweetest tone I could muster. In truth, I felt anything but sweet—more like vengeful.

She simply stared up at me with tears in her eyes. My heart broke for her and other children just like her, caught up in a world of violence that they didn't yet understand. Her family was nothing like mine. She probably feared her father, while I'd idolized mine.

I felt a pang of sorrow at the thought of my father. I quickly swallowed down the grief and moved on.

Kareem cleared his throat, losing patience with my split attention. "I know we don't. Do you want me to have some of the volunteers pull security and send some of our security forces out to go investigate?"

I opened the tube of antibiotic cream and put some on my gloved finger, then spread it on the little girl's cuts and scrapes.

I shook my head. "No, we need those volunteers to keep this open house going as smoothly as possible. The more volunteers we have providing aid, the sooner we can wrap up and get the compound secure again," I answered. That was the reason for the security threats anyways, to intimidate me into shutting down my open houses. The terror groups stayed in control by suppressing others, taking their hope. I wouldn't allow them to take this from the people who needed it.

"Then what do you wish to do?" Kareem asked. I could feel the shift in the air as he put all the pressure back on me. It was where it should have been in the first place. I was the ambassador, and I was responsible for the embassy and this program.

I looked over at him. I saw the exhaustion in his brown eyes. His brow was also raised in annoyance, likely due to the fact that we were once again in this position. Technically, it wasn't my job to assist those who weren't U.S. citizens, and these open houses were me overstepping my bounds—but I couldn't stand by and watch innocent people suffer, regardless of the flag they stood under. Even Syrians were attacked by their own people, those who sold their allegiance to those more powerful than them, instead of looking out for their own. I couldn't watch the women and children suffer for those decisions. My big heart caused me a lot of trouble, but I had issues with turning it off. That's not what my father would have wanted.

I wish he was here to tell me what to do. It seemed like he always had things under control, even when they weren't. Unfortunately, that wasn't something that I inherited from him. I internally panicked and barely kept a brave face when the odds were against us. It was a wonder I was appointed ambassador here after my father's death. I couldn't stand to see his unfinished business float into the wind. He had a vision for U.S. and Syrian relations, one that I'd failed to improve upon.

"Send two security personnel to investigate the car. Close the gates, and we will keep all of these people safe until we can confirm there is no threat," I answered. I wrapped the little girl's arm with a bandage and then placed a smiley face sticker on it.

"All done," I told her with a small smile.

"Thank you," she said with a thick accent. She gave a small brave smile. She was missing her two front teeth, and I hid back a smile of my own. I felt a small bit of my anxiety calm before her mother ushered the child away from me. She walked slowly to a makeshift buffet line, where they would be able to get a warm meal before leaving the compound.

Kareem had disappeared, likely barking out orders to anyone who would listen. I looked around at the room full of people. There was a line of injured, waiting to be assessed by medics, and an even longer line of those looking for a warm meal. In the back corner of the room, a station was set up to provide spare clothing to those that needed it, and by the door was a station that passed out supplies to go. They mainly consisted of first-aid kits, a few bottles of water, and a few canned goods. I hoped to do more for the community, but we were limited by our own supplies. This was not something that the U.S. was budgeting for yearly. It was more of a pet project for me.

"Thank you, Ambassador," a local said as he passed by. I recognized him. He offered his services to help protect the compound during these types of events. He'd been to the U.S. a time or two and shared his memories with me here and there. I began to look forward to his visits and the events I planned. Now, we spent more time in red alert, and he had less time to tell me the joyful stories. Maybe one day the circumstances would change.

"You're welcome," I said to his retreating back.

Kareem entered the room again and quickly approached me. He handed me a glass bottle of my favorite iced coffee beverage. He had one of his own in his other hand, with his rifle strapped to his back. His was identical to mine, but I invested in a better scope. I could feel the weight of the cold metal against my back.

It wasn't common for most ambassadors to walk around strapped, but most ambassadors didn't have terrorist organizations staging weekly attacks on their compounds in attempts to force them to leave, nor did they have an understaffed embassy. Our terrorizers antagonized me for so many reasons—including my gender. Most men in this country still believed a woman should not be in a position of political power.

"Any word?" I asked.

"Yes, the car drove away before security could get to it," he said with a sigh.

"Thank God. Is it the same car we saw last week?" I asked. I was worried they were scoping the place out for a large planned invasion or searching for the perfect place to plant an explosive. The hastily planned attacks, while dangerous, were still small in nature. But if the enemy had time to plot, well then we were really in hot water—in a pot bigger than we could climb out of.

He simply nodded.

"Well, I suppose that isn't bad news. The car is suspicious, but it's never made a malicious move yet. We just need to keep an eye out for the militant groups," I commented.

"Indeed. I think we need to start limiting the size of these open houses. It's difficult to provide security when we have so many people in the compound."

"I understand that, but if we limit the help we can provide, then the extremists are getting exactly what they want. The less aid we provide, the more they can suppress their own people, and that just isn't right. We can't let these people suffer," I argued. I couldn't let the assholes win. Altering our arrangements would feel like waving a white flag, and I wasn't going to let that happen.

"I know you don't want to let them suffer. You have a very large heart, just like your father, but you have to learn your limits, Nat. They also win if they kill us in their attack, storm the embassy, steal the supplies we have left, and take over the military equipment," he countered.

Again, another pang of sadness crashed over me at the mention of Father. A shiver ran up my spine at the thought of the enemy riding around in our Humvees hauling our supplies back to their own compounds.

"Have you been able to get any more aid from the president?" Kareem asked, switching topics. His words were the perfect distraction and he knew it.

"No, the president has not promised any further aid or security." I was filled with anger and dejection at the same time. "I have a feeling we are going to have to look to crowd sourcing and donations to keep these going." Really, it was the secretary of state's fault. She was in charge of reviewing my request for an increased budget, and she refused my multiple requests to discuss it.

I even went over her head and placed several calls to the White House. I was denied a call with the man several times, but finally last night my request was granted. I did my best to convince him to send us some aid to assist the community. "I can't help you, Ambassador Ali. Spending is already crazy as it is, and we're in the middle of an economic recession. I in good faith can't explain to the American people that we can't assist them with a meal on the table, but we can help those across the globe. Not to mention we are getting pressure from the Syrian president to stop meddling in the affairs of his citizens." I opened my mouth to formulate a reply but he cut me off. "You went directly over the secretary's head by calling me, and if she already told you no, there was a good reason. I know you are still somewhat new to politics and political offices, but you are walking a very flimsy tightrope. Between my conversations with the Syrian president, and with my party, there is just no room to help any further than we already are. I'm terribly sorry." When I asked about at least sending some U.S. military personnel to help pull security, he also denied that request. "If we increase the military personnel any further, it would be considered an aggressive action and escalate issues further in the area." Yet the Syrian government didn't have to denounce the acts taken by their radicals?

I freaking hate politics.

"So he's not stopping us from continuing our work, but he can't fund it?" Kareem asked.

"No. He said the Syrian president wanted it to stop, but the president doesn't care about making him happy. That's not the concern, it's the money. He commented that if the tax payers wanted to help my cause, they could donate directly," I said with a bitterness in my tone.

"I know you didn't want to do another public press tour, but that might be the best way to continue your mission, Nat." Kareem was my friend, and when no one was around, he called me by my first name. Right now, no one was listening to us, hidden in the back corner. Everyone was too worried about grabbing food or aid before they would be forced to return home.

I sighed. "I know. I hate doing them, but you're right, I may have to." I got a knot in my stomach when I thought about reporters entering my space. I didn't have a great experience with reporters after my father died. They were pushy and their questions were way too personal. Not to mention I hated public speaking, which was ironic given the very public nature of my job.

"You remember what happened the last time? There were several large shipments of supplies sent by the Red Cross and other organizations. If we can get more supplies, then the mission continues," he reminded me, not that I needed it. I was well aware of the possibilities, but also the consequences.

Our storage closets had become pretty bare, and full reserves would be worth the wrath of the secretary.

"Okay, go ahead and contact the press. Get as many news organizations as you can. I want to only do this once." We needed enough supplies to last us for a year. If I could get that, I could shift my mind out of survival mode and start concentrating on why I took this position in the first place: finding the person responsible for my father's death.

He nodded his head and took off toward the exit. I had no doubt that he'd be in his office until late tonight, contacting every U.S. news organization that he could, and possibly some European as well.

"Father would have handled this so much better," I mumbled to myself.

He was more charismatic than I was, and those in charge respected him more because he was a man. A woman in politics always had an uphill climb to earn respect, especially in a country in the Middle East. Everything about this job was more difficult for me, but I still did it, hoping that where my father was now, he was proud of me. I'd walk next to his ghost if it meant I got to feel him still.

My thoughts were interrupted by the sound of gunfire. Those who had been seeking help immediately began to run around in panic. Tables were knocked over, and food and supplies went flying. People knocked each other over to try to get outside and away from the gunshots.

I rushed to pick up a toddler who was about to get trampled. She was barely in my arms before someone plowed right through the space she had been occupying. The child cried in my arms, and I never related more to a small human. I wanted to cry, too, but I couldn't. I had to be strong and show the assholes that they would not win. As long as I kept pushing through, my mission would continue on.

Within minutes, the large area room that had been set up for the event was empty, aside from my staff and the gunman they had subdued on the ground. I pulled my gun from my back as the man started screaming curses at me. I slammed the buttstock of my rifle on his head, knocking him out cold.

❧

Two hours later, I sat in the soaking tub of my small home on the embassy compound. The water had long gone cold, and I sat with my arms wrapped around my legs. My face rested on my knees, and tears ran down my legs as I cried.

I was beyond frustrated that my life had come to this. I thought back to my time in the U.S. and how happy our family had been while we were there. When my father felt the call of civic duty, we all answered. When he was kidnapped, we had all thought the worst, and I had prayed that he'd come home to us safely. Somehow, our prayers had been answered when a special team of U.S. soldiers brought him home. My family had a few more months with him before he was taken from us again, but this time it was permanent. My chest ached at the void his loss created.

My mind flashed back to the team of soldiers who rescued him—one in particular. I thought about him often. I hoped he found a nice, quiet life somewhere. A man like him deserved everything they wanted out of life. He not only helped rescue my father, but gave me an idea on what to expect from him post-kidnapping. He had been right, Father was pretty messed up for a while, but eventually he found some peace. I could only imagine the ghosts that haunted that soldier and his friends. I hoped that my father was looking out for them, too, somehow.

I pulled the drain from the tub and stood. The cold air nipped at my skin before I was able to wrap myself in a towel. My house was silent as I moved from the bathroom to the kitchen to grab a glass of wine. My mother and my brother were both in the States. It was too much for them to stay here after Father died, and I couldn't blame them. Sometimes I could still feel his ghost walking through the halls. Sometimes I wanted to give up, tuck my tail between my legs, and go home. Each time I was ready to pack my bags, I got sucked right back into my personal mission.

I didn't bother pouring my wine into a glass. Instead, I drank straight from the bottle.

"Good night, Father," I said, speaking to the empty house. I brought the bottle with me to the bedroom, where I proceeded to finish the whole thing before falling asleep.

isaiah

I sat down on my couch with my beer and my dinner, deep in thought. Guy called to brief us all—it was brief, no signs of the other Rickett's brother, Brent. His younger brother, the one who had been running his operation in the Bahamas, wasn't giving up any info. I know Strong and Wells would have loved to get their hands on the fucker with sandbox rules where almost anything goes. Unfortunately, he was in FBI custody. Bob Dempsy's team was still trying to make him talk, but there were rules about cruel and unusual punishment here, so it could take a long time for them to get any real leads.

Guy was doing what he could to try to track down the Brent fucktard, but so far there had been no luck. He's left no digital footprint in ages, so there's nothing to track. With no leads and a long waiting game ahead of us, our mission was suspended. That meant everyone went back to their jobs and were just skating along until there was a new development. The situation reminded me of my time in the army, hurry up and wait.

I didn't have a job to return to. I was between private security gigs. They were all right, but I was looking for something a little more exciting, like a firefighter. While the doc said I needed to cut action out of my life, I still craved it. I was like an addict, I needed it to feel alive, and saving lives as a firefighter was a good job for an adrenaline junky—I think. I was in shape, and I'd have to work twice as hard to prove that I could do the job, given my pirate status. My prosthetic made me very mobile, and with enough PT and practice, I gained most of my pre-amputation speed back. It felt like my last obstacle was my nightmares. The doc's words came back to me; maybe I'd eventually share them with the guys, but not now. I wasn't ready, and they'd just talk me out of any job that would help me fill that void.

I leaned back on the couch and clicked on the TV; a news program flashed on the screen. "And now, we are back in the Middle East with a cry for help from Syria, and our station was granted an exclusive interview with Ambassador Natalia Ali, the U.S. Ambassador to Syria. Tracy, take it away." I sat forward in my seat with my elbows on my knees, my eyes glued to the screen. I knew that name.

"Thank you, Nancy. This is Tracy Townes with News Ten. I am here in Damascus, Syria, with Ambassador Natalia Ali. Ambassador, thank you for having us. It's no secret that tensions have been escalating here between two extremist groups. What is surprising is how little the U.S. is doing to stop that or assist U.S. citizens here. Can you comment?" The reporter put her microphone in Natalia's face, and I wanted to reach through the TV and smack the journalist. Couldn't she see how uncomfortable Natalia was?

The air left my lungs in one whooshing motion and left me with a sense of déjà vu. It felt like only days ago I sat at a bar with my friends and Natalia gave an interview on the conditions of those living in Syria. She'd recently become the ambassador after the death of her father.

"Thank you," Natalia said, clearly looking uncomfortable. "Yes, things have escalated here. There are two extremist groups fighting for control over the area, and one is just as bad as the other. Both groups like to suppress aid from the western world. They antagonize those who come to the embassy seeking help and threaten anyone who wishes to apply for sanctuary in the States," Natalia said, looking straight at the camera. Her eyes were glossy and she nervously bit her lip. Her tan skin was glowing in the sunlight, and her dark hair looked silky smooth.

She was just as beautiful as the day we met, but different. When we met, she was youthful and excited, happy to have her father home. She was a last-year college student, with a whole life to live, things to look forward to, I was sure. Now, she was a U.S. ambassador in a very conflicted area in the Middle East and likely still mourned the loss of her father. It was a shame that he was gone. We risked our lives to bring him back to his family, and he had what, a few months left with them?

The poor girl.

"What kind of antagonizing have you experienced?" Tracy asked. She wasn't the best reporter, but at least she seemed just as empathetic to the situation as I was, and attentive.

"Cars drive by, often—some with bombs, and others shooting rounds at the wall or ground to scare us. These terrorist groups shoot at our gates, leave dismembered animal body parts on our wall, and hijack shipments of supplies. Tracy, that's just the tip of the iceberg. It doesn't include what they do to individuals who they suspect are coming here seeking asylum," Natalia answered.

My back stiffened. I didn't like the idea of her dealing with this. Hell, her father had been kidnapped, and ultimately he couldn't escape the extremists' clutches. Who knew if they'd try the same thing to her? I imagined she'd be treated even worse than he was, for obvious reasons.

"Why are they targeting the U.S. embassy and not one of the other European nations?" Tracy questioned, her eyes wide and alert. She was leaning in toward Natalia; she had her full attention.

"There are a number of reasons. One, I'm a woman. All the other nations with embassies here have male ambassadors. Secondly, I'm providing aid to everyone who needs it, not just the U.S. citizens. Those who can't feed themselves or can't afford medical treatment come here when we have clinics. I call them open houses. We give out supplies to take home when we have them, but now our supplies are scarce, and with the extremist groups terrorizing those who try to help us, we are falling on hard times." I could see just how all of this haunted Natalia. She looked like a woman with the weight of the world on her shoulders, and for some reason, that speared me through the gut. I felt like her tired eyes were staring straight through the glass of the TV and into my soul. I'd seen her be so joyful, happy for her father's safe return, and now she seemed like she was struggling just to keep it together.

"That's awful, and I'm so sorry to hear about the difficulties you've faced since you filled the empty ambassador seat your father's passing created." I watched as Natalia flinched at the words. The motion was just barely noticeable, but I was looking for it. The words were harsh, meant to incite a newsworthy reaction. Unfortunately for Tracey, Natalia didn't give her what she was looking for. "What do you want the people back in the States and around the world to know?"

Natalia swallowed hard, her hand squeezed the microphone she was holding tighter, and her knuckles turned white. "The Syrian people need our help. They are being suppressed by a bunch of groups vying for power, and innocent lives mean nothing to them. They want me to die for the work I am doing, and I haven't left the embassy in six months because of the escalation in force they've shown. I want the world to know that we need help," she hesitates a second before she adds, "and that the U.S. government isn't giving us the help I've requested." She tilted her chin forward, as if she said the last line defiantly. For her to speak badly about our government, one she represented...things must be truly awful. This interview was likely a metaphorical last stand for her. I could only imagine the hell that would rain down on my head if I bad-mouthed our country or government while in uniform. I'd pick up an article fifteen for starters.

"Are there any special requests you have? Is there anything you desperately need to help you continue your work, Ambassador?"

"Yes, we have so many needs. To keep it simple, we need more food, water, medical supplies, and security personnel along with weapons and ammo to defend the embassy," Natalia answered.

"Thank you, Ambassador, for your bravery in coming forward to speak about the conditions the government has left its ambassador and citizens in." The reporter then looked at the camera. "If you are interested in providing assistance to Ambassador Natalia Ali and the Syrian people, please contact the U.S. embassy in Syria by their website or the phone number that you see on screen. You can also contact our news station and contact your local congressman or congresswoman. That's all for me here in Syria. Nancy, back to you."

I scribbled down the website and phone number before they disappeared off the screen, taking Natalia's beautiful and overwhelmed face with them.

I leaned back against the couch and brought my hands up to my hair, running my fingers through it. A wave of emotions hit me, and I had a hard time making sense of them. My feelings for Natalia were completely irrational. I met her once, we had one conversation, and yet I felt an overwhelming need to protect her, to help her. I knew none of it made sense; my friends had teased me about it for a while after the mission and then again after her first TV interview. "Love at first sight doesn't exist," they used to say. I wouldn't call it love, but infatuation at the least.

It was obvious how desperate she was to get help; she defied her own government to try to help others. She was ballsy as hell, and I was there for it. The rifle strapped to her back was the finishing touch, painting the danger and desperation of the situation for the world. Most ambassadors didn't carry weapons, nor did they give interviews asking for help.

I always wondered if Natalia and I would cross paths again, and now it seemed as if maybe we could. I needed a new purpose, something to fill the time until Brett Ricketts resurfaced. I could offer my services as private security and bring her some much needed supplies. I wanted to be a firefighter, but what was one more private security gig before I jumped into a new venture?

As for the supplies—I didn't have a whole lot of money, but I could go to a large warehouse store and buy what I could and have it shipped. I might not be a knight in shining armor on a white horse, but I could be a washed-up soldier with a gun and something to prove. I could prove that the doc was completely wrong about me; I needed chaos. I thrived on it. I would prove that my past wouldn't control me.

First, I had to be brave enough to face the girl who somehow had a piece of my heart, and she might not even remember who I was. *I'm used to running head first into danger, so this should be no problem, right?*

CHAPTER FOUR

natalia

"Do you understand how terrible you made us look in that news segment?" my boss, the secretary of state, Diana Schultz, scolded me. It was so bad the president didn't even want to talk to me, even for the satisfaction of getting to scream at me.

"I humbly ask you to put yourself in my position, Madam Secretary. We don't have enough supplies, we don't have enough security, and violence has escalated here. I'm not safe, and neither are the U.S. citizens here," I stated, opting to leave out those with no U.S. affiliation. Technically it wasn't my job to assist them; that was my own personal mission.

"I understand the position you are in," she practically spat. Her tone was just south of hostile. If this were a video chat, I would be watching steam leave her ears. "If you can't handle the position you are in, then you should hand in your resignation," she retorted.

"Madam Secretary, with all due respect, you know how personal this is to me. I can't just simply hand in my resignation. The same issues will still be around for the next ambassador, and U.S. citizens would still be in danger. I'm simply asking for an increase in security and an increase in funding for supplies," I countered with a soft tone.

She was as angry as a hornet, and the only way to back her down was with a dose of soft humility.

"Throw that on top of the two hundred percent increase in asylum applications that you've endorsed. You know we can't save everyone, and yet here you are, wasting resources to try to do just that," the secretary said with a loud sigh. At least she wasn't as openly angry now. I could take the passive aggressiveness.

"I'm sorry, Madam Secretary. I see what we are doing as important. It's the best way to encourage the other nations to step in and help, to lead by example," I offered.

"Do you think you are the only ambassador trying to do God's work?" she asked.

"Well no…"

"Exactly, we don't have the resources to fulfill your request," she cut me off. "You are lucky neither the president nor I are requesting your resignation over this. You are on thin ice now, Ambassador."

"What about crowdsourcing? Am I still able to do that without making the situation worse?" I asked, biting my lip in nervous anticipation.

"Discreetly, and in good taste. If it makes us look bad, then don't do it, unless you are ready to fly back to the States and hand in your resignation, understood?"

"Understood," I replied softly.

She sighed again. "I know this came from good intentions, Natalia, but pissing all over the country you represent was not the best way to do it. If you need something, you call me, and I'll get you an audience with the president. Don't go behind my back again," she warned and then disconnected the call.

I let out a breath and then bent forward and rested my forehead on my desk. The cool surface didn't do much to calm my nerves. This wasn't the first time that Madam Secretary had been on my ass. My father had been lucky—the secretary he reported to was much nicer, and he had a lot less to prove. However, this was the worst ass chewing I'd gotten. I really screwed up this time.

"How the hell do I get help without making them look bad?" I asked out loud to myself.

The silence of my office was going to drive me wild. I couldn't stand to listen to my own thoughts. I needed to be in the hustle and bustle of the embassy. I needed to be around people. I also needed to figure out what the hell I was going to do. It'd never quite been this bad before. Sure, we got periodic shipments of supplies to keep the embassy running, but I may have mismanaged that a little. I may have used those supplies to help the community. We had a week's worth of supplies left and three weeks until our next shipment was scheduled to arrive. Most of the staff had no idea how bad this situation was. I was going to have to find some creative solutions to make sure none of us starved to death.

Rations didn't sound like they would be fun, but they may become necessary. Especially if I couldn't find a tactful way of raising money before then.

A sudden knock on my door had me quickly raising my head.

"Ambassador, you have someone here to see you," Kareem said.

I quickly took a deep breath to school my features. Kareem knew how bleak our situation looked, but he was one of only a few trusted individuals. Kareem stepped through the doorway, and I stood up behind my desk. Behind him was a young woman in an old burka. It, and she, looked like they had seen better days. On her hip was a small child.

"Ambassador, I'd like to introduce you to Fatima. She comes here seeking help," Kareem said.

The young woman took a step into my office. Her body language told me everything I needed to know; she was uncomfortable, seconds from fleeing.

"Fatima, it's nice to meet you. Do you speak English?" I asked.

She hesitantly nodded. "Not well," she admitted softly.

"That's okay. Kareem can stick around and help translate if you would like," I offered.

"Please," she said with another nod.

"Of course. Please, have a seat, make yourself comfortable," I told her.

She quickly moved to a chair in front of my desk. She barely made a sound as she sat down and shifted her son into her lap to make him comfortable.

"Fatima, how can I help you?" I asked her once she looked settled.

"Forgive me, I come here out of necessity. My husband has threatened to kill me. He wanted to negotiate a marriage for our daughter, but she is too young. The man who he had been talking with, he's no good. He beat his last wife to death. If we remain here, there is nothing I can do to help her. I want a different life for her. I've heard from others that you could help us. America can help us."

She had tears in her eyes, and her hands nervously fussed with her child's clothing. I understood why she was so anxious. Her story was unfortunately pretty common here, but it was heartbreaking to everyone that went through it.

"I may be able to help you," I told her after a brief moment. "Has he beat you before?" I asked.

She simply nodded, confirming my suspicions. That too was pretty common.

"And the children, has he beaten them, too?" I asked.

She nodded again.

"I get a very limited number of people I can help each year with sanctuary in the States. We have a lot of hoops that we have to jump through, and that process can take time. How soon was he talking about marriage?" I asked.

I watched as she swallowed uncomfortably. "The end of this year," she answered.

"That doesn't leave us a whole lot of time. I have a few people on staff who will help you fill out the paperwork you need. They will walk you through the whole process, and when they are done, I will endorse you. I have to ask a question, and it may make you uncomfortable, but it could help me help you. Do you understand?" I asked.

She nodded again and looked even more nervous than before. She had likely been prepped about what I would ask from others who had sought asylum, too.

"Does your husband or his associates have any relations to any known terrorism groups?"

She nodded very slowly.

"Okay, we are going to need to get that information from you. I will have to get someone from an anti-terrorism organization here to speak to you to get that information. If that person finds the information credible, then that may speed this process up for you. But you have to be truthful with them. Do you understand?"

"I do," she said softly.

"Okay. Fatima, you were very brave coming here to help your daughter and your other children. I'm going to do what I can to help you. Kareem will take you down to meet with the staff to get started on your application. They will give you all the information you need and will help you where they can."

"Thank you, Ambassador," Fatima said with tears in her eyes.

"You can thank me once you and your children are on a plane, but don't thank me yet," I said with what I hoped was a comforting smile. Honestly, I couldn't do much more than make sure her application was filled out; everything else was out of my control. She'd have to be vetted by officials back home, and she'd be interviewed—the whole nine yards. All I could do was start her on the path and hoped that everything worked out for her, just like the hundred other women I'd spoken with this year about asylum. I'd spoken to a number of other ambassadors, and they'd greatly reduced the number of individuals they granted asylum to. They told me if I wanted their help, I'd have to put my money where my mouth was, but most of it was out of my control.

Kareem gestured to Fatima, and she followed him out of my office and down the hall, the child back on her hip.

It was women like her who renewed my passion, made me remember why I was here and agreed to play politics in the first place. I may not have been able to help Adilah, but I could help other women here. Adilah suffered abuses so great that it hurt to think about. She had been my friend, and I should have been able to help her, but I couldn't. I didn't have the ability or the means, and I swore I'd never let that happen again. It was one of the reasons why I volunteered to step in to fill my father's position, with the president's appointment, of course. Not that there were many who wanted the position in the first place, not after the mysterious circumstances of my father's death. I wanted to use this position to help others, in Adilah's honor, and my father's, and I'd do so until I no longer held the office.

CHAPTER FIVE

natalia

It felt like hours that I stared at the computer screen, hoping for a few more zeros to magically appear behind the budget in my ledger. "Maybe I can fly to the states and have a fundraising dinner or something…" I mumbled to myself, determined to try to figure out a solution. I had to keep going, keep fighting for these women and children who wanted out, wanted a better life.

My desk phone chose that moment to ring. I let out an irritated sigh because I was not in the mood to converse; I was in the mood to put pen to paper and plot out a plan.

"Hello, Ambassador Natalia Ali," I answered, putting fake pep into my voice. One of the new hires must have patched the call straight to me instead of sending it to Kareem, who was busy with Fatima.

"Yes, um…hi. I don't know if you remember me. We met a few years back," a slightly nervous male voice replied. Despite his obvious discomfort, his voice was deep and smooth like honey. It didn't immediately bring to mind a face or name, but somehow the voice seemed familiar. It created an itch I couldn't scratch. Either way, I could kick myself for not remembering the face of someone who sounded like he could narrate a romance novel. Was he as sexy as his voice was?

For the first time in a long time, I was left speechless. It took a second, but I eventually recovered. "I'm so sorry, your voice is vaguely familiar, but I'm having trouble placing it," I said, hoping it would prompt him to share his name. God, I hope he wasn't insulted.

"Fuck, I'm sorry. I spoke to someone else and assumed they would have told you who I am before transferring me. My name is Isaiah Yates. It's actually been about five years now, but my team and I helped rescue your father when he was kidnapped. I'm sorry to hear about his passing." He truly sounded remorseful, and for a moment I was grateful for the sexy voice's sympathy.

My mind felt like it was on a delay, and after a second, it made sense of the rest of his words. The air left my lungs without warning, and butterflies wreaked havoc in my stomach. Now I knew why I recognized his voice. I spent a year fantasizing about it before I gave up hope that I'd ever hear from him again. I didn't need him to explain which one of the men he was. I knew.

"Yes, I remember you. I never properly got to thank you for what you did for my family. You gave us a few more months with him, and we are very grateful for that," I said through the burning sensation in my throat as I attempted to hold back tears. Grateful wasn't a strong enough word for what I felt about him and his team.

"There's no need to thank me. I was following orders." He cleared his throat, and I sensed his discomfort again. I wondered if it was the gratitude or if something else was the cause.

"It's still definitely necessary," I said, clearing my own throat, which had started to close up. "How can I help you?" I was extremely curious about the reason for his call. After all this time, I was surprised he even remembered who I was. If he hadn't provided his sympathies, I would have suspected he was trying to reach my father, not me.

" I saw your interview," he replied. The discomfort was gone, and his smooth voice helped ease mine. If he saw my interview, then he knew exactly how far up shit creek I was without a paddle, in a boat with a massive hole.

"You did?" I heard my own breath hitch and wanted to smack myself on the forehead. I only refrained because with my luck he'd hear it. I had no idea that my interview would prompt someone like him to reach out. Most military members wanted to put their time over here behind them completely. Not confront a reminder of it head on. I had to assume he was out of the service, because it wasn't proper for a service member to contact a government official like this.

"Yeah…I saw that things look pretty bad there. I'm between jobs right now, and I was thinking I might be able to help," he said. Those butterflies kicked into overdrive, and the urge to nervous puke was overwhelming. I hadn't been this nervous since the day of my father's funeral. What did I do right to have a man like him offer me any help?

I was lost for words again for a moment. "Uh…things have certainly been rough lately. What kind of help did you have in mind? That's very kind of you to offer any at all." *Please be rich and offer to write a fat check!*

"Well, I was thinking I could come help be a private security contractor for your embassy. You said you needed some more muscle in your interview, and I still have that. I'm still working out the rest, but I might be able to bring some medical supplies in my carry-on," he offered.

"That would be absolutely amazing!" I was unable to rein in my excitement. I tried to recover with a nervous chuckle, laughing at my own excitement. Isaiah Yates was absolutely too good to be true, even without the offer of a blank check. Then my heart sank into my stomach. I couldn't afford him. "Full disclosure, we don't have the funds to pay for your services."

"That's okay, I'm volunteering them until we can figure something else out," he countered quickly.

My lips moved wordlessly for a second as my mind reeled. "Wow. That's so very generous of you. I'm a little blown away," I admitted. I struggled for more words, which didn't come. I was sure I looked like a fish gasping for air.

"I've got a few things to take care of here, but I can be on a flight out soon. I'll bring whatever supplies I can. You know how customs can be," he said with a chuckle, as if customs wasn't the biggest thorn in my side some days.

"That sounds great. Thank you, Isaiah. If you need any help

making arrangements, just call back. I'll let my staff know that you are coming so we can make some space for you." So many of the empty lodging rooms for the employees were in disrepair, I was going to have a freak-out session just trying to figure out his room assignment. It'd been years since the budget had money for new furniture, and the staff just replaced their broken furniture with the unused pieces in unassigned rooms. I'd probably have to raid five different rooms to come up with a room full of furniture, assuming that all the mattresses weren't stolen.

He was oblivious to the new direction my thoughts had taken. "Of course, stay safe," he said before disconnecting the call. I had wanted to tell him to have a safe flight and to bring an air mattress, but it was too late. I was listening to the dial tone.

Holy freaking crap. I couldn't quite believe it. I'd dreamed about Isaiah Yates for the better part of a year, even after my father passed. But over time, my sleep was overtaken by endless worrying and fears of failure, while my waking thoughts were filled with survival. After his call, those thoughts and feelings came flooding back. I was sure most of them were caused by a white-knight complex, his charm and good looks, but feelings always started somewhere.

When we met five years ago, he was dirty, sweaty, and in uniform with his weapon strapped to his back, his sidearm attached to his hip. His eyes were soulful, and I saw so much of him in them, despite the fact that I didn't know him. What I did know was that he was the kind of guy who demanded attention with his presence, and he and his friends were extremely brave.

Now he was on his way. Here. To come help me. I was already in this man's debt, and it was going to continue to grow. The only way I'd be able to pay him back was to donate an organ if he was in need.

"Holy hell, the hot soldier who came to the rescue is at it again." I mumbled as a grin formed on my lips.

"I heard that!" Kareem said at the door.

I groaned. I did not want to gossip with Kareem about this. "I swear you have a camera in here and like to spy on me," I replied playfully.

"You know it. It's my job to know what you know," he said with a wink and a chuckle. "Now spill before I have to make arrangements for whatever this is." He waved his hand at me, as if gesturing I was the one he had to arrange. He wouldn't be wrong; I was a hot mess.

"Five years ago when my father was kidnapped, a group of US Army Special Ops soldiers rescued him and brought him home. Maybe I was just young and naive, but I thought I had a connection with one of them," I answered.

"What kind of connection?" Kareem asked as he wiggled his eyebrows suggestively.

"Not the kind you're implying!" I shrieked. "We only talked for a minute, and my father watched us the whole time, like a hawk. He was handsome and charismatic—even sweaty and gross, I still wanted him."

"So you spoke to him for only a minute, and five years later he has you blushing like a schoolgirl and this close to losing your cool?" He held up his thumb and pointer finger with only an inch between them.

"I don't know, maybe? I never thought I'd see him again…" I felt my face heat, embarrassed by my infatuation with the man.

"So what changed that? Why am I hearing about this now?" Kareem asked.

"My interview, apparently. He saw it and maybe recognized my desperation, I don't know—but he called to offer security services. He said he'd bring whatever supplies he could." I hoped he had an extra-large suitcase full of medical supplies and boxed foods.

"Why on earth would he do that? Did he remember you?" he pressed. He could try all he wanted, but there was no missing his meddling curiosity. He was just as excited about this as me, and he had some kind of plan in his head. I could practically see the thoughts behind his eyes. An offer of help from anyone was more than we'd had in a while, and he was going to read too much into it, given I had a crush on this benefactor.

"Yes, he remembered me, and the jury is still out on the first question. Maybe he is just a good person? Maybe he feels guilty about my father? He saved him once, but no one was here to do it again..." I trailed off.

"No, you don't get to think about your father right now, not when you are having a moment of joy. What are you going to do? Are you going to continue looking at fundraising avenues? Fuck what the president or the secretary says, you did what was right. Look where that interview got us. You have your own knight riding in on his white stallion," he said with laughter in his voice.

"You did not just go there," I balked.

"I did. Now seriously, go get yourself ready for this. I'll make sure the guest house is cleaned up. It's not like there's going to be anything usable in the empty staff rooms. Did you tell him to bring his own towels and sheets?" Kareem joked.

"Of course not," I said in mock horror. "Now go make yourself helpful. Don't make me fire you," I teased with a laugh.

"You wouldn't dream of it. You need me, and I have a feeling things are finally about to change around here, for the better. I wouldn't be caught dead missing it," he answered with a satisfied grin before he walked out the door. He was light on his feet with a pep in his step.

"I certainly hope so," I whispered with a smile.

We really needed something wonderful.

isaiah

The phone rang several times after I started the video call before there was an answer. Guy picked up first, followed by Garcia and Mendez. "What's up, funny man?" Guy greeted me.

"Hey, just wanted to let you know that I'm planning a trip." Normally I might have opened with a joke or insulted one of them, but I had been thrown off-kilter, which normally didn't happen.

"Hold up, what?" Jones asked as he joined the call. This was the first they'd heard of any travel plans. Usually it was Wells and Christine filling us in on their next business trip or family vacation with her parents.

"I'm going on a trip," I repeated and shot him a look that implied how stupid he was.

Strong, Abby, Wells, Christine, and Jasmine joined the call.

"Where are you going?" Mendez asked.

"Hello, way to start without us! Who is going where?" Jasmine asked.

"Yates is going on a trip. We don't know where," Guy answered, bringing the group up to speed on the last thirty seconds.

"Spit it out," Wells said. Sometimes they frustrated me like no one's business, with us all acting like siblings and not friends, but I knew they had good intentions. They were also giving me my own shit and sass back to me.

"Syria." I grimaced, waiting for the reactions of my brothers who were probably relieved they never had to go to the sandbox again. Here I was announcing that I was going right back, and with one less leg than when I left.

"Syria? What the fuck?" Strong asked.

"Are we missing something? Why would you want to go back there?" Wells asked.

"Yates, did you hit your head or something?" Jasmine asked.

"I know," Jones said as he grinned like the Cheshire Cat. He would know, he was the only other womanizer in the group, and there was nothing he wouldn't have done to impress a girl—that was before he and Jasmine got together. "A girl."

I tried to keep my face neutral, but something must have given it away.

"Yates, who do you know in Syria?" Christine asked. As if she'd know them.

"I know the answer to that one," Garcia said with a smile of his own. "Ambassador Natalia Ali."

"Yeah, all right, it's to see the ambassador." I was glad I was able to get a word in through their back-and-forth chatter. They would have found out quicker if they had just let me speak.

"I feel like there is a story that needs an explanation," Jasmine commented.

"Yes, I have the same feeling," Christine added with a smile. I could tell she was debating on how much shit to give me. I was sure she, Jasmine, and Abby would be talking about this for weeks. Actually, probably their whole damn lives. I added to the awkward situations between them and their men when they each came into our lives, teasing them about sex and shit. I was sure I was about to reap what I sowed.

"The long and short of it is we saved her dad on a mission. Recovered him from a terrorist compound and brought him back to the embassy. He used to be the ambassador. She thanked us, and she and I spoke briefly. Four-and-a-half years ago he died, and Natalia was appointed to the ambassador position," I explained.

"Don't leave out the part where you couldn't get her out of your head for a year when you came home," Jones goaded.

"I had planned on it." I rolled my eyes.

"Okay, we clearly know he likes her because he's going back to the Middle East for her. My question is why do you have to go? Doesn't she make official trips here? Can't you see her then?" Abby asked. Her eyes narrowed suspiciously. She was the newest female in our group, after pairing up with Strong, but she was easily the most intimidating. She was an FBI agent, and before that, she was in the Navy.

"Let me show you." I flipped my camera view to front facing and pointed it at the TV. I hit play on the interview I saved and made sure the volume was up. After the video ended, I flipped it back to me.

"Whoa," the three women said at the same time.

"She's gorgeous, Yates!" Christine gushed.

"Yeah, she is." I'd be blushing if I hadn't purposefully had a few beers before this call. Luckily, I was already flushed. "I'm going to provide private security and take what supplies I can get over there. We don't have anything new to track down Ricketts, right?" I asked, just to make sure. I didn't want them to think I was abandoning our mission for a girl. I cared deeply about taking down the trafficking rings. If my friends needed me, I'd be on my first flight back.

"No, nothing to report. Go, don't worry about the mission. We will let you know if something comes up. It sounds like she could use you," Garcia said.

"In fact, she could use more than just you…" Christine trailed off.

"You aren't trying to send us all back to the sandbox, are you?" Wells said, turning his head to look at Christine, who was probably in the same room as him. Yeah, I'd put my foot down at that.

"I mean, he came to help us when you called, and he came to help Jones and Jasmine. Why wouldn't we help him and his lady ambassador friend?" Christine fired back quickly.

I watched the fight leave his body as his shoulders fell. He admitted defeat quicker than his favorite NFL team's first playoff game last year.

"What does everyone else think?" Wells almost growled into the phone.

"Wait, I didn't ask for help." I stopped them. I really didn't want them to drop what they were doing to come help. Everyone had already interrupted their normal lives enough over the past few months. Things were finally starting to settle down, and I didn't want to ruin that.

"That's nonsense, Yates. How are you getting there?" Christine challenged.

"Commercial flight," I answered without hesitation.

"How are you going to get supplies there? You could take a couple of suitcases' worth at most," she countered.

"They are pretty desperate. I don't think showing up with what I can drag behind me will be frowned upon," I told her. Not to mention it wasn't like I could afford to purchase more than that anyways.

"Let us help you. I'll send the Green Oil jet over to your local airport to pick you up first thing in the morning. You can fill it with all the supplies you can, without trouble," she offered.

"I don't want to interrupt your lives any more than they already have been," I resisted. I was well aware that when I voiced my concern out loud, it didn't sound as good as it had in my head. It was a weak argument at best.

"That's bullshit and you know it," Abby challenged.

"Yeah, don't make me say something sentimental," Jones joked.

As I looked at all their faces on my phone screen, I could see they were all in agreement; they wanted to help. I knew when I was defeated. My friends were good people, and they were going to help me, come hell or high water. They knew I had selfish reasons for wanting to help Natalia, and they still wanted to be a part of this.

"Like I said, the jet will be there to pick you up at the airport tomorrow. I'm going to send the pilot your number. Do you have a bulk goods warehouse near you?" Christine asked.

I knew where she was going with this. It sent so many mixed feelings through me that I couldn't even grasp onto one and keep it there.

It was an emotional whiplash of the best kind. It was the kind that might cause silent tears of gratitude tonight when no one was watching. I had never been the best at accepting help, and it was more difficult because I hadn't asked for it. I didn't have time to prepare myself for these feelings. They just slapped me in the face like gale-force winds. I was going to show up like some prince on a horse in Natalia's time of need, and my friends were all about making that happen. I fucking loved those fuckers.

"Yeah, about ten minutes up the road."

"Send me the address. I'm going to call them when they open and prepay for fifteen thousand dollars in supplies for you. Go fill up that plane and impress this girl, and you know, maybe help some people that need it," she said with a wink.

"Christine…that's too much. I don't even know what to say, besides thank you." The knot in my throat threatened to choke me.

"Don't thank me. I'm going to write this off as a charitable donation for my taxes. It's purely selfish reasons," she said with another wink. "We will probably need a few days to a week for us to get everything in order to fly out there, but we will join you. Keep a list of anything else that's needed and we will bring it."

I stared at my friends and blinked back the tears that threatened to fall. *Don't you fucking do it, Isaiah. Don't you dare fucking cry.*

"We got you, bro. Go get some sleep. You've got a long day tomorrow. But I want to know all about how it goes," Jones said, wiggling his eyebrows suggestively.

"I love and hate you all so much," I said with a laugh.

Their laughter followed, and I disconnected the call.

As I texted Christine the address to the bulk warehouse I'd be visiting in the morning, I felt overwhelmed. Within a matter of hours, I saw the face of the woman who somehow captured my attention with only a conversation. I saw how desperate she was for help and without hesitation decided to help her. I didn't even fully know why. Part of me wanted to swoop in and save the day and have her be grateful for my help. I wanted to be her hero again. Maybe I'd get a chance to explore whatever these feelings that I had for her were. Maybe I'd get her out of my system, and then I'd be able to move on with my life.

But what if I don't get her out of my system? What if it only becomes worse?

I couldn't let myself get attached. I'd help her help those around her and get to know her better. Maybe we'd hook up, and maybe we wouldn't. Maybe I'd get there and realize she was more of a fantasy that I built up in my head. That would be for the best, if anything. Yet with my friends joining the trip, I knew that whatever was going to happen, it would be complicated by their meddling. It was a small price to pay for their help making this happen.

I went back to my bedroom and started tossing clothes into a few duffels, along with my essentials and my laptop. I hated prepaying my rent, but I'd done that several times after I was called away again. It was like being on active duty all over again. I wrote the check and left it on the nightstand so I wouldn't forget to slip it under my landlord's door tomorrow.

On my phone, I made a list of supplies I thought the embassy might need to distract myself. I was used to preparing for missions with my brothers. We knew each other like the back of our hands, and I knew how to help without them even asking. However, this was much different. Natalia was a woman, one I had only met once; I didn't know her —not really. I had no idea how to really help her or her mission.

I was in the middle of throwing together the list when an incoming call popped up on my screen. Frustration and anger instantly set in. I didn't have the number saved in my contacts for a reason. I'd never outright call him. I wanted nothing to do with my father. As far as I was concerned, he was dead to me.

I hadn't outright spoken with him in years, and I purposefully wasn't there to pick him up when he was released from jail. My aunt, the only family member I kept in touch with, was pissed that I'd cut him out of my life, but I didn't care. I hid behind the excuse that I couldn't get leave to come home, but I never even tried. I didn't give a shit if he had to go to a shelter. The man was as selfish as they came, and he didn't have a kind bone in his body. I didn't want to be associated with someone like that. I definitely didn't want to be his son.

I hit the red ignore button and waited for the voicemail notification to pop up. I always listened to them before promptly deleting them. Call it morbid curiosity; I wanted to watch as he slowly poisoned everything around him, because that was just what the man did.

This time, there was no notification. Just me and my thoughts. That was fine with me—must not have been important.

Now that I had a reminder of him, I had to work him out of my system. His calls always worked their way into my head, and I had to push him right back out. It pushed me to work harder, get stronger, or be a better person. I worked hard to be his complete and total opposite, as if that would drown out the family resemblance or the fact that we had the same last name.

I picked up my gym bag and headed straight down to the twenty-four-hour gym my apartment had. It was why I picked this complex in the first place. I was a man with a lot of demons to release, and this was the best way to beat them down and lock them away. Some would say I had PTSD, and they wouldn't be wrong. They'd also say I used my humor to hide behind the things that I didn't want to confront; they'd be right, but I didn't care much for anyone's opinion.

I unlocked the gym door and dropped my bag near the treadmill. I made my way to the bar I was going to squat. I loaded the weights and carefully positioned myself in front of it. I checked to make sure that my prosthetic was properly placed, and then I squatted that bitch. As I struggled to lift the weight, the muscles in my leg and my glutes burned. It was a physical reminder that I was still here, I had overcome a lot of odds, and I was good enough.

You won. You won. You won.

I chanted that internally. That was what I did to focus on the positives and push myself. My father, well, he was dead to me. My aunt was selfish and thought I should be responsible for my father, so she wouldn't have to be. It didn't matter that she was his older sister; she didn't want the responsibility. As if a son should be responsible for taking care of his fucked-up dad, instead of the other way around.

I dropped the weights, and a loud sound echoed through the gym.

You won, and now you will win again.

I was going to prove to whatever higher power there was that I was redeemable, I wasn't my father, and I could be saved from the sins I committed for my country. I would prove that keeping me around was a good decision. It started with helping Wells with protecting Christine and then helping Jones and Jasmine find Jones' sister, Mary. We'd helped so many victims of human trafficking since then and had seen true evil be put behind bars. Now it was time to prove myself in other ways, and I was going to meet that challenge. Natalia had no idea what was coming her way or what she was going to help me accomplish.

natalia

I couldn't remember the last time I was so nervous. I barely slept at all last night, and that fact bothered me deeply. I wasn't the kind of woman that got flustered by a hot man. In fact, there were a lot of them here, but most of them were not any kind of man I would look at twice. While I was the ambassador to Syria, I was raised mostly in the United States, and most of my ideologies came from there. The way men talked to women here drove me mad and had me considering prison time to teach them a lesson. However, orange was not my color, and nothing good happened to a woman in prison here.

I spent all night nervously cleaning not only the guest house on our compound but also my home. We were low on personnel, and that meant janitorial staff, too. There wasn't a speck of dirt left behind when I was finished, but my hands and knees were raw from my efforts. However, it did tire me out so that eventually I did fall asleep for two restless hours.

I woke up to Kareem walking through my front door. "He's coming today!" he said in a sing-song voice.

"Wait, what?" I asked as I wiped the sleep out of my eyes.

"You heard me, and you are going to be shocked as all hell when he arrives," he added. I could hear the amusement in his voice as it filtered through my bedroom door.

"What is that supposed to mean?" I asked, feeling slightly terrified. This was happening so much sooner than I anticipated. Didn't it usually take people at least a few days for commercial international travel? I spoke to him a little over twenty-four hours ago. I had a hard time comprehending how this was even possible or why Kareem sounded as excited as he was.

"I'm not telling, but girl, thank your lucky stars. Again." The smug look on his face had me re-questioning my ability to rock an orange jumper. I'd never know until I tried. If he was going to behave like this, the day would be unbearable until Isaiah arrived, and possibly afterward as well. I had a hard time handling Kareem when he was over the top. I knew it came from a place of good, but he was going to drive me crazy talking up Isaiah's arrival like he was a god riding in on a chariot. Kareem was determined to meddle in my love life. He referred to it as "helping my favorite charity." He thought if I got laid, it would be like slapping gorilla tape over the cracks surrounding my heart. One romp in the sheets wouldn't fix my broken heart, not unless the dead were risen afterward.

"When is he going to be here?" I asked. I was still taken aback by the moved-up timeline. I thought maybe I'd have one more attempt at a restful night sleep before he arrived. One last chance to ditch the dark circles under my eyes.

"A few hours." I could hear the smile in his voice through the door. I looked at the clock and it wasn't even seven in the morning yet. "Are you decent?"

"Yes," I groaned and then flopped back down on the bed and pulled my pillow over my face. I heard the door open, and he groaned in annoyance.

"Oh Natalia, your house looks great, but you, not so much," he said after I removed the pillow to stare daggers at him. He flinched when he saw my face.

"How kind of you," I retorted.

"That's what I'm here for. I got your coffee brewing. Now get out of bed. Do us all a favor and shower. After that, come to your office. We've got work to do before the white knight arrives," he ordered.

I floundered at his audacity to boss me around. "I'm sorry, but which one of us is the boss?" I asked.

"Right now me, but once you put on some clothes and enter your office, you can have the title back," he said before turning around and leaving my home.

"He's entirely too much sometimes, but man do I love him..." I mumbled sarcastically before I did what he said.

I jumped in the shower and scrubbed all of the dirt that still coated my skin from a long night of cleaning. My hands were still raw, but I pushed through the pain as the warm water assaulted my sensitive skin. Afterward, I dressed in a nice dress with comfortable flats. I grabbed my coffee from the pot and left for my office. It was just a walk across the compound, so it only took minutes to make it to my desk. Along the way, my staff waved to me and greeted me in various ways. I had a reputation for being kind to them, despite the shitty situations we found ourselves in. A lot of them had worked for my father, too, and they stuck around out of loyalty or the need for a paycheck.

Once I got to my office, there was a stack of letters I needed to review. One by one, I went through the pile. I reviewed requests for visas and formal inquiries. Once I reviewed those, I sorted through our budget for the month and approved spending for specific projects and tried not to let my mood plummet. We really needed at least a thirty-percent increase to our budget, but I had been unsuccessful in gaining any financial backers. So far, all I had was the one offer for private security services and a suitcase full of supplies.

"Ughhhh," I groaned and put my head down on my desk. I needed coffee or to win the lottery.

"Ready for a break?" Kareem said as he knocked on my office door.

"God yes," I answered quickly and stood up.

"Great, because your white knight is about to pull up to the gates. Grab your rifle. We've heard reports that he's being followed. They might try to ambush him at the gates once the vehicle stops moving," Kareem said.

I noticed that he had his side arm strapped to his hip and his rifle strapped to his back. I reached behind me for my M4 and slipped the strap over my head. I checked to make sure that my M9 was still holstered on my side. It figured that the assholes would try to do something to screw this up for us. They messed with shipments whenever they could and attacked the embassy whenever they'd inflict the most terror.

Kareem stopped dead in the doorway. "You look like you are going to be sick."

"You would, too, if you looked at the budget for this quarter," I retorted—a weak save, but one nonetheless.

"I have, and you aren't wrong," he answered with a sigh.

We walked through the halls and down to the front entrance. We exited the doors right as I heard the roar of a large engine. I watched the gates open, and in came a large box truck, and then another one behind that, and my eyes grew wide as a third truck pulled up behind the first two. All at once, the engines were cut off, and the compound grounds were eerily silent. Anyone who had been outside stopped to look at the three large trucks that just pulled in.

I was a little bit in awe as the door opened and a muscular-framed man dropped down out of the cab. The sun only made his silhouette visible, but that was all I needed to see to know that this was Isaiah Yates in the flesh. My mind had envisioned him so many times since we last saw each other, and if his silhouette was anything to go by, the man was still as fine as the desert sand.

He shut the door, and at the same time the sun disappeared behind a dark cloud. I didn't know that I'd ever been thankful for a cloud before, but I guessed there was a first time for everything. I was able to see his face, and man, my dreams didn't even do him justice. The five years since I had seen him had certainly changed his appearance, but I'd say it was for the better. His face seemed slimmer, his naturally curly hair was a bit longer, and he was no longer smooth shaven. He kept a very short scruff on his cheeks and jawline. His honey eyes took me in, and I hoped to God he wouldn't see my blush.

His dark, fitted t-shirt clung to his chest as a gentle breeze drifted in his direction, and his dark jeans accentuated what looked like muscular thighs. His combat boot was black, matching the whole ensemble. The look was completed with a pair of aviator sunglasses, which rested on top of his head.

Combat boot? I did a double take. My eyes weren't playing tricks on me; he was only wearing one boot, because where the other should have been, there was a prosthetic ending in a hook.

Oh my God. I immediately felt ashamed, knowing that my eyes lingered on the prosthetic for too long to not be considered rude. He was here for five seconds before I already screwed up and embarrassed myself. How was I going to survive spending so much time around someone I'd built up so much in my head? How was I going to avoid making this uncomfortable for us both? I wasn't sure yet, but I'd have to try. It was the least I could do to repay him for his kindness.

He had a sexy, badass aura about him, which was hard to miss as he took a second to look at his surroundings. Despite the missing limb, he had the confidence of a man who knew where he was at and what he was capable of.

After a quick scan of the compound, his eyes found me again, and I swore it was as if his glance was a physical touch. It started at my toes and made its way up my body. By the time his eyes rested on mine again, I could feel how red my face was. There was no way that I didn't look like a tomato. I was at a loss. Did I approach him, or should I wait for him to come to me? Would that be mean of me to make him walk this way when I could easily do so?

He crossed the difference between us as I stood there worried about formalities. He came to a stop in front of me; his lips were formed in a relaxed smirk, and his eyes were alight with amusement. He extended his hand like some suave Casanova, invading my personal space and making me wish he'd touch me some other way. I wanted to melt into a puddle at his feet.

"Ambassador, it's good to see you again," he said with a charming smile that made me weak in the knees. It was the same confidence he eluded last time, but there was no one else here to steal his attention. He was here for me, I thought?

I gave him the best smile I could and prayed that there were no bits of lettuce stuck in my teeth from the sandwich I had earlier. "Isaiah, it's good to see you again," I answered as I took his warm hand. I held onto it a second too long for it to be professional, and I could have sworn that my face grew even redder. *Good going, Natalia.*

"And I'm Kareem. I'm her right hand, and the left one, too." I jumped. I'd nearly forgotten that he was right beside me. I looked over to him, and he was beaming at me with a smug grin. *The cocky asshole.* He probably had my and Isaiah's wedding already planned in his head.

"It's good to meet you, Kareem. Thank you for your help with facilitating this," Isaiah said. He let go of Kareem's hand and gestured to the trucks behind him.

"Of course," Kareem answered with his most charming smile and then another knowing glance at me. My friend was going to be unbearable while Isaiah was here. *Wait, how long is he here for?*

"Well, let me show you what I've got," Isaiah said before I could ask him how long he'd be offering his help. He took only one step in the direction of the trucks as the quiet mid-afternoon air was tainted by the sound of gunfire outside of the gate. From the number of shots going at one time, it sounded like there were multiple hostiles outside of the gate engaging us. One of the truck tires hissed as it quickly deflated. It had two bullet holes, meaning it was no longer drivable, at least until it got a new tire. The back end of the truck lowered, and I hoped there was nothing fragile in the back.

"Take cover!" I yelled as I reached behind me and grabbed the M4. I flipped off the safety and aimed for the gates. The security personnel ran in our direction to provide suppressing fire with their guns drawn, probably to help me make an escape, but I wasn't going anywhere. I started exchanging fire with the men who were likely firing blindly through holes in the security fencing. My heart raced as I focused on controlling my breathing and keeping my hands still enough to aim at the gaps. I needed to make sure those got filled ASAP.

"Get down!" Isaiah shouted as something came flying over the fence toward me. I dove forward into the prone position with my gun in front of me. The breath left my lungs painfully as his body landed on mine. He made himself my human shield, and if I weren't in a life-or-death situation, I might have swooned over that fact.

I heard the brick that had been thrown my way hit the ground behind me. It shattered on the concrete, throwing brick dust into the air. If I hadn't moved fast enough, the brick would have struck me in the head with enough force to kill me.

It was only a split second in time, but it felt like minutes as I saw the barrel of a gun get pointed in our direction. There was a large enough opening in the fence that I could see the assailant's entire weapon, his hands, some of his torso, and his head peeking through. There wasn't enough time for Isaiah to roll off of me and for me to get off my feet before the hostile popped off some shots in our direction. I felt the weight on top of me shift, and I wasn't sure if it was to draw a weapon or to try to move us both out of harm's way. I felt a tug at my waist as he grabbed my sidearm.

From my prone position, I aimed my gun at the hostile. I hyper-focused on my target, pulled in a painful breath, and squeezed the trigger. There was no hesitation, no second guessing. Just an instinctual reaction to terminate a threat before a threat terminated me. Blood splattered as my .556 round took out his hand. He dropped the weapon without firing a single shot. He cursed in his native tongue and disappeared from my sight completely. He was either on the ground or left the wall completely; either way he was neutralized for now.

All around me I heard the gunfire exchanged between the hostiles and my security force. Isaiah was still on top of me, providing cover as he aimed my M9 to our right. His body jerked slightly with each pull of the trigger, somehow making this shoot-out feel erotic. I focused on keeping my head down and my eyes peeled on the situation, even though my brain wanted to hyper-focus on the feeling of Isaiah's body against mine. I'd probably dream of this moment forever, and my imagination would run away with me. What would it feel like to be under Isaiah Yates in different circumstances?

All too soon, the firefight ceased, and the attackers shouted their commands to retreat.

I tried to take a deep breath and struggled. Now that we were still, I felt his heavy heartbeat between my shoulder blades and his breath on the back of my neck. The hair on my arms raised and my nipples pebbled beneath me.

Holy crap, I think I'm wet.

"Are you okay?" Isaiah asked softly in my ear.

I shivered at the sensation. "Yes, just another day in paradise," I joked, hoping to distract him from my body's reaction to him. I felt him chuckle, and again the vibration did things to me I wasn't comfortable admitting. I was grateful he couldn't see my face because it was probably as red as the blood that now coated our security fence.

He slowly peeled himself off of me. A layer of sweat only made the task more difficult. He got to his feet, and by the panicked look on his face, I assumed he visually searched me for injuries. I missed the warmth of his body. His weight had pinned me against the gravel, which cut into my stomach and chest, but that didn't matter to my sex-deprived body. He put my M4 back on "safe" before he stood in front of me, grabbed me by my arms, and hauled me to my feet.

"So this happens often?" he asked as he gently touched my cheek. My breath hitched in response. His fingertips were smudged with dirt, which he must have wiped off my face. I was so distracted by his touch, I barely registered his question. All I could focus on was keeping my breathing even and my heart inside my chest.

He gave me a quizzical look, with one eyebrow raised. "Ambassador, are you sure you're okay?" he asked, snapping me out of my physical reaction. "Did you hit your head?"

I was so embarrassed, I couldn't wait to put some distance between us and possibly drown myself in a bottle of wine. "Yes, I'm fine. Just having a hard time hearing after all that gunfire," I lied. I brushed dirt off the front of my dress. "Please, just call me Natalia." I put my rifle on my back.

"I have to say, that was impressive shooting. If I didn't know any better, I'd say you had some formal training," he praised. God, the only way that statement could have made me more eager to please him was if he added, "Good girl."

"Oh, I did. My father saw to that after he was kidnapped. He wanted us all to be able to defend ourselves. Security personnel are nice to have, but he was kidnapped once, and it was easy to presume that it could happen again to any one of us," I answered. He'd put me and my brother in a two-week bootcamp to learn all about gun safety, how to take care of our weapons, and most importantly how to use those guns in possible scenarios, including a multi-attacker situation.

Isaiah nodded. "I'm sorry again about your father. I wish there was something I could have done."

I swallowed hard. I could see the regret in his honey-colored eyes. "Thank you." I did my best not to show any emotion. I refused to cry within the first fifteen minutes of his arrival, especially after I'd had one embarrassing reaction to Isaiah himself.

He glanced around us. "What typically happens after the embassy is attacked like this?"

"Some of the security crew will inspect the area for any damage, and we will remove any bodies if the attackers were able to get through. Otherwise we leave their dead outside the walls. They usually come to collect them at night," I answered.

"That's so…"

"Strange?" I said, cutting him off.

"Yeah, well, we have a skeleton crew here. It isn't like what you are used to. We don't have the resources to dispose of their dead, nor has the Syrian president requested we treat them any differently. We don't have resources to accomplish a lot of what the other embassies do. I swear the local extremist sympathizers attack us just hoping that one day we will run out of bullets," I added.

"I'll make sure to add more of that to my list," he said, and then he turned to face the trucks. They looked a little worse for wear, but they were all still locked up tight.

He called over his shoulder, "Come take a look."

I took a hesitant step toward him, and then another. Before I knew it, I stood next to him but attempted to keep my distance. He leaned forward and lifted the door to the back of the truck. The back of his shirt lifted, and I saw lean muscle and the edge of a tattoo that came down his back. The sight had me involuntarily licking my lips like I was looking at a juicy snack. He was definitely a snack, the best kind.

He took a step back and rejoined me. He caught me checking him out and sent me a knowing smirk. I quickly snapped my head to the left to look straight ahead. I would not acknowledge anything between us. I couldn't; I was a freaking trainwreck.

It took me a moment, but when my eyes focused on the sight in front of me, my knees went weak again. I took a step forward and grabbed the back of the truck to keep myself up right.

Holy Hades in Hell!

There had to be hundreds of boxes of food stacked in there. Easily thousands and thousands of dollars' worth of food was parked right in front of me, and it was all ours. The packaging detailed large cases of canned veggies, fruits, large boxes of prepared mixes, and even what looked like styrofoam coolers.

I wanted to say something, but the sight of this food and his generosity stole the air from my lungs and any bit of common sense I had left. I was floundering like a fish, with no hope of regaining any form of composure. *How embarrassing!* How the flying fart did he get all of this?

"Wait, that's not all," he said before he grabbed my right wrist and dragged me toward the next truck. I felt the loss of the warmth of his touch again as he let go to open the next truck. In the back was even more food and what looked like medical supplies. There were tanks of oxygen, boxes labeled as saline, first-aid kits, and more.

Before I had time for my knees to give out, he dragged me to the back of the next truck, which was where I found all kinds of survival equipment, boxes of linen, and clothing.

"I think I need to sit down," I finally said before I leaned against the back of the truck.

He put his hands on my hips and lifted me so that my bottom rested on the bumper of the box truck, as if I was a child that needed assistance.

"Are you okay?" he asked for the third time today. Pretty soon he was going to piece together the fact that I was not actually okay, so I might as well stop lying.

"No," I answered honestly.

"What's wrong? Did I do something wrong?" I wished he wasn't hiding his eyes behind his sunglasses, because I'd love to gaze into them as I struggled to gather words.

I scoffed in response. "You did nothing wrong. I'm just in complete and utter shock of your generosity."

"Well, to be fair, my friend paid for much of this. She allowed me to open a tab at a large warehouse and for me to use her company's private jet to get it all here," he said. For just a moment I saw a touch of vulnerability, and I couldn't figure out the reasoning behind it. Was it embarrassment because he personally didn't pay for the items, or was it feelings for this woman who so selflessly sent us thousands and thousands of dollars' worth of supplies?

I felt a brief pang of jealousy. *Did his girlfriend buy all of these? Suck it up, Natalia! Even if she did, wipe the disappointment off your face and be thankful!*

"That was extremely kind and generous of you both. I'm having a very hard time wrapping my mind around the scope of this," I admitted.

He smiled, and it was genuine, with no trace of arrogance. "I'm happy to help. Let's get all of this inside somewhere so it's not tempting any more bad guys, huh?"

"Good idea," I replied with a small, grateful smile.

Now I saw exactly why Kareem had been beaming. Maybe I wanted him to plan a wedding after all.

He lifted me off the bumper, put me on my feet, and then we got to work.

isaiah

The morning was way more eventful than I had ever anticipated. I thought I'd roll in, the ambassador would be super impressed with the goods, and then I'd have a nice, relaxing evening before diving into security-related tasks tomorrow. Man, what the fuck was I thinking? I wasn't; I'd been delusional. Kareem warned me that they'd had previous shipments of supplies hijacked by locals, and for that reason they'd started scheduling shipments at all sorts of crazy times, avoiding any semblance of a routine that could be tracked. My whole ride from the airport to the embassy was spent clenching my ass cheeks hoping that no one decided to attack the small caravan. I wasn't sure if I had the lack of organization between the competing local terror groups to thank or the element of surprise for the safe passage to the embassy. I'd been a civilian for too long, because I forgot an important lesson: the moment you unclenched your ass and took a breath, someone was going to stick a bullet in it.

Luckily the bullets were in the truck's tires, not my ass.

After the tantalizing exchange of gunfire, the large effort it took for me to stay in the here and now and then helping unload the trucks, I was fucking exhausted. Actually, I was beyond exhausted. It was so bone-deep tired that it reminded me of the days shortly after my amputation. Add the fact that I was back in the Middle East and the hostiles I faced weren't much different from the ones responsible for my missing leg, it was a struggle not to want to turn around and haul ass home. I'd be too prideful and a liar if I couldn't admit—at least to myself—that I severely underestimated what being back in the sandbox would do to my mental health. I was too proud to admit that to anyone else, though.

Truth be told, when the small convoy of trucks loaded with supplies pulled up to the embassy, I was hit with a sense of déjà vu. Except instead of returning an ambassador to an embassy, I was bringing supplies to an ambassador with a different need.

I still scratched my head as to the reason the hostiles even bothered to attack the compound once the vehicles were behind the closed gates. There weren't enough of them to overrun the compound. In my assessment, there were maybe twenty of them. My only assumption was that they wanted to terrorize Natalia and her staff; they knew the goods were out of their reach. Didn't matter what the end goal was, they did a number to the vehicle, and rounds penetrated the cargo area of the trucks, destroying a few cases of food and supplies, but luckily none of the gas or oxygen tanks were penetrated—meaning no bonfire at the U.S. embassy.

I might have been embarrassed that I let my guard down, but my instincts were still sharp. I threw myself on top of Natalia, shielding her body as best as I could. If we weren't being shot at, I would have paid attention to how warm she felt beneath me and how our bodies fit together just right, with my front melding to her backside. Some of the guys used to joke that the sound of gunfire, the rush of adrenaline used to make them hard, and I never quite understood it. Don't get me wrong, I liked the rush—you had to enjoy it to survive in the infantry —but I'd never gotten hard from the rush like I had with Natalia under me. I'd also never been so worried, either. It was a weird mess of confusing feelings that I'd never be able to sort through, even with a therapist.

What was really my undoing was the level of confidence Natalia exuded with her M4. There was no hesitation, only precision decision-making skills and the confidence to follow through with pulling the trigger. Her body jerked beneath mine despite the eerie calm she'd fallen into as soon as she hit the ground.

She shot off a hostile's hand! The accuracy that it took for a civilian to make a shot like that from our distance, and with almost no time to aim, it was impressive. It was like a woman out-dunking a man on the court with an auditorium of witnesses; it was that level of awesome. Thoughts of an ice-cold shower were the only thing that saved me from a very awkward conversation and apology after the fact. I was sure she didn't want to feel a raging-hard boner against her ass while she was returning enemy fire.

We'd spent hours unloading the trucks full of supplies and putting them in their prospective places. The medical supplies went to an infirmary type room, and the food went to a massive closet near the kitchen. It was scary to see how much food was left on the shelves before we started stocking it. They didn't have much in reserves at all, even for an understaffed embassy.

"Here's my office," Natalia said, ending the tour of the embassy. She opened the door, and I peered inside. The office looked clean and organized, like the office of some stuffy government official in Europe, not the youthful woman who stood in front of me. She didn't strike me as someone who enjoyed opulence; she seemed like the practical type.

I whistled. "Nice digs." I wasn't able to keep all my sarcasm to myself.

She actually laughed. "It looks like it was decorated two hundred years ago by a rich white guy, doesn't it?"

I nodded and chuckled. "I pegged your taste for something a little more feminine, laid back maybe?"

A sad smile crossed her face, and her eyes softened before the expression was gone. "It is, but I didn't want to change it. This is exactly how my father left it. It's like a monument to him. The only thing that didn't stay is the dust." I could understand that reasoning.

"Again, I'm sorry about that." I hoped she could feel the sincerity of my words. I didn't think her father liked me much. I was a smartass young man, not very sympathetic to what he experienced. After all, he was only a civilian, and I was desensitized to some of the crueler aspects of the sandbox.

"Thank you," she said softly, looking sad.

Before catching the Green Oil private jet, I tried to get more info on what happened to the former ambassador but hit nothing but dead ends. It was as if one day he was ambassador, and the next he wasn't, like it was a normal occurrence. He was a political figure; certainly there'd be some kind of over-the-top obituary that might mention his fate—but there was nothing of the sort. The official obituary was a paragraph and mainly mentioned the family he left behind. I wanted to understand what series of unfortunate events caused Natalia to end up as the youngest ambassador in U.S. history, but I also didn't want to be the prick that forced her to talk about it.

Regardless of what either of us wanted, I needed to know. If there was a security issue that led to his demise, then it really was my concern to fix it. I didn't want the same thing to happen to Natalia.

I cleared my throat uncomfortably. "I don't want to be rude, and you can tell me to get lost if you want—but can I ask you what happened?"

Her body language changed, and it was as if she stepped into a pool of sorrow. I instantly regretted the question. Surely I could have asked around to see if anyone knew. Kareem, Natalia's assistant, seemed like the chatty sort. "Yes, but let's take a walk first." She pulled the office door shut and silently walked ahead of me to the end of the hallway. She pushed open the door, and then we went up another set of stairs. At the top of the staircase was a heavy-duty white metal door. The rooftop. She opened the door, and the light of the setting sun washed over her.

The golden rays of light gave her an angelic-like glow that practically took my breath away. She walked over to two lawn chairs that were perched close to the ledge of the roof. She took a seat in the one to the left and then gestured for me to take a seat in the other. She crossed her feet in front of her and leaned back into the chair with her rifle on the ground beside her.

There was an uncomfortable silence between us as I waited for her to blurt out something, anything. She looked down and nervously played with her hands. I suddenly felt bad about ever asking the question. My curiosity shouldn't be answered at the cost of Natalia's pain. I was about to tell her to forget my question completely when she spoke.

"We don't exactly know what happened or why he left the embassy that day without one single security guard or without telling anyone where he was going. My mother realized that he was gone and checked his calendar. He had no meeting scheduled that would have required him to leave the safety of the embassy."

She shifted nervously and avoided all eye contact with me. I wanted to reach out and grab her hand, but I wasn't sure if that form of comfort was wanted, and it certainly wasn't professional.

"When hours ticked by with still no response, the security teams led a small search party through the closest town to see if anyone could tell us if they'd seen him. The next day, he was officially a missing person, and the Army got involved in trying to track him down. Two days later, they found his burned body in a charred car. We still don't know who did it. We flew him home, he received awards and honors from the president for his public service to his country, and that was it. We buried him, and Mom never returned. Neither did my brother. It was too painful for them to even think about coming back here to collect their things." Her voice had a haunted quality to it, as if she was reliving the worst parts of her life over again, just so I would know about her biggest vulnerability.

Fucking hell. I was a dick for putting her through it, but I wasn't done. My curiosity was a bastard of a beast and something I couldn't control even if I wanted to. "How did you end up taking his place?" I cringed as soon as the words left my lips. I could have phrased that better.

Her eyes closed briefly, and I heard her sharp inhale and exhale before she spoke again. "I volunteered. The secretary and the president both attended his service. As they shared their condolences, I asked about taking over as the ambassador." I read her body language. She was so close to shutting down this conversation, but I desperately held onto it, no matter how much pain it caused. She looked ready to stand up abruptly and storm back over to the door and down the stairs to her office. I couldn't let that happen; I needed to learn these things about her. I needed to know what compelled Natalia to volunteer to come back here, to fill her father's shoes, despite how painful that task would be.

I watched her closely as I asked, "Why would you want to come back here?"

She sunk down further in her seat and let out a sigh. I imagined that she was regretting answering my questions in the first place. This couldn't have been easy for her to talk about with a stranger.

"His killer is here somewhere, and I can't find out who murdered him from the States. Someone has to find out the truth. The president assured me he and the government were still investigating his death, but I can assure you they aren't." Her tone was bitter. She had remained tear free to this point, but now a few escaped her eyes and left trails down her cheeks. I sensed open hostility between her and her superiors, although I imagine I'd feel the same in her situation. "I would know, because they'd have to provide the ambassador with updates regarding high-profile investigations like that, it's required, and it directly affects our security here. Yet there's been nothing." She quickly wiped the tears away with angry forceful motions. "I've spent my free time searching, and I haven't found anything, either. I'm starting to think that the idea was stupid. I went to school for politics, not criminal justice. I'm not a detective. I just know conflict management and how to speak politely."

My heart hurt for her. That level of self-down took time to fester. "You can't give up."

She just shrugged nonchalantly and angrily wiped away some more tears. She chose to stay silent as opposed to lying to me. I recognized a soul on the brink of despair; I'd been there, too.

"So you're looking for your father's murderer and you are helping the people who are likely hiding him?" I asked to redirect the conversation.

"Funny, isn't it?" she asked and finally turned her face to look up at me. My eyes met hers, and I could feel so much passion there, it nearly knocked me out of my seat. Natalia Ali was a hurricane, and I had no idea she had been hiding such power.

"There's nothing funny about it. It's only heartbreaking and a complete shame," I answered instead. I felt so bad for her that I could barely stand it. Professionalism be damned, she looked like she needed some form of comfort, and I'd help her if she'd let me. I reached across the arm of my chair and grabbed her hand from her lap. I laced our fingers together and gave them a squeeze.

"I'm sorry I made you talk about it. I only wanted to understand what happened and what kind of threats we may be up against and your motivations for staying in a war-torn country that killed your father," I apologized.

She sniffled and then shook her head. "No. No, don't be sorry. I owe you so much, for what you brought with you today, for offering to assist us. It means so much. The least I could do was answer your questions, even if the answers hurt a little." I watched as she took in a deep breath and her face relaxed, some of the tension disappearing. Her shoulders relaxed, too, more composed than she'd been minutes ago.

I still couldn't help but feel bad that I caused her to be so vulnerable with someone she barely knew. It was never easy to open up to a stranger. My therapy sessions were a stark reminder of that. I wasn't naive to think that our brief encounter years ago meant that I knew Natalia in any way. People changed, and neither of us were the same people we were back then. I was missing a leg, and she was missing her father. She wasn't a woman in her early twenties enjoying life. She was an ambassador trying to find the person responsible for her father's death and trying to save the people she should resent.

"I'm a complete asshole to put you through that, though, so let me make it up to you. Ask me anything you want. There's nothing off-limits," I offered.

"Tell me about your leg," she fired off with no hesitation. I smiled because that was the obvious, and I didn't have a problem talking about it. I'd much rather talk about my leg than my PTSD or my own father.

"Let me set the scene first. I was on a mission with my team, the same guys you met before. We were in a village on a high-profile mission, searching for the leader of a terrorist cell. We had orders to kill him on sight and then to get the hell out of there." I felt her eyes on me. It felt intense, as if she were trying to memorize my every word. "The sun was setting on a day a lot like today. We were following our translator, who was talking with a local. The man explained he knew where to find our target. He offered to take us right to him. We grilled him mercilessly, looking for any inconsistencies with his story, anything that would identify him as a hostile leading us into a trap, but we couldn't find any. I still don't know if it was an accident or if we were led that way on purpose, but the translator stepped on an IED, and I was the one standing directly behind him. I took a majority of the blast, protecting my unit behind me."

Natalia gasped, her fingers clutching mine in a tight squeeze. "Unfortunately, the IED ripped a hole open in my leg, and I was bleeding out. They made the determination while transporting me to Germany it was either me or my leg. By the time our bird touched the ground, they already had the operating room ready for me."

"Wow, I'm so sorry." Her hand still squeezed mine.

"I'm not," I replied quickly.

"Really?" she asked. Her eyes searched mine, as if searching for a lie.

I nodded my head. "Really. It was either my life or my leg. It's a no brainer. The Purple Heart and the no federal taxes are just a bonus," I joked. I actually hated the Purple Heart, and I'd gladly pay taxes if it meant that me and my leg could have survived, but it just wasn't meant to be.

She looked confused by my words for only a moment before she asked, "Are you a glass half full or empty kind of guy?"

"I couldn't tell you. I do like to make light of situations, though. I'd rather laugh than cry over things I can't change. I'd rather make jokes and bring joy to others than wallow in self-pity," I answered.

"Wow," she said a little breathlessly.

"What?"

"You are not what I expected at all, Isaiah Yates."

I smirked. "And what were you expecting?"

"Maybe someone a little jaded like me," she answered honestly. That surprised me. Was she looking to compare pain?

"I'm plenty jaded, I won't lie—I don't dwell on it. I choose to push past those thoughts and focus my energy on something more purposeful." It wasn't a lie; that was how I spent my waking hours most days now. Although my nights were a different story.

She nodded as if she agreed and was going to do the same—like my words were solid advice. I hoped she did. Someone as beautiful and selfless as she was didn't deserve to be a haunted soul.

I glanced back up at the sky. All the oranges, pinks, and purples faded into a dark blue night sky. "Should we get back inside?" I asked.

"Yes, we should get you set up in the guest house." She stood up and stretched her back for a moment. It took everything I had not to check her out while she wasn't paying attention. Normally I'd have at least snuck a peak, but even smooth-talking Isaiah Yates sometimes had some shame.

I followed her lead but stopped to look back at the chairs. This was her safe place, and she brought me here. This connection I felt to her wasn't a fluke; she must have felt something, too. I was once told there was a rhyme and reason for everything, and now I finally understood. There was a reason I saw her interview. I was meant to be here with her. I was meant to help her find answers and keep her safe while she looked for them. And she was going to show me what it meant to care for a woman.

natalia

After my rooftop conversation with Isaiah, I felt raw and exposed. It had been a while since I had to talk about what happened to my father. Half of the staff here had been working here when he died, and they knew the vague details. If someone had a question about the circumstances of his death, they'd whisper about it in hushed voices when they thought I couldn't hear them. I'd never gone to therapy to process his loss, nor had I really confided in any family or friends. It hurt talking about my father, so I usually avoided it and internalized my feelings and talked to myself and, when I felt like being spiritual, my father's ghost.

Talking about my mother and my brother, Tal, hurt almost as much as talking about my father. I hadn't seen them in two-and-a-half years, which was the last time I was in the States. Things were so crazy at the embassy all the time, making it difficult to take off enough time to travel back home. We talked on the phone occasionally, and Tal would send me a text here or there, but it wasn't the same. We were a shell of what we once were. We didn't get time to grieve together, and we grew apart as we grieved alone. I had no idea how they were really doing, and they had no idea how heartbroken I really was. In fact, accepting this position caused strife between my mother and me. She couldn't understand why I had to take on this job, why I needed to endanger my life to help the people of a country that had wanted us gone. In one night of brutal honesty before I left the States she told me I had a death wish, just like my father. I didn't know how to respond to that, because from the outside, that probably appeared to be true. All I could do was walk away from her so she wouldn't be able to say more hurtful things she'd regret later. Grief did terrible things to those suffering, and in my mother's case, she lashed out at everyone she cared about. Tal hadn't fared much better. She was on his case about settling down, and he was far from ready. Tal was angry with me because I left him all alone to be the center of our mother's attention.

I walked Isaiah to the guest house, and he thanked me at the door. He had one duffel bag slung over his shoulder and a box of supplies that he took from storage. He seemed like the independent type. He wouldn't rely on the staff of the embassy for his every need like I did. He'd probably do things himself, like making his own food and doing his own laundry. Self-sufficiency was an important trait in a man.

We stood at the door awkwardly for a moment. I stared up at him, and his eyes glowed in the porch light. He could have turned the knob and left me in the dust, but he didn't. He stared down at me, as if he were reading his favorite book in my eyes. It felt like maybe there was something that needed to be said or something we needed to do.

Like kiss!

No, that would be wrong for me to kiss him. While he hadn't formally discussed the role he'd be playing here, I was still the official that governed over the embassy. That wouldn't be professional of me, and on top of that, he could have a girlfriend back home that would be awfully pissed. Especially since she spent so much money helping us out.

No, Isaiah Yates was off-limits, no matter how much my body wanted him or my heart called out to the man who seemed to like saving others.

"Make sure you let me or Kareem know if you need anything. Good night." I turned to walk away, thankful I'd have a moment to get my thoughts together. Distance would help me make it through Isaiah's stay without starting something I couldn't finish—like a kiss.

"Wait," he said, and butterflies formed in my stomach.

Go away, pests!

He spoke to my back with a gentle hand on my arm. The sparks that ignited with the contact had me wanting to combust. Jumper cables might be less of a shock. "I just wanted to say thank you for opening up earlier. I promise I won't make things awkward or uncomfortable for you again. If it's all right by you, I'd like to speak with your existing security team. I know I can't order them around, especially since they are military, and I know they won't take kindly to being bossed around by a civilian." He paused as if he needed to rethink his words. "Doesn't matter that I have a lot of prior experience, they won't see it that way. Maybe I can work with them to identify areas that they think need improvement, and maybe I can help fill those gaps in some way, or I can follow you around and be your personal bodyguard. I don't know if you have a need for that or not..."

Personal bodyguard? Hell no. I'd throw myself at him within two days; I was sure of it.

He was absolutely right about one thing: the troops already here would not appreciate him trying to boss them around. I'd send out a memo that he could be trusted and that I was contracting him to help with security needs. Hopefully that would prevent him from hitting a brick wall in his efforts. It would keep him busy outside so that I could stay inside, far away.

He remained silent, his hand still on my arm. It made it difficult to formulate words that didn't sound breathless or embarrassing. I was glad my back was still to him. "Of course, we can discuss that further in the morning. I'll make sure that the security teams know you are here to help at my request. They'll work with you in what capacity they can without violating their rules," I replied.

I mentioned nothing about his suggestion to be my bodyguard. If I did, I might accidentally say something too embarrassing to walk back. How could I not? Look at him, tall, dark, and handsome, with a kind heart. What was not to love? He'd unravel me in no time.

Stop thinking about him, Natalia! You are only setting yourself up for heartbreak.

"Great, and one last thing," he added, making the butterflies flutter even harder in my gut. I wouldn't be able to take too much more of this. No way would I be able to make him my personal bodyguard. I wouldn't survive it. The pesky insects would chew a hole through my stomach within a week.

"What?" I asked.

I felt his body heat against my back. Oh my God, this was it. I was going to actually explode and paint the outside of the guesthouse with my guts. What a way to go.

His breath was warm and tickled the back of my neck as he leaned in to whisper. "I want to help you find who murdered your father. Any information you have on that, can you get me a copy?"

His words hit me in the gut like a freight train striking a bicycle. I stood absolutely no chance of not falling for this man. He was a white knight formally dressed in camos. No one had ever offered to help, aside from the lies that the president and Madam Speaker made. I'd never seen a shred of their investigation. Yet the man, who came riding on his white box truck wanted to help me find my father's killer. I wanted more than anything to kiss Isaiah Yates. I wanted to thread my fingers into his hair as I jumped on him and wrapped my legs around his waist. I wanted to swallow his tongue and sink into his chest, only to stay there forever. The thoughts were completely and totally insane. I wasn't some creep who obsessed over a man. In fact I didn't pay most of them any mind—but if Isaiah Yates had a fan club back home, I wouldn't be surprised in the slightest. I'd pay the dues and join.

The few people I previously confided in told me that I was delusional to think I could find my father's killer, especially in an area of the world such as this. I was sure he knew the odds were stacked against me...us. Isaiah was different; he wanted to help, not dissuade me. What did I do right for someone like him to walk into my life not only once, but twice? Did my father send him?

Yeah, right, he'd know better than to send me a man currently in a relationship with another woman. My heart deflated at the thought.

"Uh…yeah, I'd like that," I answered lamely.

"Great, I'll take a look at what you have. Have a good night, Natalia. Sleep well." His body heat disappeared, leaving me shivering. I counted his near-silent footsteps—ten. The door closed behind him, leaving me by myself outside. I let out a sigh of relief. I was alone and could process my thoughts without his curious gaze making me nervous. I could think without the smell of his chocolate and citrus cologne clouding my head.

I took cautious steps back to my house, which I could see from the front of the guesthouse. I was afraid that I might collapse from sheer exhaustion. I nearly celebrated when my heavy feet brought me to my porch. I unlocked my front door, grabbed a bottle of wine out of my fridge, and popped open the cork. I didn't even bother with a glass. I was going to need the whole damn bottle to settle myself down anyways. What was the point in dirtying a glass? I put my lips to the bottle and took a large gulp of the sweet white wine. It soothed my throat as I swallowed. I let out a sigh as the liquid cooled my raging hot insides. The butterflies could drown in the bubbly for all I cared.

I hesitantly walked over to the safe, which was hidden behind a portrait of my father. I entered the combination, his birthday, and the door swung open. Inside was a jar of coins I had been collecting, my personal savings, and a thin manilla envelope.

The feel of the crisp paper in my hands brought me some peace. Inside was all the information I gathered on my father and his death. I had an electronic copy saved on a USB drive, which was in a safety deposit box in the States. The envelope itself wasn't filled with much, but it was the fruits of years of searching. In this thin envelope were the names of several suspects, photos taken of the burned car. Tucked inside another envelope were the photos of my father's body—not that you could tell it was him. The body was unrecognizable, and the car didn't belong to him. Officials identified him from the scraps of clothing not torched. They matched the fibers to what he had been wearing that day, nice expensive clothing. No locals would be riding around in a nice Brooks Brothers suit, not here.

The weirdest part was the vehicle he was found in. It was registered to the embassy, but it had been missing for months. No one had seen it or done more than a few random searches for it since it went missing. Afterward there had been an investigation into the embassy's resources and who had access to what. Those with access to the vehicles were questioned, but nothing ever came from it. The Army closed their investigation, just like they had my father's murder investigation.

The last item in the envelope was a recent addition to the file. Background checks on the three possible suspects. They were leaders for three different terrorist organizations, but there was just no telling who did it, nor any evidence linking them to the murder. They were only suspects in the first place because each one had made direct death threats to my father via social media after he was rescued from a compound and brought home by Isaiah and his buddies. I wasn't sure if I even had any of the right guys; I had no access to any letters or phone calls my father might have received. The three leaders could be a small drop in a large bucket. That realization alone was enough to be disheartening most days, but I held out hope. Eventually someone would take credit, or I'd piss them off enough that they'd try to get rid of me, too. *At least then I might get some answers.*

I took another gulp from the bottle of the wine and walked upstairs with the envelope in hand. I set it on my nightstand, crossed my room to the bathroom, and turned on the water to my soaking tub. I dropped in a bath bomb and watched as the bubbles formed. Within minutes, I was soaking in clean, warm water and chugging wine like it was water. This bathroom used to belong to my parents, and my mom used to soak in this tub after a rather stressful day. I took up the habit, if nothing else to keep my parents' memory alive in this place. As if I could still live with the ghost of happier times.

What had I been thinking?

I had no skills that would help me identify a killer. I was a grief stricken daughter, too angry to grieve. Anger and vengeance were my crutch so that I wouldn't go to bed crying at night. I couldn't handle the chest ache and sobbing that came with losing a parent. I could only handle the plotting and dreaming for the day when I'd be able to bring the killer to justice.

The fact that Isaiah didn't tell me I was stupid or in over my head told me a lot about his character. He recognized what hope meant to someone like me. That or he really didn't want to be the asshole to waltz into my home and burst my bubble. Either way, I couldn't quite find the words to describe the feelings that Isaiah drudged up in me. I began to lose hope a long time ago; it faded each year like the ink on an old newspaper article. Now that he was here, that he even cared about my mission, it felt as if he flipped a switch and renewed my spirit.

It was as if I was trapped in the woods in pitch blackness, and Isaiah's presence was like a candle in the distance. I'd make it through the scary red eyes, brush, and thorns, as long as I kept my eyes on that tiny speck of light. He briefly mentioned what he'd been up to since he got out of the Army: bounty hunting. He and his friends solved a friend's kidnapping and then caught two human trafficking rings. If anyone could help me solve my own mystery, it was Isaiah.

Now if only I could figure out why the hell Isaiah Yates was really helping me. Why would he leave his life in the States behind to come to my rescue with tons of supplies and offer to be my bodyguard? I was practically a stranger. We met once, had one small conversation about my father, and then we parted ways. It'd been five years since we met, and yet somehow he recognized me still. Was he truly just a kind person who saw a need that he could fill, or did he have an ulterior motive? He could've been hiding from something in the States. Although if he was running from the law, then he was pretty stupid. The embassy was considered U.S. ground, and he could be arrested here.

No, I didn't think he would make a mistake like that. And after everything he did to bring criminals to justice, he wasn't the type to get himself into trouble in the first place. He was a highly trained U.S. Special Forces soldier. He had a reputation to uphold and brothers for support.

What if he did come here to help me? If that was truly his only purpose for showing up like a Sam's Club on wheels, what was the reason? Did he feel a sense of responsibility for me, given the death of my father, a man he saved only a few months before his death? Did he see the interview and feel sorry for me? Or maybe I wasn't as naive as I thought; maybe he had felt a connection in our brief moment meeting five years ago.

What if he likes me, too? What if he is here because he feels that pull that I feel to him?

That couldn't be it. He had a girlfriend back home. One who was nice enough to spend tens of thousands of dollars on the supplies. Kareem had let it slip that the private jet he flew over on was practically another Air Force One. His girlfriend was absolutely loaded, so there was absolutely no way he'd risk something so good on romantic feelings for little ole me.

My head hurt from all the hypothetical questions. I could torture myself for ever trying to figure out motives for the actions of those around me. My head felt like it was a bass drum, pulsing as it reached the end of what it could take. I was sure the only way to get rid of the headache was to hold my head underwater until I passed out. Instead, I closed my eyes.

I concentrated on a mental inventory of our full stock room and pantry. Most of the supplies survived the attack. The man thought of everything, from nonperishables, to first-aid kits, to survival kits, and more. Cases of water took up shelves upon shelves, and we emptied out janitor's closets just to make more room for supplies where they could be protected under lock and key.

I was already dreaming of the next open-house clinic and how blown away those attending would be. We'd be able to serve an alternate meal option, make more to-go boxes to feed families, and our on-site doctor might be able to provide more than basic first aid for those in need. There was honest to god professional medical equipment here. Surgical tools, over-the-counter pain medications, lots of sterilizing materials, and even a few medical books.

With all the joy and excitement also came the dark cloud. Most of the different local terrorism groups were likely aware of the three trucks of supplies sitting here, ripe for the picking. I wouldn't put it past them to try to take it from us or destroy it, just so we wouldn't have it. I had some choice words for the assholes.

I'd have to be careful about the capacity in which we helped those in need. I had been doing that all along, but I needed to be even more cautious now. I couldn't advertise just how much we currently had in supply, and I couldn't afford to anger the groups by providing so much help that they felt they had to step their game up. I only had one more person added to the embassy's security rooster. It wasn't like I had a whole Special Forces team here to help. No, we'd have to operate as if everything were normal and hope that everything else remained status quo.

After washing off the dirt from my earlier play date with the ground, I pulled the plug on the tub and dried off, trashing the empty bottle of wine. I not so gracefully made my way to my bed and climbed under the covers. I didn't even bother with my robe before dreamland took me.

CHAPTER TEN

isaiah

I should have kissed her. It was the perfect moment, but I chickened out. A first for me. I was a suave motherfucker. Women loved me; I'd never been worried about the possibility of rejection or upsetting a woman if I was coming on too strong. When a woman did reject me, I took it in stride and just moved onto the next. But it was different with Natalia, and it frustrated the hell out of me. I was far from a coward, yet I acted like one.

I was a Special Forces soldier, for fuck's sake. I lived in a kill-or-be-killed world for so long, and I came out on top. The fact that I let my nerves get the best of me and passed on the perfect opportunity to see if these feelings for Natalia were real or not really lit a fire under my ass. I was determined to see if my head built the woman into some fantasy I thought I'd never have or if she really was that perfect. This was my chance to figure out first hand if love at first sight really was a true phenomenon or if it was just infatuation with a woman off-limits. Infatuation sparked because of the dirty looks her father gave me when he saw us together. If it was the latter, I was as shallow as a ditch, but at least I'd be more self-aware, and I'd finally have my answer.

I tossed and turned for hours before I threw the suffocating covers off of me. The circulated air from the ceiling fan cooled my burning-hot skin almost instantly. I wanted to get up and march across the grounds to Natalia's front door. I wanted to knock until she threw open the door and then grab the back of her head and bring her lips to mine, like I imagined doing years ago.

Instead, I satisfied myself with a trip to the bathroom and rubbed one out in the shower.

It's going to be a long fucking stay...

My phone alarm screamed at me at six in the morning. It was about time the bastard went off. I was lying in bed wide awake for thirty minutes, just waiting for a reasonable time to get up and move. It was enough time to plan out my day. I wanted to speak to the security team and identify and address any weaknesses I found. We were going to run a tighter ship around here. They might have had budget issues that limited their capabilities before, but we were going to work past that. Holes in a stone-and-brick perimeter fence that could be shot through were unacceptable. No, I was going to turn this place into Fort Fucking Knox. I'd find and repair the vulnerabilities and make suggestions for better security equipment. And if the embassy's budget didn't have the room for a few fucking high-tech cameras, a drone, and a upgraded radio system, then I'd ask Christine to buy them. Her parents networked with all kinds of government officials. Fuck, their company sold fuel to the military for a discounted rate; they could ask the president to kiss their ass, and he probably would. The U.S. was in a recession and Green Oil saved the U.S. taxpayers millions of dollars each year.

Christine's family would certainly have the connections to convince the budget makers to increase Natalia's budget, but would that hurt Natalia's job in the process? No one wanted to be undermined.

During Natalia's tour of the embassy, she brought me to her office. It was like a shrine to her father. It was sad but also convenient. He might have left behind clues about those who were after him or why he was targeted. I was sure that an investigator likely came through the room before moving on with their investigation, but unless I knew them personally, I didn't trust their work. I had a feeling that Natalia wasn't given access to their findings anyways, so if there was a clue left behind, then that was better for us.

Determined to get started on the day, I slipped into a white t-shirt and a dark-colored pair of jeans. I pulled on my boot, brushed my teeth, and made sure my short hair looked presentable before I even turned on the coffee maker. Without realizing it, I brewed two cups. I was presumptuous in assuming that Natalia even drank coffee; at least if I was wrong, I'd have a second cup to myself. There was no such thing as too much coffee.

With two steaming-hot mugs of coffee, one in each hand, I walked across the yard between my quarters and Natalia's. I didn't have any place to set the cups down without placing them on the ground, so like an idiot I used my head to knock on the door.

I stood there for a while looking like an idiot. I used my forehead to knock on the door a second time, and a startled-looking Natalia opened the door in nothing but a robe. Her eyes focused on my forehead. "What's wrong?" Her eyes drifted down to the cups of coffee, and her shoulders relaxed. Nothing could be urgent if I had time to make coffee, right?

"Relax, nothing's wrong." I shot her my best charming smile. "I came to bring you coffee and get started on our day. There's a lot to cover, and I'm sure you have lots of things you have to accomplish." She looked at me like a sprouted a horn in the middle of my forehead. "Is it a bad time?" I asked as I remembered my manners.

Her face was flushed pink. Her dark hair was wild, and I could see crease marks on her face from the bed linens. She shivered as a gentle breeze blew between us, causing the steam from the cups to dance away.

"Uh…sort of. I'm sorry no one told you, but I am not an early riser," she answered as she pulled the front of her robe tighter. She reached for the cup of coffee in my left hand.

I chuckled, because there we were opposites. I was often up before the sun rose. "Sorry, I should have anticipated that. I'll come back later." I took a step backward, prepared to head over to the embassy and find something to keep me busy.

"Wait! No…it's okay. Come on in. We can talk while I get ready," she said.

She used her ass to push the door open behind her, and I stepped into the living room. The space smelled like her. It was something fruity mixed with something floral, and it was intoxicating. Whatever it was, I wanted to add it to my coffee cup and drink it right up.

The home wasn't large, but it was decorated in a style similar to her office. The wood tones were deep, the rugs were plush, and the couches looked unused. Artwork from different centuries hung on the walls, and gold accents surrounded the room. A dark green wallpaper covered the walls, and the front windows let in a lot of light. "Let me guess, your father also lived in this house, and you didn't want to change it?" I asked.

She gave a tiny smile, and her eyes twinkled. Her expression was so cute that I wanted to see it again and again. *What the fuck? I'm never this sappy. What is this girl doing to me?*

"Well, it's nice. Doesn't suit you, though."

"And what is my style?" she asked. Her eyebrow raised in curiosity, and her eyes twinkled with the challenge. Then she brought the coffee mug up to her lips as she waited for my answer. I'd never been jealous of a coffee cup before, but there I was, experiencing something new.

"Light pinks and neutral colors. Soft cottons with delicate patterns. Open and airy, with nothing imposing in sight. Instead of century-old paintings, you'd have photographs of nature or people laughing or something."

Her eyes lit in amusement, and her forehead crinkled as she laughed. I must have been spot on. "So if the whole bounty hunting and private security thing doesn't pan out, you could go into interior design, because that sounds lovely."

I chuckled because I never saw myself doing anything artsy. A three-year-old could make a better stick figure than I could. "Yeah, that would be a heck of a sight. I have the artistic inclination of a fly. I'm just good at reading people." *Especially women.* "Anyways, I was hoping to search your office today to see if your father left behind any clues. I don't have the luxury of knowing much about your father, but if his disappearance and death was premeditated, if he had any inkling he was still in danger, maybe he would have left something behind," I explained.

She nodded, and our lightheartedness was gone. "Have at it. Feel free to look around wherever you need to. Some officials came in and did a search while he was missing and again after he was found. If they found anything, they didn't tell me." She took another sip of coffee and scanned the room.

Her eyes studied the coffee cup as she pulled it away from her lips. "Mmm…this is good. What kind of blend?"

"Specialty from back in the States. I'll bring you a bag tomorrow." I had a whole stash in one of my duffel bags. "Can I start looking around now, maybe starting here?" I gestured to the living room we stood in.

"Be my guest. I'm going to go get dressed. I have a few meetings today, but we can work around those. My door is at the top of the stairs and to the left." Her statement sounded more like a warning that her room was off-limits.

I nodded. I wouldn't barge in without knocking. While I'd love to see her in less than a robe, I wouldn't be rude. If I did get to see her naked, it would be a decision she made, not an accident. After all, I was not an animal. Every woman that screamed my name did so of their own free will.

I watched as she padded softly up the stairs. Her pink satin robe swayed behind her. From the light at the window at the top of the stairs, I could see her silhouette through the fabric. I had to quickly look away to keep my thoughts from wandering. The last thing I wanted was to sport a painful boner all morning.

I searched couches, under rugs, inside trinkets, closets, and drawers. I came up with a resounding nothing. I felt a little frustrated, but what did I really expect? To find what I needed the first time I looked for it? Nothing ever worked out that way, in the movies or real life. I'd need to comb the place with a fine-toothed comb, and I didn't have that kind of time while I waited on the beautiful ambassador to get ready.

I walked up the stairs and searched the other rooms that weren't occupied by Natalia, and I found no answers there, either, although there were plenty of drafty windows, squeaky floorboards, and a slew of other needed repairs. I was about to knock on her bedroom door when it suddenly opened.

"Oh, hi," she said, looking a little startled. She was dressed in a women's pants suit, and her long dark hair was curled. If I wasn't mistaken, there was just a smidge of makeup on her eyes, and of course she smelled incredible.

"Sorry, I was about to knock. I just wanted to let you know I didn't find anything," I shared.

She let out a disappointed sigh. "I should lower my expectations."

"What?" I asked.

"Wait, I didn't mean that the way it sounded. My hopes are too high. I spent the whole time in the bathroom getting ready hoping I'd come out here and you would have found some clue that we all missed. I need to lower my expectations. You aren't a magician. You can't just pull clues out of the air if they aren't there in the first place," she said quickly. Almost too quick for me to understand.

"I wish it worked like that." I put a comforting hand on her shoulder. I couldn't ignore the urge I had to touch her.

She nodded. "Me too. Let's head to my office and get started on your to-do list."

She carried a briefcase and the rest of her cup of coffee with her rifle strapped to her back. The pistol I used yesterday was concealed on her hip. I felt the cold, unforgiving metal as I gently moved her out of my way when we both tried to walk through the door at the same time.

She'd shivered at my touch, and I wondered why. Was she uncomfortable with touch in general, or was it just me?

Whatever the reason, she was just going to have to get used to it. I wasn't going anywhere.

CHAPTER ELEVEN

isaiah

Wе made it to her office, and I resumed my search. It was as if he designed everything in the space to blend in with its surroundings. Half the pieces in the room probably belonged in an art gallery or a museum. Not in the middle of the sandbox where they were vulnerable to those who would destroy them on sight. The room was a deep red, almost the color of blood, with a dark wood wainscoting covering the bottom half of the walls. The dark wood floors were covered by a red-and-gold area rug. There were golden trinkets on shelves, an old-looking globe near the solid wood desk, and a tall bookshelf stuffed with old books in the far right side of the room.

I meticulously combed through the office, pulling paintings off the walls, opening books, and trying to take apart the globe. All I found was a bunch of dust. Natalia cleared her throat from where she sat at her desk. I paused what I was doing, trying to shove the bookcase away from the wall, to look at her.

She looked endearing in her suit and firm *I mean business* attitude. "I'm getting ready to join a virtual meeting." I had the impression she wanted me to leave, but she didn't outright say it. "Oh, before I forget, this is what you asked for about my father's murder. This is all I have, so be careful with it. Maybe you can give it a look while I'm occupied," she said as she pulled an envelope out of her briefcase.

"I'll sit over there and go through it, quietly," I said, hoping she'd let me stick around. I didn't want to part ways with her, and that seemed totally irrational. I went five years without seeing her. I could go thirty minutes, couldn't I?

"Fine, but do not make a sound. It's a meeting with the secretary of state, and I'm already at the very top on her shit list," Natalia conceded.

"Scouts honor," I said, holding up my three center fingers and flashing her a goofy smile. She simply shook her head in response and handed me the envelope. I sat down in the chair on the other side of her desk and quietly opened the envelope. Once she was sure I was actually going to keep my promise, I heard her click her computer mouse. The sound of a connecting video call filled the space between. I scanned the contents of the folder as the secretary joined the call.

I wasn't a fan of the woman. She always seemed cold and closed off. Someone had asked her to comment on the death of a Navy SEAL once, and her response had been cold and impersonal. From there, I lost respect for the woman holding the office.

"Madam Secretary," Natalia greeted her.

"Ambassador. Thank you for agreeing to speak with me so late," she relied.

"Of course it's early morning here," Natalia responded, sounding friendly enough.

"Yes, that's right." Her words were clipped. As if she had better things to do and she wanted Natalia to know it. "I wanted to meet with you because we've heard some chatter. It seems as though a private plane from the U.S. flew into a local airport, and there was a delivery at the embassy yesterday," she said stoically.

I looked over at Natalia. Her eyes went wide for a moment before she caught herself. "Yes, ma'am. A friend of mine from the States flew in and brought some supplies with him."

"You do realize that this makes your government look very poorly.

You having to go to private citizens to fundraise makes it look like we aren't doing our jobs," the asshole on the other end said.

"Well, to be fair, I've combed through our budget, and frankly we aren't getting enough funding. I've compared our budget to those embassies in neighboring countries, and we are receiving twenty percent less. On top of that, my friend was responding to my news interview. I didn't go seeking this out. Not to sound long winded, but if you had agreed to at least review my request for additional funding, I wouldn't need outside sources," Natalia said with a resolve I'd never seen from a government official before. I was pretty put off by anyone that held a public office, but Natalia showed her backbone, and I was proud of her.

I tried to skim the documents in front of me, but this conversation had captured my full attention. It was a window into why Natalia's situation had become so desperate. Her boss was being a bitch, on purpose.

"I should just ask for your resignation now," the secretary retorted. Her voice was full of malice. I wanted to jump up through the computer screen to intimidate the hell out of her, but I made a promise to Natalia that I would be silent.

"You could ask for it, but I won't give it. I imagine the only thing that might make you look worse in the public's eyes would be for me to have to leave my office. Then they'll really think badly of you and the administration, and I definitely don't want that. Do you?" Natalia asked sweetly.

Well, I'll be damned. Natalia was clever, found a way to make herself comfortable while she was backed into a corner.

An angry puff of air escaped the other woman's lungs. She knew that Natalia was right, and she didn't like it. "Fine, do what you want. I'll take a look at the budget if it means you shutting the hell up about this to everyone. In the meantime, no one needs to know that you privately sourced those supplies, do you understand?"

"Yes ma'am. My friend won't say anything," Natalia promised.

"Good, who is this friend?" the secretary pressed.

"An old friend with strong ties to us. He served in the Army," Natalia offered, not identifying me directly.

"Ah, a patriot." The words were clipped in annoyance again. What did she have against the Army?

"Yes, ma'am," Natalia answered.

"Well, keep your patriot on a tight leash. I assume he's still in Syria with you. Make sure he stays out of trouble. The last thing we need is a news story about some rich soldier getting kidnapped by the terrorists. We have enough going on in your region right now." Yeah, a whole lot of chaos.

"I will keep him close," Natalia promised. I liked the sound of that.

"Good. Now onto other pressing matters. Have you had any luck in your conversations with the Syrian president?"

"Unfortunately, no. He's just as stubborn as you'd expect. If he isn't moved at the sight of his people starving, then it was too much to expect him to consider my request," Natalia said, sparking my interest in this conversation further. The papers in front of me were all but forgotten.

"Keep pressuring him. I need these results. Do whatever you have to, even if you have to wine and dine him," the secretary demanded.

"How can I wine and dine him when we can barely afford a bottle of wine?" Natalia countered.

"I already told you I will look at the budgets. Maybe throw something together using all those supplies you just got. I've got another meeting I need to prepare for. Keep me posted on your progress with the Syrian president, and make sure your friend keeps his yap shut."

Natalia nodded her head, and the call disconnected.

"Well, she's a real peach," I quipped.

Natalia rolled her eyes. "Yeah, tell me about it." An exhausted sigh followed.

Did she know she was going to get in trouble for privately sourcing the supplies? I was sure she had to have known. It seemed like they probably went head to head a lot. "I didn't mean to get you in trouble," I apologized.

She shook her head furiously. "There's no need for that. I meant what I said. This is all her doing."

Things fell silent between us for a moment as I looked at the documents I was still holding. "Is this really all you have on these guys?"

She nodded.

"All right, I have a friend who is an internet sleuth. I'm going to make an inquiry to see if he can find anything out for us, if that's okay?" I asked.

"Do you trust him?"

"With my life. He was actually one of the guys on my team that you met," I offered.

She hesitated for a moment. "Okay, bring him in on this. Anyone who can help is welcome to try."

"Perfect. In the meantime, I'll go speak to the head of the security here and come up with a plan for some improvements." Natalia narrowed her gaze at me briefly but then nodded and then returned back to her work.

CHAPTER TWELVE

natalia

Where did he go? I hadn't seen Isaiah since my meeting this morning with the secretary of state. He had said he was going to go speak with the head of security for the embassy, which I knew he had done. I spoke with Tom at length about their conversation an hour ago. He'd left Isaiah to his own devices because, "I am not a babysitter." I actually begged to differ; he babysat the whole embassy. Naturally I just kept my mouth shut and chose not to argue.

He wasn't pissed at Isaiah, so to speak; he understood his suggestions were made to make everyone safer, but he wasn't happy that someone twenty years younger had waltzed right in and started pointing out flaws. I had assured Tom that I asked for Isaiah's help, because the new shipment of supplies made us more vulnerable. I bribed him with the promise of a homemade batch of chocolate chip cookies, made only for him by the cook. He groaned, but he accepted the terms of the deal: accept Isaiah's help and enjoy warm delicious cookies that he didn't have to share.

I wandered aimlessly, looking for Isaiah, probably looking like I was lost. He wasn't at the house, my house, or anywhere in the embassy building as far as I could tell. Unless he was hiding in one of the staff member's rooms or a janitor's closet somewhere. If he wasn't in the embassy, then maybe he was outside of it or on top of it. I walked back through the building and to the stairs that would take me to the roof. There was no sign of Isaiah. My chairs were undisturbed.

"What the fuck, Natalia? The secretary told you to keep him close, and you've already lost him. No wonder she doubts you as an ambassador," I mumbled the insult to myself.

I walked over to the edge of the roof to see if it would at least give me a better vantage point of the grounds. I spotted a shirtless man over by the perimeter fencing. Jackpot. None of the embassy's staff would dare walk around shirtless; that just wasn't professional.

I sighed. At least I'd located him.

After taking off my suit jacket and dropping it off in my office, I stalked across the embassy grounds to reach him. As I approached from behind, I saw the muscles in his back, shoulders, and arms as he lifted rocks into place. He was repairing a weak section of our wall. Someone had detonated a car bomb there three years ago. While the fence held, there was no denying that the holes left behind were undesirable and a safety hazard.

I couldn't help but lick my lips as I watched Isaiah move. He was oblivious to my presence as he put a mortar-like substance on a large rock and lifted it to waist level. I couldn't help but check out his ass as he had squatted to pick up a new rock. His capabilities amazed me. Even with only one leg, he was lifting rocks that would throw my back out if I even thought about lifting them. I was fit, but I was not the Hulk.

"Are you going to check me out all day?" he suddenly asked without looking behind him. His voice jarred me. I hadn't expected to be caught staring red-handed.

Shit. How do you recover from looking like a creeper? Humor, maybe?

Yes, he liked humor. "No, I only blocked off an hour."

He let out a deep laugh that made me smile in response. I liked the sound of his laughter; it did things to ignite those butterflies in my gut.

God. I was so in over my head. I barely knew anything about him. The little I did know made me like him even more.

"What are you doing?" I asked. I stepped forward so that I was standing to his right, looking at his work.

"Are you really going to make me say, 'What does it look like I'm doing?'" He chuckled, the sound deep and sexy. After seeing him doing hard work while shirtless, sweating in the sun, I was going to need new underwear.

I scoffed. "No. I'll rephrase: why are you repairing the wall? We have contractors we hire to do this."

"How do I put this nicely? Was it in the budget to pay for them? Was the work already scheduled?" he countered.

He had me there. I shook my head gently as I admired the masonry work. "No, but the secretary is reviewing the budget. We may actually get money for some repairs." I was unable to keep the wistful hope from my tone.

It was his turn to scoff. "Don't kid yourself, Natalia. You're smarter than that. She's stringing you along. What was it she wanted you to do, something about the Syrian president?"

I felt a slight hint of anger at his accusation. Did he think I couldn't see right through my boss? She'd only been a nightmare to deal with since I took over. I knew she was trying to use me. I recognized her manipulation and self-serving attitude. I'd attended plenty of virtual calls with other ambassadors. She liked to pin us against each other, make us compete to be the apple of her eye. It was the work of a callous woman, but she didn't care. Not when the work resulting from our competition made her look better. She had more successfully negotiated trade deals than had occurred during any other administration.

I knew how cold she was, and I didn't need him on my case for doing my job. "Hey, I don't need you repeating what I already know. I appreciate the help, but remember that playing politics is my job. I have to play nice, even though I don't want to," I said pointedly. I hoped I was giving him my best version of a stink eye.

"Oh, I know. But what does the secretary want from you involving the Syrian president?" he asked me again. He must have realized that I purposefully avoided that topic.

"I can't say. That's a matter of national security," I answered.

"Really?" He scoffed again. He angrily placed another rock into place. He used the butt-end of the trowel to beat the rock into the perfect position.

"Really," I said with a quick nod.

What the secretary wanted was more like an act of espionage, and I was still on the fence on whether or not I could go through with it. What she wanted was very complicated and could get us both in a lot of trouble should anyone catch on, but it could also make us heroes if we were successful. I originally questioned why she wanted my help in the first place—I knew she was far from my biggest fan—then I realized how much of a win-win it was for her. I was to use my intelligence and good looks to seduce the man, capture a recording of him admitting that he was purposefully mismanaging U.S. aid, aiding and abetting terrorists to plot against the U.S., and that he was encouraging the civil war within his country. And if I couldn't get a confession, then I needed to find the hard proof and turn it over. If I attempted and got caught, then I was her scapegoat, and she could just fire me. It would be possible that I could end up in a Syrian prison, or much worse. If I didn't agree to help her, she was just going to continue to blow off my requests regarding the budget and helping Syrians. The situation I found myself in was seriously fucked up. I couldn't share that with Isaiah; that would become a national scandal if anyone found out. He'd tell me to walk away from the job and tell the secretary to go fuck herself.

"I don't know if it's occurred to you, but my security clearance level is probably just as high as yours is," he said, also narrowing his gaze.

"You might be right, but you all of all people should know how important it is that we protect the information we keep and act ethically with its knowledge," I answered.

"I'll concede for now, because you make a valid point, but I'm going to be your bodyguard, so you'll need to let me know if it's something that can become dangerous."

Absolutely not. Fuck no. To hell with that. "Did we formally discuss that you'd be my bodyguard? I don't have the budget to pay you for that." It was a weak argument, but I had to try. God, I wouldn't be able to stand that. Having him this close all the time and trying to boss me around would have me ruining every pair of underwear I owned in no time. Not to mention my blood pressure wouldn't be able to take it. I called the shots here; this was my embassy. If he wanted to up the security, so be it. But he didn't get to appoint himself anything. He was a volunteer.

"You don't need to pay me. And I don't know, I just assumed you wouldn't have a problem with it. Did I assume wrong?" he asked. His eyebrow raised quizzically, challenging me to stand up for myself.

Yes, yes, you did.

I hesitated, and his eyebrow raised even further.

"Uh…" I blanked out. I was looking for any other reason I could give him aside from saying, "Because I want to ride your face."

"Do you think it's because I can't keep you safe?" he asked as he took a step closer to me, and I took a few backward. He backed me into the wall that he had been repairing. He placed a hand on either side of my head, trapping me.

I began gasping like a fish, looking for any response to save my pride.

"It's a simple yes or no, Natalia," he said. His face dipped lower toward mine, making my mind short-circuit.

"I trust you with my life!" I blurted out. Hopefully that was the answer he wanted and he'd give me the space I needed to think properly.

"Then what's the problem?" His right hand left the wall to grab a piece of my hair. He rubbed it between his fingers but never took his eyes off mine. Good god. I could feel myself becoming aroused, and there was nothing I could do to stop this train wreck. We were about to nose dive off the cliff of maintaining a professional relationship.

"This!" I blurted out. I felt my cheeks get hot, the telltale sign that I was blushing.

"This?" His eyebrow shot up again.

"Yes, this. I'll explain due to the very real possibility that this is all in my head. I feel this chemistry between us; it's so thick it's difficult to breathe, especially now." His eyes lit up with a spark that could have ignited us both like a bomb. I didn't trust us not to take this whole section of the perimeter down. "I'm sure you probably have a girlfriend at home, and I'm super appreciative of what you've done for us, but I can't be tempted by what I can't have. It would be like torture having you follow me around all day. Spending so much time with someone I can't have, it's not right. Therefore no, I'm fine. I'm more than capable of protecting myself, in case you forgot about yesterday." My breathing was heavy with the effort it took to voice my words and the adrenaline that kicked in while I waited for a response. I was going to lose it. He needed to go back to the U.S. pronto.

He leaned a little closer, and I waited for the top of my head to explode into a mushroom cloud, but it didn't happen. Instead, I felt the tickle of his breath on my cheek and neck as he said, "Who says you can't have me?"

I sputtered for a moment. I completely short-circuited. I frantically searched for my reset button. "Don't you have a girlfriend at home? Isn't she the one who bought all the supplies?"

He had the nerve to smile like he was the cat that caught the canary. "You thought I had a girlfriend?"

Duh. "Of course. Why wouldn't you? And what female friend donates thousands and thousands of dollars' worth of supplies to someone she's never met just because her guy friend asked her to?" I countered. I felt an eyebrow raise in an accusatory manner. If he was going to lie, he had to lie to us both.

"My rich friend is married to one of my best friends. If I ask for help, she gives it, because she's a lot like you. Has a bleeding heart and wants to help everyone." His smile grew wider, and I wanted to smack him in the chest. The words hung between us as I waited for more of an elaboration. "She's married to one of the guys who was with me when we rescued your father. She's rich as hell. Her family owns Green Oil Industries. All of that," he said, gesturing toward the embassy, "was pocket change to her. She'd literally do it for anyone. Don't read too much into it."

I struggled to intake air. I had been so, so stupid. The Daniels family had to be one of the wealthiest in the country, and they just made a private donation to the embassy. If the secretary found out, she'd skin my hide and make me into a ugly-ass purse. Now I was really up shit creek—no paddle, no life vest, and no freaking boat. Holy crap. Naturally, that wasn't what my brain wanted to circle back around to. Isaiah wasn't with her. They were just friends.

"So you are single?" I shouldn't have cared. A relationship between us still wouldn't be right.

"Mhmm…" I wasn't sure if I was imagining things, but I could swear his face got millimeters closer to mine.

"Oh," was all I could muster up.

"So you like me, huh?" His voice was low and slightly raspy, like he couldn't believe my previous words, and he was questioning them, even as he reiterated them. Before I could do anything other than nod, he reached forward and put his hand behind my head and brought my lips to his.

I swore someone could have opened fire at us and I wouldn't have paid attention. I was so lost in the feel of his luscious lips on mine that I was worried I was going to combust, right there in his arms. Too soon, he pulled back, and I struggled to take in oxygen. I was in danger of passing out.

"Damn, I've wanted to do that for such a long time," he said as he continued to play with my hair. I could see the sincerity in his eyes, which surprised me even further. He only got here yesterday.

"Since when?" It was my turn to ask the questions.

"Since the moment I met you," he answered without a second of hesitation.

The butterflies kicked into overdrive, and I swore they were about to come up my throat or out my ass. The jury was out on which was going to happen. "Really?"

"Absolutely. Occasionally, I'd see you on the news, and it would take me weeks to stop thinking about you obsessively. I believed you were off and living your life. I wasn't in a great place myself, and you didn't need to hear from a miserable man like me. But when I saw your interview, I knew I had to do something. I like the man I am now, and I hoped that maybe you would, too."

My heart was beating like a bass drum in a high school band's drumline.

"So you came here, with thousands of dollars of goods and a private jet that you convinced your friend to provide, purely to impress me?" There was no way I somehow got so lucky.

He simply nodded.

Call me the Grinch because my heart grew five sizes too big. "Color me impressed."

"I see that." He lowered his hands, and they grabbed my hips. "So how do you feel about me being your bodyguard now?" he asked.

Hell yes. "Consider my mind changed. Guard me all you want." My smile never faltered.

"Good, I take my job seriously. I just want you to know that. I also have a request," he said.

"And what's that?"

"Let me see more of that body I'll be guarding," he said with a wink.

I slapped his chest playfully and then leaned in to kiss him.

Finally, something went right.

isaiah

I wanted to keep her pinned against this wall and fuck her brains out. Even though she would have enjoyed it thoroughly, that kind of stunt could force her to hand in her resignation if anyone saw us. This was public property, and someone was sure to witness a show like that. I was positive she wouldn't be happy with me once it came out. So instead of taking her hard and fast until the stone rubbed her skin raw, she sat and watched as I finished repairing this section of the wall. She didn't speak much, but neither did I. The most important things had already been said. Five years ago, a brief conversation between the two of us was enough to totally captivate us. It brought me across the Atlantic Ocean for her.

Shortly after I placed the last stone, she helped me clean up the supplies and suggested that we go back to her place. I took a shower to clean off all the dirt, and she cooked dinner. After I told her how good the meatloaf was, which I may have exaggerated a bit, we made out.

Her lips were a drug I could lose myself to. Her fruity-floral scent was so divine that I wanted to devour her. And her eyes, they seemed so alive for someone who was under so much pressure.

It was common knowledge that many combat vets lost themselves to a crutch, something that made them feel alive. Natalia had such a strong hold on me, and it happened in such a short amount of time. I'd do anything she asked of me, except get lost. I couldn't walk away from this, even if I was held at gunpoint. This relationship-type feeling was so new, and if I thought about it hard enough, it would scare the shit out of me.

I laid on the couch, and she laid on top of me, her tongue tangled with mine, and it was better than I could have ever imagined. Pining over her for years was totally worth it, but we weren't finished yet. I was going to make Natalia mine in every sense of the word. *Mine.*

But that started with introducing her to my friends and fitting her into my life. Would they like her and she them?

"So I have something I want to talk to you about," I told her. We'd taken a break from making out to come up for air, not that it was much air; she still laid on top of me.

"Uh oh, you're secretly a serial killer, aren't you? Something about you was too good to be true," she joked. Her face scrunched up like she caught a whiff of something bad.

I laughed even with her weight on top of me. "No, no. I'm absolutely perfect, God's gift to mankind. In fact, I was so good, he had to take a piece of me back," I joked as I lifted my prosthetic leg.

She rolled her eyes at me and then smirked. "I'm glad you have such a good sense of humor."

"Only the best. I wanted to talk to you about my friends. They want to come help you with your project." I watched her closely to see if she'd be upset.

"Come help with which one?" she asked, looking confused.

"Giving aid to the locals in need. I do think they could help us in the search for answers about what happened to your dad, though. They are a lot to handle, so I want to prepare you for them, but I don't even know where to begin." There was so much to my group of friends. But most importantly, they were like fleas: where you found one of us, you found us all. Except we were way better company—and presently they wanted to hitch a ride on Natalia's hide.

"The beginning is a great place to start," she said with an encouraging smile.

"Well, my friends are kind of a package deal. Where one finds adventure, the rest come riding in like the cavalry. No, that's a bad analogy, fuck the cavalry. Those bastards think they are the best part of the Army, when they are like the fourth best, if that. At least what's left of them. Did you know they stopped using horses in combat in 1942? They are just ceremonial now."

"No…I didn't know that, but now I do. So what about your group of rough riders?" she asked.

"I should punish you for that one," I said with a smirk. I could easily get carried away in my punishment, and it would start with throwing her over my shoulder and carrying her up the stairs to her bedroom, and it would end with us in a sweaty mess, both suffering from the aftershocks of an amazing orgasm.

"Yates, back to your friends," she encouraged firmly. My punishment would have to wait. *That's unfortunate.*

"Anyways, we're kind of a package deal. They called when I was out repairing that wall before you came over. I was explaining to them everything you're up against. Low budgets, hostiles trying to sabotage your ability to help their people, and your search to find answers about your dad. Christine asked about what you do to help others, and she wants to help further. Once she volunteered, the rest were quick to step up, too."

Her jaw dropped, and I gently pushed it closed. She shook her head, as if to clear some cobwebs from the inside of her head. "So they want to come help me?"

I smiled. "Yeah, the guys can help with repairs, upgrading security, and investigative work. Jones's girlfriend Jasmine actually speaks Arabic. Her skills might come in handy with speaking to locals. Christine has plenty of resources to help upgrade your tech, and Guy is the tech expert who will make it happen. We can do all of this without it ever getting back to the secretary. We run it all through Tom so that he knows it's legit, and they can continue running the operation, even if we aren't here," I explained.

She smirked at me in defiance. Uh oh. What did I do? "Do you think I don't speak Arabic?" she asked.

I hesitated. "Actually…I don't know. Do you?"

"Naeam," she replied.

"Okay, then she'll be happy to have someone to practice with. Anyways, what do you think?" I asked, feeling nervous. What if she didn't want anything to do with them? What if she rejected my help?

"They're your friends. I'm not going to say no to you. You know that I'm on very thin ice with my boss, so I need them to stay out of trouble. Anything they do is going to be a direct reflection on me. Can you set that expectation with them?" she asked.

"Already done," I answered quickly.

"How many of them are there?"

"Nine."

Her eyes widened with surprise. "You're bringing a whole party. Where are we going to put them all?" Her heart beat sped up against my chest.

"They can all stay in the guest house with me, no big deal." I already had this all figured out.

She shook her head. "Ten people in that small house isn't going to go well. I also don't think it's safe to just put them in a hotel, not now with the political environment here getting worse. Once people get word that they are American tourists, they'll be mobbed—by people either asking for help or wanting to harm them. They have to stay here. You can stay with me at my place. That will free up a little room at the guest house," she offered.

"I'll take any excuse to shack up with you," I said with a wide grin. I leaned forward and kissed her again. Then there was a loud pounding on Natalia's door.

"Madam Ambassador, open up! There's been a security threat!" someone called urgently from the other side.

I pulled Nat off of me and immediately sprung to my feet, or foot, and grabbed my side arm from the coffee table and tucked it into the back of my waistband. Nat pulled a blanket around her and joined me as I walked to the front door.

"Tom," I said as I swung the door open. The embassy's head of security stood on the doorstep. He barely looked put together, and that was worrying. His face might have been neutral, but his eyes were panicked. No, this couldn't be good news, especially since it was eleven at night.

"Tom, what's going on?" Natalia asked before I could.

"We are upgrading the security threat level to red alert," he said, speaking directly to her. I might as well be chopped liver.

"What? Why?" she demanded immediately.

This would not be good news.

"There's been a direct threat made on your life by Faris, the leader of the worst terrorism group in the area. He posted it on Twitter. He all but hinted that anyone who assassinated you would be deeply rewarded."

Rage threatened to rip through me like a tornado, not that it would help. It'd only make Tom even more wary of me, and it might upset Natalia. I needed to swallow back the acid-like feeling in my chest and focus on how to keep her safe.

Tom passed over his phone. I looked over her shoulder at the phone in her hands. The tweet was in Arabic, with Natalia's photo attached. Over her face was an angry-looking red X.

"Holy shit..." she breathed out. I felt her panic like it was a pillow that just smacked me in the face. The tension in her shoulders and her shaky hands told me everything I needed to know. This threat was real, and she believed that someone out there would try to act on it. I might have patched up a hole in the stone wall, but the embassy was still far from Fort Knox.

"The tweet has already been taken down. This is a screenshot. It was only up for fifteen minutes before it was flagged, but fifteen minutes is a long time on the internet," he commented.

"So red alert—does that mean that Natalia is getting more security?" I asked.

"Yes. I've made a request to the secretary of state and the Department of National Security. Given the larger-than-normal target with what they referred to as a surplus of unsanctioned supplies, and the direct threat, they will be authorizing the temporary deployment of military personnel for the surrounding areas. They can only move around so many troops without pissing off the Syrian president. You know that," Tom said to Natalia. She gave one nod of acknowledgement.

"We are going to close up the embassy, no one in or out. Mr. Yates, I suggest you make a decision now on whether you have somewhere to be in the next few days or not. If you do, I suggest you leave ASAP."

"I'm not leaving, but I have friends who are flying in from the States. They are supposed to arrive tomorrow evening. We need to let them in." I understood what he was doing by closing up the embassy, but my friends would only help us.

"We don't need to do anything of the sort. We need to protect the ambassador," Tom countered.

"My friends are my buddies from the Army. We are all former Special Forces and trained in counter terrorism tactics. If there is anybody that can help keep the ambassador safe, it's them. I'll give you their names. Do full background searches if you want. You'll find just how highly decorated they are and just how badass they continue to be, even in civilian life," I argued. I took a step closer, hoping I could intimidate him.

"That's great and all, but don't you think getting them into the country is going to be dangerous enough?" Tom countered.

"It's nothing we haven't handled before," I countered.

"Yeah, sure, but you don't have the uniform or the resources to back you up anymore, Mr. Yates. You don't get to waltz in and play the hero because you think you can. Civilian life doesn't work like that. You and your friends may think you can just parade yourselves around and do what you want, but not here. This ground belongs to the United States government. You take orders here. You don't give them." His voice was low and full of contempt.

I wanted to clock the guy in the face. It took a lot to get under my skin the way he did, but he managed it in only a minute.

"Noted. But this 'civilian' would still give his life to protect Natalia, and so would that plane full of civilians you want to abandon. We won't do anything rash, and we will follow Natalia's orders, since she's actually the government official in charge," I said, reminding him.

"Guys," Natalia said, stepping between us. I think she knew that someone was going to start swinging fists real soon. "Tom, I agree. We will lock down the embassy for now, no one in or out, except for us. We will allow his friends inside, and that's it. A small compromise. We won't hold any open houses for now until we get a better handle on this."

He looked like he wanted to argue, but he gave one nod of his head. He walked away a winner: the embassy would be closed, he would be getting more operational support from the military, and there'd be no open houses. I knew for a fact he thought they were an unnecessary risk. He'd said as much when he didn't know I was listening.

"We're going to put a guard outside your front door," he insisted.

"That's fine, and I think it's best if Isaiah moves into this house. It's one more level of protection," she said, making the decision sound professional.

"If that's what you think is best. The friends will be in the guest house?" he asked.

She nodded.

Tom gave a simple nod in acknowledgment. It was done, and he wouldn't argue further. "You should call the secretary. She's waiting to hear from you," he warned and then stalked away.

"Now?" she called out after him.

"Now," he answered without turning around.

isaiah

"**F**uck," she mumbled as she pushed the door closed.

"This is fantastic," I added as I tried to figure out our next steps.

She took a deep breath, and her exhale tickled my face. "Tell me about it. I have to speak to that bitch twice in twenty-four hours. Let's get this over with," she countered.

She moved over to her laptop and opened the screen. Seconds later, the call connected and the harsh voice of the secretary filled the room.

"Looks like you are getting what you want after all," she said snidely in greeting.

"Excuse me?" Natalia asked. Her head jerked back, as if she'd been physically slapped.

"More resources. We are mobilizing a National Guard unit to be at the embassy and surrounding areas. I'm sure you know that we are limited in what we can do without pissing off the Syrian president. Not that that's ever seemed to bother you before."

Nat rolled her eyes but schooled the rest of her facial expression. "Yes, I'm aware. Anything else would look like a possible declaration of war. Although calling for my execution sounds like it to me," Natalia replied.

"If you were the president, I'd agree, but you're not. To the Syrian president, you don't mean much. However, he just released a tweet condemning the calls for your assassination, though frankly, I don't feel like his heart is in it. I think that's just to save face. If he had supported it, we'd cut off all his resources for encouraging the assassination of a U.S. official, and he'd be fucked. Pardon my language."

"Yeah, our last meeting wasn't pleasant. He referred to me as his babysitter, and he indicated one day I wouldn't be needed," Natalia answered, and I clenched my fists. I was already considering a plot to kill the man.

"Do you think there is still the possibility of getting him to admit to his support of the radicals and the embezzlement of U.S. resources?" the secretary asked. I could feel my jaw involuntarily lower. This must have been what the secretary had referred to earlier, what she wanted Natalia to do. She wanted Natalia to play double agent to get info, but what would that do? Give grounds for the U.S. to declare war or give evidence for them to send in a Task Force Black Ops unit to assassinate the man? I knew that our leaders took out dictators all the time and put puppet governments in place. Hearing it being plotted out was way different than being sent in as the gun to do the deed.

"I don't know, honestly. He's a sexist pig, so I'm sure that I could take advantage of that, but Madam Secretary, what we are discussing here crosses so many ethical boundaries. So many accuse us of creating and destroying regimes. This would only be evidence of this," Natalia replied. I could tell just how anxious this had her. She was an ambassador, not a CIA spy. If she was caught, it would surely mean her death.

"Who gives a flying fuck what they think, Natalia? You are a U.S. citizen, and your loyalty is to your country above all else. Correct?"

Natalia nodded.

"I don't give a damn what any other country thinks of us, especially the Syrian president. You and I have a duty to protect our people, just as those who put on the uniform do. We have different duties, and unfortunately this is one of them. While they plant bullets in bodies, we plant ideas, and we share information. I am telling you, if you are able to get confirmation of what we suspect is taking place, you'd be a national hero. If the Syrian president is harboring extreme terrorism instead of denouncing it, then he's a direct threat to national security, especially if he is using our taxpayer dollars to do it." The secretary's passion couldn't be missed; in her head, this was the right thing to do. That still didn't make it any less of a nightmare to execute.

I was deeply torn by the situation that Natalia found herself in, and I by default. If I took a logical step back and removed us from the situation, I might actually think this was cool. This was comparable to the colonial founders of our country sitting in a Boston bar in secret planning the revolution. I was witnessing the beginning stages of a plot to overthrow a presidency and possibly the start of a new war.

The other part of me was scared shitless. I didn't know that I'd ever felt this scared. Not when my dad beat me as a kid, not when I was sitting in his trial, and certainly not when I served in the Army. I wasn't afraid of dying, not even when my leg bled out and my vision went dark. Now everything was different. I was terrified for the woman sitting in front of me. She was about to be thrust into a plot that could get her branded as a traitor to her country if it went south. While the secretary was in on it, I had no doubts she'd point her painted claw in Natalia's direction if this blew up in her face. The White House and the Office of the President couldn't be caught up in another scandal, not during a recession and an election year. It would hands down be worse than Watergate.

Holy fuck.

I sat down as I tried to take in the rest of their conversation.

"So you are officially asking me to use my office to spy for my country? Does the president know?" Natalia asked and released a shaky breath.

"No, I can't involve him until we have results. Yes, we are talking about treason, but there is no reward without risks," the secretary countered. "You're focusing too much on what could go wrong and not enough about what it would mean if you are successful."

Nat's back straightened, and she held her head high. "What's in it for me?"

The power dynamic suddenly flipped, and I wanted to high-five my girl. *Mine.*

"Excuse me?" The secretary's shocked words echoed through the room.

"You heard me. What's in it for me? No doubt that if all of this goes well you're going to swoop in and receive all the credit for this and be branded a hero. You'll receive medals and glory for discovering that another nation was plotting against us, and you authorized the obtaining of that information. But what do I get? I'm still the ambassador in a war-torn country and the daughter of a dead man. In fact, if you get what you want, and we cut off federal funding to the Syrian government, or worse go to war with Syria, I'm even more at risk. I have nothing securing my protection or the safety of the staff. We're stuck between terrorists and a government that may turn its back on me." She paused and swallowed hard. "I don't win in any of these scenarios, but I get to do a good thing for my country." Her sarcasm was heavy but effective.

I hadn't known her for very long, not really, but I was so fucking proud of her. I wanted to close the laptop screen, pin her down on the table, and fuck her brains out. I wanted her to know just how smart and brave she was. She was so selfless, and everything about her drove me crazy. I wanted to communicate all of that with my lips, my fingers, and my dick. I wanted to make her feel so good that she forgot all about the shitty cards she'd been dealt. I could say what I wanted about my lot in life with a dead mom, shitty father, and a missing leg—but Nat was dropped into a real life Tom Clancy novel with the very real possibility of not getting a real-life happy ending.

The pause in Nat's conversation was becoming enormous and awkward. Finally, the secretary broke the stare-off. "I may have some information on your father. It's classified, of course, blacked out in official records and all, but I can get you that, if you get what I'm asking for. I'll even get you more funding. I'll make sure the president knows just how essential you were, and you'll get more than you asked for in your report. I can promise that."

"Assuming that war doesn't break out and the embassy isn't closed because it can no longer be protected," Natalia added.

"Naturally." The words were ice cold but confident, as if there was no possibility this would backfire. Nat could do everything right and still lose her position as ambassador, the embassy closed, and those she'd spent years trying to help would be left in an even worse position.

Natalia let out a shaky breath. "I need time to consider. Between this and the hit out for me, I've got a lot going on. The fact that you're implying there is more to my father's death than you told me doesn't make me trust you any more than I did before. You lied to me and said there was nothing, and yet here you are admitting to lying."

"Oh, Natalia, grow up. It is above your clearance level, even if he was your father. There are plenty of national secrets you will never learn of. Be an adult about this. Don't let your attachment to your father cloud your judgment." She paused as if she was considering an apology, or maybe she was concocting a new bribe or blackmail.

"Let me make a suggestion, woman to woman, and not boss to a direct report. Go get laid. When everything seems like it's too much, I feel much better after a good fuck and a cigarette. You have forty-eight hours to think about my offer. Natalia, this is a career move that others could only dream of. Take this by the balls while you can. You may spend the rest of your life regretting it if you don't, especially if it's all true and the evidence exists. The National Guard unit will be there in six hours. Use that time to make the right decision and come up with a plan. They'll be at your disposal."

Natalia completely ignored the comment. "I'm bringing in some friends of mine to help me with my security issues. They were already on the way. I'm assuming you will give Tom and any other security personnel the orders to not stand in my way of anything I'm planning. If I were to even try to go through with your plan, they are a barrier," Natalia countered. Honestly, I couldn't believe how brilliant she was. She was using one situation to gain leverage in another while she thought about her options. No one backed Nat in a corner, at least not without her gaining something from the encounter.

"Of course, anything you need. Get a good lay. Tom told me about that friend of yours. Screw him, think about my offer, and then get back to me. You could get information vital to keeping our country safe. I get that's a lot to put on someone's shoulders, but you are a tough woman. None of the other ambassadors fight against me the way you do. That's how I know you've got what it takes."

With that, the call was disconnected.

What the fuck? The secretary was telling Nat to sleep with me? I mean, I hated the woman, but I certainly wasn't opposed to that suggestion. The rest of it still had me completely on edge.

"Are you okay?" I asked.

She was silent for a moment before she answered me. "Just…processing."

"Do you want to talk about it?"

"No, I need to mentally unpack this," she responded.

"Do you need anything?" I sensed the retreat of the strong woman I just witnessed standing up to her boss, one of the most powerful people in the country.

"Wine, a big freaking bottle," she said.

"So…you want to get drunk? That's the solution for a time crunch?"

"The secretary has her way, and I have mine. Alcohol makes you lose your barriers, and I need mine to figure this out. In the morning after a whole bottle…or more, I'll wake up with the answers," she shared.

"That's a weird ability, but all right, I'll bite." I walked over to the fridge and pulled out two bottles. "I have a feeling you won't be sharing yours."

"Not a chance," she said with a small smile. We popped the corks and drank straight from the bottles.

natalia

lcohol was a fascinating invention. Wait, was it an invention…or a product?

Whatever it was, it was amazing. I lost my mental blocks, and I knew somewhere in the back of my head my issues were being analyzed. I would wake up with a hangover but also an answer. The downside to losing my mental blocks was that I lost them completely, including the physical ones. When I was alone, that wasn't a problem, but for the first time in a long time, I wasn't alone.

There was a hot-as-fuck man in front of me, and somewhere in the middle of finishing our bottles, he lost his shirt. The man was sculpted, and I had to give him credit. If I lost my leg, I wouldn't be a gym rat. I'd be eating bon bons in sweatpants double my current size. Yet here he was, sexy as a real life Freyr, the Norse god of fertility.

The secretary's words bounced around in the back of my head. I had to admit, her recommendation to sleep with Isaiah didn't seem like a bad idea. In fact, the longer he and I stayed in the same room, the more I wanted it. Wanted him.

He occasionally touched my thigh as we talked, and he twirled a piece of my hair around his fingers. His soulful eyes left me feeling flush, as if their heat was transferred directly to my skin. It was as if he'd undressed me ten different times with his eyes, and I felt them each time. Like silk slipping over the skin, leaving expectant shivers in its wake.

God, I wanted this man, consequences and expectations be damned.

Who cared if I let alcohol be the deciding factor? I'd wanted to jump his bones long before I started this bottle. I had no doubts that this was not a one-time deal. Sleeping with him once would not be enough to get him out of my system. So was there really any reason to regret it? To my sloshed brain, absolutely fucking not.

I leaned forward and put my lips on his for another drunken kiss. We'd shared several since he decided to indulge me in my quest to consider the secretary's offer. Those kisses were fun, lighthearted, sweet even, but this one was different. I was different; I wanted this. There was an underlying passion that I was going to bring to the surface.

I pushed him backward with my hands on his pecs, and his head found the armrest. I leaned over top of him, my ass resting on his lap. I felt his arousal beneath me, and this time I planned to do something about it.

I ground my ass into his lap, and his chest rumbled beneath my hands as he let out a groan. He broke the kiss. "You can't do that to me. I am a strong man, but you will have me undone in no time. Don't tease, please." He sounded like he was physically in pain, like saying those words, asking for me not to tease him, was hurting him.

"What if I'm not here to tease? What if I figured out an answer already to one of the secretary's suggestions? What if I want to see if a good fuck clears my head?" I asked.

It was as if someone lit a blazing bonfire in the room right next to us. His skin became hot to the touch, and his eyes were molten pools of lava. There were no words to describe what exactly happened to them. One minute they were slightly hazy, and the next he was sober. He looked ready to devour me, and I would willingly let him.

"Then I'd have to say please continue," he said in a low, gravelly voice that had me ready to melt.

I grinded my ass against his pelvis again. Isaiah only allowed me to do that for a few seconds before he growled and flipped us in one quick move. He was on top, his chest pressed to mine, and our tongues danced and swirled. His hands roamed down my body. My nipples turned hard, and my underwear became wet. His fingers found the edge of my waistband and teased the skin there. I let out a small whine.

If he was anyone else, I'd have been embarrassed that he heard me whine. Isaiah seemed to like the sound, because he rewarded me by moving his lips to my neck and sticking his fingers lower into the waistband of my pants. When his finger entered me, I cried out. I was ready to shred my clothes off my body with my nails, I was so desperate for more of his touch.

As if sensing what I wanted, he used his other hand to unbutton my pants and then slide them down my hips, giving him more room to work. I grabbed the bottom hem of my shirt and pulled it up and over my head and then tossed it to the floor. Isaiah leaned forward and licked the skin on my chest, just above the edge of my bra. While it felt sensual, I was done with the teasing.

"I need you, now," I said breathlessly.

I heard him groan, and then I felt his hand leave me as he moved to unbuckle and kick out of his pants.

"Fuck, I don't have a condom with me. There's a few in my bag… back in the guest house," he said, almost dousing the flaming inferno of need that had taken over.

"I'm on birth control," I told him.

His only response was to spit on his hand and coat his dick. It was so big that I knew this was going to hurt before it felt good. It had been a long time since I had gotten laid. After a few pumps into his hand, he lined up with my entrance and slowly pushed his way in.

I winced once, and he stopped moving. "Are you okay?" he asked. He sounded slightly panicked. It felt like such a vulnerable moment between us that I smiled.

"I will be. Just start out slow," I answered.

He leaned forward and put his lips on mine, and very slowly I felt his lower body shift. He slowly pushed further into me and waited a moment. Then he slowly pulled out and then re-entered.

It was starting to feel better, so I shifted my pelvis to get a better angle, and I let out the softest of moans. Isaiah took that for the positive reinforcement it was and slowly began to pick up his pace. His thumb landed on my clit, rubbing it just the right way to create the best friction.

In no time, he thrusted with no restraint, and I latched onto his arms with my nails, riding the wave of pleasure that Isaiah brought me. The building pressure was too much; I arched my back as stars erupted behind my eyes and my nerve endings lit up with pleasure. I let out a mewl that I had no idea was even possible for me to make. No one had ever brought me to this height of pleasure or done so with such skill.

A few thrusts later and Isaiah was roaring his release. When he finally stopped, I was still floating out on cloud nine, waiting to catch up with my body. I had no doubt that I'd be sore tomorrow. It had been a long time since I had a sexual partner. Every bit of pain would be worth it.

"I think I like the secretary's suggestion," Isaiah said as he looked into my eyes. There was a lighthearted smirk plastered on his face. *I think I like you.*

"Me too," I replied with a smile.

He pulled out of me and picked me up off the couch. "Let's go to bed. We can worry about everything else that needs to be done tomorrow, once we are sober."

"Yes, let's let my drunk mind figure out the rest." I giggled. Then he playfully smacked my ass as he fireman-carried me up the stairs.

CHAPTER SIXTEEN

natalia

It was amazing what booze and six hours of sleep could do for me. I woke up knowing exactly what I needed to do. For now, it was the path of least resistance. It certainly wasn't without risk. In fact, most of the plan was riddled with unnecessary risks. I was taking a huge one by trusting the secretary at all. While she was my boss and she had ethical boundaries she had to maintain within her position, I didn't trust her to remain within those boundaries completely. She was like an octopus who couldn't escape her tank completely but could get her tentacles loose and wiggle them around for all to see. She was doing what she could to make sure I saw her waving them. Whether that was a good or bad thing was up to how I interpreted it.

I would agree to her plan, but she was going to have to do it my way or it wouldn't happen at all. I was the one taking all the risk. I was putting my career and my life on the line. There was no doubt that if I was caught in a failed act of espionage, the Syrian president would have me killed or my own government would arrest me. Whoever could get to me first. The worst part was I was involving Isaiah and his friends in this. I'd give him and them the chance to bow out, to completely pretend they had no knowledge of this and go home. Hell, I wouldn't blame them a bit. If it weren't my skin in the game, I might do the same.

However, if I was successful, I'd be rewarded, according to the secretary, and I'd finally figure out who killed my father. Again, that was assuming that the secretary was being honest with the carrot she dangled in front of me. It was cruel, but it was effective motivation, and we both knew it. I had to wonder just how highly classified that information was. It was the first I was hearing about it, and it was only offered so she could prove she was going to bend the rules for me. She'd take a risk and leak classified information if I gave her an equal trade.

I despised the woman most days, but there was no denying that she was highly intelligent and always a step ahead of me, even when I thought I was winning.

Isaiah softly snored beside me, and it pulled me from my thoughts about the secretary. I had a feeling that he would not like that I was going to go through with this plan, but I also knew that he would do his best to help me. He'd only been here for two days, and I had only met him briefly years ago, but I could tell without a shadow of a doubt that I could trust him. I was not some itch that he scratched. I could see it in the way he looked in my eyes last night, even through our drunken haze. Whatever this was between us, it was the real deal. He'd keep me safe, just like he and his friends had protected my father. I just had to hope that if I was successful, the information I gathered wouldn't send a whole bunch of men like him into war.

It was funny how fate had cruel tricks and twists. The sight of Isaiah should have brought me so much pain, and yet he brought me strength and joy. I'd forever link him in my mind with my father, but that didn't feel like such a bad thing. It helped keep my father's memory alive.

He shifted. "Good morning."

"Good morning," I echoed and then stretched my legs and back.

"How are you feeling?"

I sighed. "Hungover, but good. I know what I'm going to do."

"I think I know it, too. If the situation was reversed, it would be the same choice I would make," he said with a small sigh of defeat.

I rolled onto my side to look him in the eyes. "So you won't fight me on it?"

He gently shook his head, and his eyes roamed my face. "Nope, I understand exactly what's at risk and why you want to go through with this. I don't like it, but I can't tell you what to do. All I can do is make sure that you are safe and aren't caught. My friends and I will be here to help you every step of the way," he promised.

I felt myself smile. God, he was too freaking good to be true. I pinched myself, and Isaiah watched. "No, you aren't dreaming." His wink was playful and a reminder of the dirty deeds we did last night.

"Thank God for that. Speaking of your friends, will they be here soon?" I asked.

He looked at his watch. "I think their flight is about two hours from landing. At least, that's what they said at their last check-in. What do you say we get up and get ready for their arrival?"

"Okay," I agreed and gave him a brief kiss before we got dressed and left the comfort of my room. It was the same room my father once shared with my mother. It hadn't felt like anything other than a room full of memories until now. Now it felt full of hope.

We moved Isaiah's things from the guest house into mine. He made us both to-go cups of coffee, and then we met up with Tom. The National Guard unit had already arrived and was waiting for orders. They were two hundred men strong, and the sheer size of that number felt overwhelming but at the same time comforting. With two hundred men in addition to my security staff, Isaiah, and now his friends, we had a shot at actually keeping the location secure.

Again I thought about the secretary. Sure, I wanted to throat punch her, but she was an opportunist nonetheless. A direct death threat with a hundred comments prior to the deletion of the tweet was enough for the military to respond in kind, beefing up embassy security. These weren't wartime numbers, but it was enough to fill the security holes here and defend against any small terrorism groups that took a shot at me. The groups had a hard time organizing in long numbers and working with other groups. There was always a power grab, which meant the attacks we had in the past were usually organized by groups of twenty-five or less.

If I were to take a page out of the secretary's book, I'd be using this opportunity to score a meeting with the Syrian president, Faris. I could ask for his reassurances that he doesn't condone this behavior and see what information he could provide regarding these small hostile militias. If he provided information, great. If not, then I knew he was aiding them. There was no way that he didn't have files on them the size of novels. He wasn't a stupid man.

I may have drifted in and out of Isaiah and Tom's conversation, but I was fully invested in the end result. We were going to meet the plane at the runway of the airport and then give the crew an escort back to the embassy. Tom didn't like that we were leaving the embassy, but he didn't try to stop us. There was a sizable security team now and plenty of soldiers to help escort us to the airport.

He hustled out of the security office, ready to give the orders. The plane was thirty minutes out, and they would be in danger if they didn't make a quick entrance and exit. I spent ten minutes on Twitter as I was getting ready for the day and saw the uptick in anti-American sentiment being spewed by some of the more influential Syrian citizens and those with connections to President Faris.

"This is the only time we are leaving the embassy until things de-escalate. Things are only going to get worse before they get better." Tom's order when he returned sounded more like a complaint. He moved to the other side of the office to make some other sort of preparation.

"Are you nervous?" Isaiah asked me after he took a sip from his coffee cup. I'd kill to be that cup right now, with his hands wrapped around me and his lips on my skin. *Get your mind out of the gutter, Natalia. You have more important things to focus on!*

"You'll have to be more specific. To meet your friends or to leave the compound while there is a hit out on me?" I asked.

"Both," he said with that charming smile of his. He was using it to distract me, and it almost worked. But I could sense the same nerves from him, so it only worked so much.

I nodded. "Yes to both."

"Well, don't be. Tom, the soldiers, and I will make sure you are safe. The embassy will be fine, and my friends are going to love you," he said. Then he leaned down and gave me a quick kiss on my forehead. An overwhelming feeling of contentment washed over me.

"Thanks," I said and grabbed his free hand.

"Ambassador, we're ready for you," Tom called out to me.

But was I ready for this?

natalia

Isaiah and I walked hand and hand over to him. "You'll want to put this on. It will make you blend in with the rest of us. Pull your hair back, and tuck it into either the helmet or the uniform," Tom said, handing me a set of multi cams.

I did what I was told as Isaiah slipped into a set as well. A set of armor plates were placed over my shoulders to rest in front of my stomach and my back.

"Holy fuck," he said as I was tucking my ponytail into the back of the uniform.

"What?" I felt myself blanch.

"This is honestly a fantasy of mine. A hot girl in uniform about to go put herself in danger. I'm saving this for my mental spank bank." He winked as he took a quick photo of me on his phone.

I groaned in annoyance. "I'm glad to be of service." I took the weapon that Tom held out for me. Isaiah bent forward and tied the laces on the boots that were a size too large for me.

"Perfect, now you'll blend in. No one will know it's you from a distance. They'll assume you are still back at the embassy. Let's go. The plane is touching down in ten," Tom said, throwing around more orders.

Honestly, Tom wasn't a bad man. Sure, we had a few disagreements, but that was just because he took his job seriously, and protecting me was important to him. I didn't always make it easy when I was focused on trying to help others. I knew now just how much risk I had taken in doing that. Now I was about to take an even greater risk and expose the Syrian government.

We loaded up into the five vehicles. Three were to transport ourselves and Isaiah's friends, and the other two were to lead and pull rear of our little convoy. The ride to the airport was nerve wracking. Occasionally someone pointed to our convoy as we made our way through the city that sat between the embassy and the airport.

No one fired at the vehicles, which was a relief. Although I could see the curiosity on the faces of those nearby. They were trying to figure out what we were doing there. It wasn't a normal thing, only done on rare occasions, such as the arrival of another government official.

When we made our way to the airport, the environment was completely different. The curiosity from those in the city had changed to hostility. There were men with guns outside the airport fence chanting, "Death to America." It gave me chills every time I heard that, no matter how many times I had been forced to hear it over the years.

The airplane was trying to land, but those shouting outside of the gates took turns shooting at the plane, trying to either damage it or scare it away.

"Mother fuckers," Isaiah groaned, and his hands tightened on his weapon.

Our vehicles sped up to the gates, nearly running over several chanting men. "Leave or you will be shot," Tom ordered over the speaker of the vehicle. Then a translator repeated the order in Arabic.

The men chanted angrily again, but this time toward our vehicle. One of the security personnel shot at him—purposefully just missing the man. The group scattered, and it was like complete and total chaos. They yelled and threw rocks at our vehicles. I jumped when one smashed against the window next to Isaiah. When the group finally reassembled, they were on the other side of the airport, a safe enough distance as long as they weren't shooting weapons at us.

The plane took advantage of the distraction and lack of small flying bits of metal, landing on the dirt runway. Several of the National Guard soldiers left their vehicles and ran to the plane door as it lowered. They ushered the occupants off and led them over to our vehicles. Isaiah's friends had duffel bags slung over their shoulders, while the three women pulled two rolling suitcases each. The men were bogged down with black hard cases that could hold weapons or expensive computer equipment. They exchanged a few words, and then soldiers, along with a few more, went back to the plane to grab boxes.

More supplies. Why wasn't I surprised or any less impressed than the first time they were promised?

When his friends made it to the convoy, Isaiah stepped out of the vehicle. He directed me to stay put. "We don't need you exposed. We can do proper introductions back at the embassy," he reasoned.

He one by one hugged his friends and then ushered them to the three center vehicles. Two men who looked vaguely familiar climbed into ours.

"Natalia, this is Garcia and Mendez," Isaiah said, introducing me to the first of his friends.

"Good to meet you again, Ambassador," Garcia said, extending his hand.

"Same here, glad to see you again," Mendez added along with his hand.

"The pleasure is all mine. Welcome back to Syria," I said with a smile after shaking their hands. I could imagine they had a million other places they'd rather be, but there they were, helping their buddy. It told me a lot about their character.

The two men were very good looking. As their names suggested, they were both Hispanic or Latino. They had classically handsome good looks, and I could see that they had large, muscular arms, at least the parts that I could see under the rolled-up sleeves.

"I'd say it's good to be back, but I never imagined that I'd find myself back here," Mendez replied with a forced smile that showed just how uncomfortable he was being back in the country.

I felt a pang of sympathy for him. For all of them, really.

"I can only imagine. I can't promise it's going to be good times and good vibes, either. We've had some recent developments that are pretty unsettling. We can explain more once we get back to the embassy," I said.

Garcia sighed. "I wouldn't expect anything less. It's not a real mission unless it goes off the rails somehow." Then his head turned so he was speaking to Yates. "Just a heads-up, Wells, Strong, and Jones plan on getting retribution."

Isaiah coughed as if the statement caught him off guard. "Of course they are. I wouldn't expect anything less from those little shits." He rolled his eyes, which told me that whatever they were referring to didn't worry him too much.

The ride back to the embassy was relatively smooth. There was more chanting, and some people threw rocks at the vehicles, but we made it back to the compound relatively unscathed.

I was nervous to step out of the vehicle and meet the rest of Isaiah's friends for the first time, but I had to have faith that they'd like me. They huddled in a semi-circle around me after exiting the vehicles. "Everyone, I'd like to introduce to you Ambassador Natalia Ali," Isaiah said, introducing me. "You've already met Garcia and Mendez. This is Wells and his wife Christine. She's the one who lent me her private jet and footed the bill for the supplies. This is Jones and his girlfriend Jasmine, Strong and Abby, and last but not least is Guy. He's our tech expert, and I haven't found anything that he can't hack into."

"It's nice to meet you all," I said and shook everyone's hand. "Christine, thank you so much for everything you provided for us. I'm still in shock by your generosity." I was also in shock at her beauty. Her dark, wavy hair cascaded over her shoulders. She was dressed cute but comfortably in a ribbed sweater and jeans, which probably felt more than a little warm now. Don't get me started on the men. They looked older, more mature, and even more delectable. I felt guilty for thinking that about Isaiah's friends, but facts were facts.

"The pleasure is all mine. What good is all that money if you don't use it to help others? I have a foundation to help women and children who are the victims of abuse, but I'm always looking at ways to help beyond that." It was a good thing that she was married to Wells, because I'd be no competition for her if she wanted Isaiah. The other women in the group were just as gorgeous. I felt inadequate standing among them, especially in an oversize Army uniform and a helmet and boots that were a size too big.

"We have plenty of women and children who fit the bill for that. The best way to help them is to get them out of their abusive situations and into other countries. We don't have time to talk shop now, but maybe later?" I suggested.

"Oh, absolutely," Christine answered with a grin. It was clear to say she meant every word. I was sometimes sensitive to the vibes others gave off, and hers felt pure. She loved helping others. I had a whole slew of people she could help.

"Why don't I show you the guest house you'll all be staying in, and then we can talk about recent developments?"

Everyone chorused their agreements, and I led them back to the guest house. Tom had wandered off to take care of the vehicles and get everyone back to their stations. Apparently, there was a lot of work that had to be done to get the National Guard unit situated for a more long-term stay. There wasn't enough lodging so they had to send up heavy-duty tents and temporary structures. I wished I could house them all inside the embassy main building somewhere, but the building wasn't very large in the first place.

The couples called dibs on three of the four bedrooms, and the single guys decided to rotate out between the couch and the last spare room. They took a few minutes to get situated, make coffee, grab some snacks, and change into comfortable clothes before we all crowded into the living room. The women took up the couch while the guys perched on the armrests or joined me on the floor.

Ten eager faces were looking at me expectantly, and I couldn't keep them waiting any longer without being rude. I was sure that they wanted to get this out of the way so they could rest and regroup. "So

Isaiah told me he showed you guys my interview. So much has happened since then. Now that the supply situation isn't nearly as desperate, we've had other problems arise." I took a deep breath and waded in the deep end. Isaiah trusted them with his life, and I trusted him. I had to hope they wouldn't let me down. "To make a long story short, my boss, the secretary of state, is furious that I did it, along with the president. I've been working on community outreach since I took this job so that I could help those in need, even those who aren't U.S. citizens. The radical groups don't like my help or interference, and it's gotten to the point when they've put a hit out on me. They are calling for my assassination."

The group collectively gasped. If only that was the worst part. "No, you don't understand, that's only the tip of the iceberg." I explained to them what the secretary had asked of me and what she was holding over me to do her dirty work.

"Ambassador, I'm so sorry to hear about your father. What you are doing is amazing. You remind me so much of me. You can't stop what you're doing because of this. If you do, then those radicals win; they are getting what they want. You can't let this slow down or stop your open houses," Christine pushed.

"Please, just call me Natalia. And I'm not stopping entirely, just re-evaluating to find safer ways. Not to mention I'm going to have to shift my priorities, at least for a little while. I need to figure out the best way to get a confession or evidence that Faris, the Syrian president, is in league with—if not organizing directly—the local hostile groups and inciting and supporting terrorism against his own people. There's been chatter that another large scale terrorism plot is being planned right here within our borders, and I need to figure out what it is so we can prevent it. If I'm successful, then I'll still need to come up with a plan for continuing to operate the embassy and open houses in an active war zone." I was breathless from explaining exactly what I faced, and when I explained it out loud, it felt more overwhelming.

"So if you succeed, the U.S. could withdraw its aid to the country, and either country could declare war on each other for espionage or any other number of reasons. If you don't give it a shot, then you remain underfunded and at risk of the radicals attempting to carry out the assassination plot, and the Syrian government uses U.S. funds to secretly support terrorism?" Guy asked.

I nodded.

"And if you do try and fail…"

"Then any plans I've made won't matter anyways. I'll be in a U.S. prison cell for trying to conduct espionage and abusing my position. Or…I'll be dead." It was hard to deliver the words with a flat tone, but I didn't want to show just how scared I was.

"Talk about a rock and a hard place," Strong mumbled. The muscles in the heavily tattooed man were bulging as he crossed his arms in front of him.

"I can't win here, so I have to figure out exactly what I can live with. My father, if he was here, would remind me of the obligations of the office I hold. I have to look out for America first and then figure out the rest later."

The room was silent for a moment. Most of them understood what type of sacrifice that could end up being, but it was Jasmine that broke the silence. "Then let's do that. Do you have a plan for exposing this bastard?"

I shook my head. Nothing concrete, anyways. "No. He's a peculiar man and doesn't invite many into his inner circle. He does host a monthly dinner. It's the only time that I'm aware of when he invites others into his home. Otherwise he conducts all his business by phone and video. Occasionally he hosts wealthy individuals from the area or representatives from foreign governments to see if he can schmooze them for money or trading agreements or insider information. If I could somehow get an invite, that would be the best opportunity to snoop through anything he might be hiding."

"What about you?" Garcia said as he raised an eyebrow at Guy. "Could you hack the president's computer?"

Guy nodded. "Most likely, given enough time—but there are a couple of problems with that."

"Your contract," Mendez commented.

"Yes, my contract. I accepted a contractor job for the government, and there is a list of things I can't do while under that contract. Hacking into the computer of a foreign government is on that list, unless I have specific orders from my superiors to do so."

"And the other problem?" Isaiah asked.

"That right now you have the complete element of surprise. If I hack his computer and he has some kind of security system that alerts him to a breach, you lose that entirely. He likely becomes a recluse, might force him to push up some timelines, and the situation could become more volatile."

"So back to the ambassador's plan. It might work, but it doesn't guarantee that he's going to share anything useful or even give you the opportunity to snoop. If you are going to go full double agent, maybe you should leave some bugs behind. Gives you a greater window of collecting useful information," Strong suggested.

"Assuming he doesn't have a full sweep of his home done each time he has visitors," Wells countered.

I grimaced. "The idea of leaving any trace that someone is onto him worries me. He's eccentric, and I wouldn't be surprised if that was his cover for paranoia. There is a lot at stake here—including my life. Faris is practically looking for an excuse to start shit. He wants me to leave his people alone. He's just not as openly critical. If he really is in league with the localized terror groups, supporting them and organizing them, then he's likely just waiting for me to fuck something up," I countered. It could be an alternative reason for the bounty placed out on me, with the idea to freak me out so badly that I'd panic and make a big mistake.

"What if we add more players into the mix? Are you friends with other ambassadors to other nations?" Abby asked. She was the FBI agent, right?

I nodded. "Yes, we all talk. It helps us keep a handle on the environment around us and share security threats. I'm sure Tom, my head of security here, has already notified their security forces."

Abby looked thoughtfully at me. "The British and the French aren't too friendly with President Faris, either. I've been doing some research on the area. He's made some comments lately that maybe he might want the opportunity to walk back. What if we can get their ambassadors an invitation to this dinner, too? They can provide a distraction for you to slip away, but also they are present to become suspects should he become aware that someone's looking into him. Who knows? They might have their own chatter regarding security threats from the region and be looking for their own intelligence."

"How do we get all of us invited to dinner at the same time without bringing them into the loop? There's no way I can really tell them my intentions, what I'm looking into. That elevates the risk and gives them more leverage in negotiating deals with me." I sighed in defeat. "I'm already taking a huge leap of faith by bringing you all in on this. We could all get in very deep shit. When you start bringing in other governments, well, then shit really gets complicated."

"We need a cover, a real reason for the dinner. Something that would interest all the parties, like lifting trading bans. If we lift bans on some of the products we import from Syria, that makes a very lucrative deal, one that the other countries might want to prevent or, even better, get in on. What if we get the secretary to reach out to the other countries to see if they are willing to lift bans on certain products? If President Faris thinks there is a shred of hope of increasing his exports, think of how much he could exploit his people to increase his profits? It would be a deal he couldn't afford to refuse," Isaiah elaborated.

"That actually has really good potential. I've heard the man has an ego the size of Texas. If he believes that the countries are willing to put aside differences for small concessions, then that might be the perfect in," Abby said.

I agreed. With a solid reason to get everyone together, money, we might just be able to get everyone into the mansion. It was set. "I'll make a call to the secretary and see if we can make that work," I offered. It really was the best shot at making sure I made it out unscathed, whether I was successful in getting information or not. It was like the game where you hid a ball under the three cups, shifted them around, and then tried to find the ball. I just had to hope that he and his staff wouldn't know we were playing a game and that they wouldn't be watching too closely.

"Now, are you ready to talk about what other needs we might be able to assist with? Hopefully nothing else espionage related?" Christine asked with a teasing smile.

"Gladly." My own grin broke free. It was a much better subject change. For once, I didn't feel alone in this. Fuck the secretary. Doing that interview was the best decision I had made in a long time.

isaiah

It took hours to catch my friends up on the multiple issues that Natalia faced between Nat's deceased father, the strong likelihood of foul play, the secretary's special assignment, and the issues facing the embassy. After all of that, Christine wanted to talk about what could be done to help Nat with the open houses she ran. The open houses served the demographics Christine aimed to help back in the States, women and children who were being abused.

There was a lot of bickering about unnecessary risk. There was no easy way to help those who needed the open houses without opening ourselves up to risk. We were forced to evaluate priorities, and unfortunately investigating Faris, the Syrian president, had to come first. This frustrated Natalia and Christine to no end, but they were outvoted. Security and laying under the radar had to take priority.

The idea of Nat walking into the home of a possible enemy, searching for his secrets, was enough to throw me through a tailspin. Thanks to Abby, I knew exactly the power a woman could have when she was highly trained and hot. Nat was very hot, and with Abby, a trained FBI agent, she was going to get a crash course in espionage and possibly the art of discretely seducing. The plan wasn't for Nat to straight up seduce the guy, but it wasn't completely out of the picture, either. I wasn't a fan, but if it was a desperate attempt to keep her out of trouble, then I'd have no choice but to support it.

I wanted to go into the house with her, but that was vetoed. "Absolutely not. He won't let his guard down around an outsider. He knows the ambassador, and it will be easier for her to sneak away by herself." Abby's reasoning made sense, even if it sucked for me.

We discussed it until we were blue in the face, and I lost. Divide and conquer seemed to be the motto of the day as we all broke up into groups. Natalia gave another tour, and we all found areas we could help. Garcia, Mendez, and Guy were upgrading security systems, placing cameras, and working with Tom to identify any other weaknesses.

Wells, Jones, and Strong helped Christine and Jasmine with fixing the rundown areas of the embassy, although I didn't see the point. Call me a pessimist, or call me a historian, but most countries would track down and kill spies if they could. Natalia wouldn't be able to remain here after she got the information the secretary wanted. Part of her had to know that, so any work we did was really benefiting whoever took over the role of ambassador next. Assuming we didn't declare war and close the embassy entirely. If we did, the compound would get taken over by the local groups anyways. But I digressed. If they wanted to spend the day painting, or whatever the hell they decided on, that was their wasted time.

Instead, I was focused on what I'd consider the important mission: figuring out what the fuck was going on so that I could convince Natalia to leave this place.Abby, Natalia, and I combed through Natalia's office, skimming through all the information we could find on President Faris.

So far, we'd only come across the blatantly obvious—Faris wasn't really an elected official; he took over from his father. He called himself a president, but he was definitely a dictator. The elections held every term were just a sham, and most of his political opponents, when they dared to face him, ended up dead.

President Faris' wife died recently—it was likely she was murdered. She didn't seem like the sickly type. His children were adults, with the oldest male being groomed for his future role to fill his father's place. They lived in the presidential mansion, which was just him flaunting his power over his people.

The more we dug, the more I hated the guy. He wasn't directly related to terrorism cells from what Abby could see in her FBI database. While she was no longer a full-time agent, she still worked closely with Boss to help the agency when she could, meaning she kept her clearance and resources.

While Faris might not have known direct links to terror groups, it didn't rule out the possibility. There was still a lot the intelligence teams didn't know. One thing was certain: President Faris did nothing to stop the local groups from inflicting fear. The more frightening they were, the less power the rebels had and the more control he and his sham of a government held. After all, the rebellion started as a call to remove him from power. He benefited from the chaos the smaller groups created.

"I'm pretty sure this asshole killed his wife," Abby announced. Her eyebrows were pinched together in disgust as she stared at the computer screen. It was the same conclusion I already came to, but it was just a hunch. Did Abby find concrete evidence?

"Why do you say that?" Nat asked.

"Look at this news clip," Abby said as she turned the computer screen our way.

A beautiful woman wearing clothes just as beautiful as she was got out of the passenger side of a Ferrari. She was approached by several lower-class women. Their clothing was smudged with dirt at the bottom hems, and they seemed tired, thin, and barely hanging on. They placed their hands over their hearts as they spoke to her. Faris' wife was not what I expected in the slightest—she nodded her head, pulled jewelry off her body, and handed it to them. They bowed to her with their hands over their hearts, with grateful expressions on their faces, then they quickly disappeared into the streets. Men who looked like a security detail surrounded Faris' wife before they ushered her into a market.

"This was broadcast all over the news at the time, and shortly after that, the Syrian president announced the death of his wife. He reported she had been ill for some time, but she doesn't look ill to me," Abby commented.

"She looks like the picture of health and youth," Nat said as she shook her head at the computer.

Dread filled my gut. The man had no decency or sympathy for his own people, let alone his wife. To have her killed for helping those less fortunate, there was a special place in Hell for him. I'd like to see him head there with a one-way ticket, but I knew me and my friends couldn't be the ones to send him there. We'd plunge the country into a war, and even our long list of good deeds wouldn't save us from the wrath of our own government.

My eyes met Nat's. "Yeah, that's definitely suspicious," I commented. "I'm liking this plan less and less." I was sure she could see my hesitancy with the plan, but she only strengthened her resolve.

"I already knew the man was responsible for many deaths. This changes nothing. It just makes me want to do this more. He has no business being president," she declared.

Abby jumped in. "All right then—pull your strings and get yourself and the other ambassadors invited to his home, and I'll teach you everything you need to know to get in, sneak around, and get out safely."

Natalia called the secretary to let her know that she'd do what she could to spy on President Faris and listed her conditions. The secretary agreed without any hesitation, almost sounding surprised that Nat was agreeing. Nat requested authorization to negotiate the lifting of an embargo against Syria, mainly the one on oil exports.

"You realize that one's going to be hard to swing, right?" Her tone didn't rule out the possibility, but it hinted at the difficulty the secretary would have in getting that authorization.

"Yes, I know. You'll have to go to the UN for clearance, but it gives you the perfect opportunity to address both Britain and France, because I want to get them all in the same room and talking."

"Are you telling me that you are going to use these discussions as an incentive and distraction to search President Faris' home?" the secretary asked. Her eyebrow was raised, but her face didn't appear concerned. If I wasn't mistaken, she almost appeared impressed.

Natalia nodded. "That's the plan. I need a way to get into his home. What better way to do that than to hint that I'm interested in possibly having an embargo or two lifted? Having ambassadors from other UN nations in attendance only makes it seem more legit and will hopefully lower his guard. Meanwhile, when he's privately discussing terms with them, I'm searching his house hoping to find something we can use."

The secretary played with a pen in front of her, staring at it long and hard, like it was the secret to world peace—or it held all of President Faris' secrets. If only it was that easy.

"I'll see what I can work out. We might not be able to get a full embargo lift, but maybe a limited one under the guise of a staged fuel shortage. Possibly a temporary thirty-day lift. Let me take this to representatives of the UN. If I do, there may be more countries interested than just Britain and France. Will more ambassadors in attendance be a problem?"

Abby stood behind the computer out of the secretary's view. She shook her head and mouthed, "Not a problem."

Nat repeated the same, and the secretary ended the call to work out whatever she needed to. She promised to call back once the plan was set in motion. I just hoped that our plan wouldn't unravel before we could even get started.

CHAPTER NINETEEN

isaiah

Three days later, the secretary called back. She secured permission from the UN for limited discussions on a temporary pause on the embargo for oil. There would be all kinds of terms and stipulations, to be drafted and sent to Nat's email, but the mission was given a green light.

Of course, many of the other countries wanted to be present for the discussions, so seven or eight ambassadors wanted to be present, regardless of if their countries were negotiating a deal or not. Even as joining members of the UN, they were untrusting of each other.

The kicker—these discussions were to take place within a week or there would be no discussions authorized. Abby assured Natalia that would be enough time to learn the basics of espionage and the getaway. Guy wanted time to teach Nat how to use the gadgets he was going to give her. He and Abby went back and forth on the gear she would need. Nat tried to keep up with the conversation but quickly gave up.

I could only imagine what Natalia was feeling. I tried to put myself in her shoes, and I didn't like what I felt. I wanted to steal her away from here and take her where I could keep her all to myself, but I couldn't be selfish. Instead, I'd have to settle for playing spies by day and playing with her at night.

I remembered the feel of her body squirming under mine as the pleasure was too much and she lost control. The way her toes curled against my calves as she rode the waves of an earth-shattering orgasm. The feel of her fingernails scratching my shoulder blades as she called out my name. I wanted an encore every night. I wasn't sure how I ever could have thought she might just be an itch to scratch. Natalia Alia was the real fucking deal, and I was going to do what I could to hold onto her for however long I had.

My phone vibrated in my pocket, pulling me from pleasant thoughts that were getting me dangerously close to boner territory. When I saw who was calling, I wished I hadn't bothered to look. My semi deflated like a sad circus balloon.

On my flight to Syria, I swore I wouldn't answer any more calls, but my conversations with Nat had me second guessing that choice. She'd give anything to have a conversation with her dad, and if she knew I was actively avoiding mine, it might upset her. The man was lucky that I found a woman who I wanted to stay in the good graces of.

"Hello?" I answered, pretending I didn't know who was on the other end.

There was a second of hesitation. "Isaiah?"

"Yes? Who is this?"

Another second of uncertainty. "It's your father… Sorry, I didn't expect you to answer. You've been ignoring my calls for two years. I've just been planning out voicemails, not actual calls," he replied.

"Ah yes, two years since the last time I asked you not to call me. I see you changed your number and kept trying," I retorted. I sounded like a dick, but he deserved it, honestly. All of the misery he put me through as a child, all the lives he'd destroyed. He deserved a lot more than prison time and then some harsh words from the son he had fun making but did little to raise.

I felt Natalia watching me, despite the rapid-fire conversation between Abby and Guy, who were arguing the pros and cons of a certain type of listening device. They were right next to her, and their voices certainly carried louder than a whisper. Even with that as a distraction, her eyes were glued to me, and I could tell she was trying to read my lips.

I wished I'd gotten up and left the room before answering the call. I was sure she'd ask me about the call later, and I'd feel like an asshole explaining that I couldn't stand my father when she'd do anything to have hers back. I didn't want to see the pain that explanation might bring her. I never should have taken the fucking call.

My father's voice came through quietly, his tone melancholic. "Look, son, I know saying I'm sorry won't ever be good enough… I'd love your forgiveness, but I won't expect it. But there is something you need to hear from me and not your aunt."

What the hell had he gotten himself into now? Was he going back to prison and wanted me to know before I got a call from his crying sister? Regret tugged deep in my gut. Whose life had he destroyed now?

"Out with it, then," I barked.

He paused for so long I wasn't sure if he was still on the other end of the call. "Well, there's no easy way to say this… I'm dying. It's cancer, and it's inoperable."

Guilt twisted a knife in my gut for the assumptions I'd just made. The news caught me like someone hitting me in the back of the head with a board and a rusty nail. The wind involuntarily left my lungs, and I struggled to regain it. I wasn't sure exactly where these feelings came from. How many times had I told myself I wouldn't care if he fell off the face of the planet? Yet here he was, about to do just that—and it didn't feel how I had imagined it would, not at all.

He continued to talk, giving me time to recover. "Don't feel sorry for me. I know that this is karma catching up to me, and I've come to terms with it. The only thing I haven't come to terms with is leaving this earth without having a man-to-man conversation with you."

I sat down on the couch on the other side of Natalia's office. Natalia, Guy, and Abby were all staring at me. I simply shook my head and turned my back to them so that they couldn't read my face. I wished they'd leave the room.

"Are you still there, Isaiah?" my father asked.

"Yeah, I'm still here," I answered, letting out a shaky breath.

"It's a lot to take in, huh?"

"Yeah, especially because I told myself that I wouldn't care if this ever happened," I said, not sparing his feelings. He wanted a man-to-man conversation; that meant brutal honesty.

"I can't say I'm surprised. I've done a lot of wrong in my life, and you might have suffered the most. I laid my hands on you, I said vicious things to you when I wasn't myself, and I did unspeakable things." He couldn't even admit that he was responsible for my mother's death. "I did things to others that brought me shame, which I'm sure you felt, too. I want to say I'm sorry, and I want you to know that I've done something with my life since I got out of the slammer. I didn't want to go to the great abyss knowing that you thought I never turned my life around. I stayed clean. I started helping others, and I got an honest-to-God job. Not selling drugs, not pimping out women. It's a legitimate job. I pay my taxes just like everyone else."

I felt a pang of something that I couldn't quite comprehend. I wasn't sure if I was proud or relieved or angry. Was I proud that he finally began to right his ways, relieved that maybe he was redeemable, or angry that he wasn't this way to begin with? Or was it that he put me through thirty years of shit before finally figuring out how to be a normal person?

"I'm happy for you," I replied. The words were true enough, I was glad he was finally getting his act together, but that happiness was tarnished by so many other thoughts and emotions. Things that would take me years in therapy to sort through, long after he was gone. The doctor was going to have a fucking field day.

"Thank you, son. I wish I had done it much sooner, but I'll answer to my maker soon enough. I'm putting together my will, and I'm leaving you everything I have. It's not much, but it's something, and I want you to have it." I let out another involuntary breath. I didn't think the man had two nickels to rub together. How did he have anything to leave to me? "It's not millions of dollars, but it's enough to bury me and then some change. There's a house, it's not very grand, and it's got a mortgage, but it's decent. You could sell it or move in. I don't really care. I've got two life insurance policies that would help you pay it off if you want to keep it."

He was throwing a lot at me. He was giving me a house? A whole fucking house. And his life insurance money. How did he fix his life enough to be able to obtain any of that? The statistics about former felons were unforgiving, and I expected no different for him.

"Your aunt isn't doing well, and I was hopeful that maybe you could make the arrangements for me, whenever my time comes. You won't have to pay for a single thing, but I'd like to have some family there for me," he said, his voice hitched at the end. I could hear him fighting back the tears of a lonely old man. I struggled to hold back a sob of my own. I was not a crier, but damn him. He made me cry as a kid, and now he was going to make me cry as a grown man, for different reasons.

Before I had much time to think it through, I answered, "Yeah, I can do that. Do me a favor and spell out your wishes, okay? I'm not good at this sort of thing. I don't know you well, and I don't know what you'd want. I'm used to taking orders—make it simple for me."

"I will, son. Thank you." I heard a sob of relief on his end of the line. The sound nearly choked me. He must have wanted so badly to make sure that he had the opportunity to have this discussion before the cancer took him. Now he'd done it, what was left for him?

I knew that he wanted to see me. Wanted the chance to reconnect. Did I want that? If you asked me thirty minutes ago, I would have told you there was a snowball's chance in hell, and I had a better shot of regrowing my leg like a starfish. But now? He somehow managed to scrape his life together into something somewhat meaningful. All without my watchful eye—meaning he did it because he wanted to, not to impress me. So somewhere, somehow that had to count for something. The longer I spent on the phone with him, the more regret settled into my bones. I could give him one face-to-face meeting, couldn't I?

"Do me a favor and hold on for a while. I'm in Syria, and I can't leave." I didn't know what his doctor told him about his life expectancy, and I didn't ask. They were often wrong anyways.

"I will, son. I'm not asking for you to come home. I know that's a big ask that you may not be ready for. Maybe we can have another call sometime soon? It was so good to hear your voice, to be able to talk to you." He sobbed again, and somehow I found my heart breaking for a man who did a whole lot to break my heart and not much to mend it.

"Yeah, you can give me another call when you need to," I answered, but I couldn't let this call drag on. I had an audience, and I needed time to process this. He and I weren't buddies, and I had no idea what I even wanted to tell him during our next call.

"That would be great, thank you, son. I've got to get going. I have a doctor's appointment. I'm going to speak to my attorney about getting the will in order, and I'll let the sheriff know that you are still my next of kin." I could imagine the sheriff's pleased grin. He pestered me to check in on my father for a while after his release, until eventually he got the point and stopped trying.

"Before you go, I forgive you." The words came out in a rush before I could change my mind. I knew they were the words he needed to hear—whether I meant them or not. Even if I didn't mean them, it was a lie that would do good, right? They would bring a dying man peace. I wasn't the judge, jury, and executioner, so who knew if he'd actually be forgiven for his laundry list of sins? But what I did was a reflection of my character—logically, I knew that.

"Thank you, son," he sobbed and disconnected the call.

I blinked back tears as I pocketed my phone. I was sure my eyes were red and slightly puffy. I needed to pull myself together; I needed to process the conversation and what that meant for me when I left Syria. I felt like my whole world was shifted out of orbit by a stray meteor, and now I had to figure out how to shift myself back into place. How could I pretend that everything was as it had been thirty minutes ago? I wasn't sure that I could.

"I need a minute." I simply stood up and walked out. I was almost to the door when Natalia tried to take a few steps toward me, but Abby put her hand out to stop her. Abby wasn't a very emotional person, I knew Strong struggled to get her to open up to him, and it took her a while to acknowledge that she was emotionally stunted. But I appreciated her recognizing that I had the same walls, the same struggles, and that I needed space. I'd have to come up for an explanation for Nat later, something that wouldn't break either of our hearts.

I left the office behind and then the building. I needed to do something, anything. I had this build-up of emotions festering, creating pressure in my chest. If I were home, I'd be going to my spot in the woods. I'd climb my favorite tree, and I'd read a biography or autobiography of a general or military hero from long ago. I'd lose myself in the problems of another man until mine didn't seem as significant. But I wasn't home. Instead, I was back in the sand box, only a few hundred miles from where I lost my leg.

Did my father even know about that? I imagined that somehow he did, but he hadn't brought it up. I considered asking Strong or Jones to box with me, to let off some steam, but I was sure neither of their girlfriends would appreciate their busted-up faces, although Abby might be slightly more understanding.

Doc would have a field day if she knew about all of this. Instead, she was completely in the dark, put off by an email that I was out of the country and unable to attend in-person visits. I was sure she was peeved, but I didn't care. If I came back with some kind of self-revelation I could share with her, or some measure of progress, I was sure all would be forgiven. One thing was for sure, she'd probably appreciate the disappearance of my bedroom eyes. After having Nat, no one else could compare. Not even a smoking-hot therapist with a rockin' bod, designer shoes, and a high IQ.

I wished I'd thought about bringing one of my books with me on the trip, but I didn't— and that was a stupid mistake. Luckily, I had a small reserve in audio format on my phone. I pulled my earbuds out of my pocket and popped them in. I located a small cluster of oak trees in the corner of the compound, near my patch job in the wall. I climbed the biggest one and stopped halfway. I did a few pullups, just to expel some physical energy, before I settled on a branch and leaned my back against the trunk. I closed my eyes and listened to the narrator give the introduction to a Ulysses Grant biography.

natalia

"What was that?" Abby asked Guy before I could. Whatever it was, it had Isaiah in all kinds of distress. He kept his voice low, but I could still hear the pain and sadness in his tone. It was impossible to hide that in his tone.

Guy stared open mouthed after Isaiah, only cementing my belief this was completely out of the blue for Isaiah.

"I'm not sure." He shook his head, but his thoughts seemed far away. I suspected he was lying, covering for Isaiah, and that only upset me more. Whatever it was, it was a big deal. Isaiah was a happy-go-lucky free spirit, despite everything that happened to him. He liked to joke and tease and flirt—so to see the opposite had caught me off guard. He told me that he had moments in the past where he struggled with darkness, which was to be expected after one almost died, but this seemed entirely different. This was a pain caused by someone else, not his leg.

I went to try to follow him again, but Abby simply shook her head. I knew if I tried to leave this room, she'd stop me. She was solid muscle and curves, I knew I wouldn't win going up against her, and what was the point? She knew what Isaiah needed, didn't she? She'd known him longer. Guy pulled out his phone and sent out a text, unfortunately not one I was copied in. I'd kill to see what he was texting the others.

"We're going to give him his space. In the meantime, Ambassador, why don't you and Christine shop for a dress for dinner at President Faris' house?" Guy suggested. He pulled up a website for evening dresses.

I shook my head. "No, that won't do. I'm going to have to show up in traditional clothing," I answered, temporarily distracted. I hadn't forgotten that Isaiah was hurting, but his friends knew him better than I did. If both Guy and Abby thought space was what he needed, then I'd just have to trust them. After all, Isaiah trusted them with his life.

"Do you already have one?" Abby asked.

"Yes, I have a few. You never know what occasion might arise that you get invited to," I answered.

"Show me," she said and then grabbed my hand and dragged me back to my house. Christine and Jasmine were there waiting. I was sure they knew that something was up with Isaiah and I was to be kept busy to let him have his space. Did everyone else know what was going on besides me?

Christine and Jasmine both ogled over my selection of colorful beaded Abayas while trying to pick out the perfect one to wear.

ða

Three hours later, I was really starting to worry. Christine had asked me to show her how to make a traditional Syrian dish, Yabrak. It was meat and rice stuffed into leaves. They were delicious and time consuming. We'd spent the time chatting about Green Oil, her foundation, and she told me about her frustrations with the last mission. Mainly that they hadn't yet captured the man at the top of the trafficking operation they were trying to end. I saw right through the distraction, even if she was trying to be friendly. After we finished the last one, I couldn't allow them to babysit me anymore.

"Okay, so tell me what the hell is going on with Isaiah before I lose my ever-loving mind," I demanded.

Jasmine's eyes grew wide for a moment. "We don't know. I've never seen him like this. The guys said he just needs space to brood. He will figure things out and then come back as good as new." That didn't tell me anything. Did the guys know what that phone call was about?

"Do we at least know where he's at? Is he still in the compound?" I asked, feeling worried for his safety.

"I believe so," Abby answered. The embassy and its grounds were still locked down, and there was a whole National Guard unit here to enforce the restrictions, but that didn't mean a former Special Forces soldier couldn't pull the wool over their eyes and sneak out.

Isaiah walked through the door looking exhausted, but better than when he stormed out of my office hours ago. His eyes looked tired, his posture was slouched, and his mouth was downturned. "Can we have a moment?" he asked the girls.

They quickly got up and left, all putting a hand on his shoulder in a show of support before they left.

"Are you okay?" I asked. I wanted to rush over to him and wrap him in a hug, but truth be told, I didn't know what he needed or what he'd want from me. We'd only spent a few days together. We barely knew each other in the grand scheme of things, even though he knew all about my darkest days. That didn't quite seem fair.

He sighed. "No, but I will be. I don't really want to talk about it. I just needed them to leave. I don't want a bunch of eyes on me, watching and trying to figure out what's wrong. Those women…they are fixers. There's nothing wrong with that, but I don't want to be fixed. I just want to forget about it for now."

I could understand that he was still full of angst and didn't want an audience or anyone telling him how he should feel. How many times had I been thankful for the same thing when my father died? "That's fair enough, but promise me that when you are ready, you'll talk to me about it? I'm here for you. I won't say a word if you don't want me to. I'll let you vent and not offer one word of advice or sympathy if you don't want it," I offered. I was a fixer, too, but I could take a hint. I wouldn't prod him, and I'd let him open up to me at his pace.

"Thank you," he said with a half-smile that didn't quite reach his eyes.

I needed to distract him or at least give him a safe place to be in his own head. "Do you want to watch a movie?"

He looked relieved. "Yeah, sure." He plopped down onto the couch, and then I snuggled in next to him. He smelled like trees, but I didn't bring it up. Instead, I inhaled the scent as I clicked on a movie. I really didn't pay much attention to what it was—it was background noise for us both.

I reflected on the day, and I had to admit to myself his friends were a lot. Not in a bad way, but it was overwhelming having so many strong personalities in one space. I could tell how close they all were, and I felt a bit of jealousy. I didn't have many close friends, mainly because most of them were back in the States. It was rare to get phone calls and emails from them. Out of sight, out of mind, right?

My closest friend was Kareem, and while he was a great friend, I felt sad about that. My friend was on my payroll. Isaiah had a solid friend group who had his back, people he had history with. I wanted that…desperately.

"You okay?" Isaiah asked. "You look like someone just took a piss in your cup of coffee." He was one to talk.

My arms were folded in front of me, and I was slouched down into the back of the couch with my feet propped up on the edge of the coffee table. "Yeah, I'm fine," I lied.

"Where do you keep your fire extinguisher?" he asked suddenly.

I sat upright and sniffed the air. I didn't smell any smoke. "Why?"

"Your pants are on fire. I need to put them out," he said with a wink. Good, a small bit of the Isaiah I knew was coming back.

I bit my lip to hold back a smile. "You are so corny," I groaned.

"That is not an insult. I take that as a compliment, thank you very much. Don't let Jones fool you. He thinks he's the funny one, but it's really me, and everyone knows it."

He gave me a pointed look that indicated he wasn't going to let this go until I truthfully answered his question. It was kind of hypocritical for him to hit me with that look when he wouldn't talk about what was bothering him. Instead of mentioning that, I decided to trust him with my thoughts, in hopes that he would do the same with me. Not knowing what happened with that phone call earlier today had been eating away at me.

"It's just…your friends. They can be a bit much. It just reminded me that I've pretty much closed myself off since my father has been gone. Until you came here, Kareem was like my only friend. The ones I had back in the States lost touch." I shrugged my shoulders like it was no big deal. But maybe I was partly to blame for that; maybe I should have made more of an effort to visit or invite them here to come see me.

He reached out and snagged my hand. His thumbs massaged the palm. "I'm sorry, I know they just like to come in and own the space," he apologized.

"No, it's not a problem. They are doing me a favor. I don't know. It's just a reminder of some of the things I missed out on to be here. I've lost a lot more than my father, but in a way my youth, too."

"Do you really not have any friends back in the States? You've lost touch with them all?" he asked in disbelief.

"I haven't seen them in several years now, and not even a phone call was exchanged within the past year. We grew apart, and with me out of the picture, no one has made much of an effort to keep in touch," I clarified.

"I'm sorry about that. I hope you know that my friends are yours now. All three women in our group are outsiders, and it seems one by one we are all settling down. With each new relationship comes a new friend, so they are going to induct you into the group. It may take some time to get to know them, but be patient. They drive me crazy, too, but there is no group of people more loyal or determined as they are," he said with unmistakable pride. His hand left mine and traveled to my thigh, rubbing it, as if he was reassuring me.

"I appreciate that. I knew they were good people when you told me they wanted to come here to help," I said with a small, reassuring smile. I didn't want him to feel sorry for me. I just wanted him to understand what I was feeling. "Let's just watch the movie," I suggested so that we could move away from depressing topics. Unless he wanted to address the elephant in the room, then I was all ears.

"Or we could do something else," he suggested with a wag of his eyebrows.

"Hmm, maybe we could recreate last night?" I countered.

"I'm game, as long as you don't have to call your boss again," he replied.

"Deal."

He flashed me a seductive smile. "I'll grab the wine."

CHAPTER TWENTY-ONE

natalia

"Natalia?" Isaiah called from the kitchen. The change in his tone had my stomach in a free fall. What was wrong and why did he sound like someone kicked his puppy?

I got off the couch and cautiously walked over to him. He held a piece of paper in his hands. He looked up and held it out to me.

Stop looking into your father's death…or else.

I turned the note over, looking for anything else I might be missing. The handwriting was unfamiliar, sloppy even.

My head began to spin, and my heart started racing. "What the hell?" I asked between deep hills of air. "Where was this?" How did they get into my house on secured embassy grounds?

"Taped right here to the fridge," Isaiah answered.

"So whoever left this got into my house…"

"It would seem so," he said. He put his hands flat on the kitchen counter and looked down at the floor. His head dropped down so it was in line with his shoulders, and his knuckles were white as he squeezed the edge of the marble counter. He seemed to be teetering between on edge and deep in thought. His arms bulged and his veins were more noticeable the longer he stayed in that position. His eyes closed as he controlled his breathing.

We were in the middle of something seriously fucked up, but all I could manage was staring at Isaiah. He looked like a wrathful god, and if he wasn't careful he was going to crush the marble in his hands. I wanted to rub my fingers up and down his arms as I plastered myself to his back, but now was not the time for seductive thoughts. It was time to figure out where to go from here.

I pushed the thoughts of Isaiah in this position naked to consider the situation unfolding. I had so many immediate questions my head might pop off from all the pressure. I could already feel a headache forming. I liked thinking about Isaiah better.

Did the person who left this work for the embassy, or did someone get through our beefed-up security? Either way, this was a colossal fuck-up to the status quo that needed to be addressed. We'd need to interview staff to see if they saw someone enter my house and identify who it was if there were witnesses. If not, then we needed to assume that someone working for me either killed my father or knew who did. Not many people knew that I was still looking for my father's killer. Only the secretary, Kareem, and Isaiah and his friends.

"Your friends aren't into pranking, right?" I asked. I just had to make sure for my own piece of mind.

"Yes, they prank, but not about something like this. They know I'd beat their faces in over a prank like this. This wouldn't be funny. This would be cruel," he answered right away. I believed him, even though I didn't know them well. His trust in them was unyielding, as was mine in him.

"So that means someone is spying on us and knows that I was investigating my father's disappearance and death or the secretary is trying to scare me," I tried to reason. I got a cold chill at the thought of a stranger rummaging through my house and leaving me a note like this. How were they spying on me in the first place? When did this note get there?

"While I can't rule out the secretary is messing with us, I think at this time it might be unlikely. Should we maybe see if someone is spying on me?" I suggested.

"Yes, that's what I was thinking, but I was considering the options," he replied.

"What other options are there?" I asked.

He took a step closer to me and then leaned down so that his mouth was next to my ear. I shivered at the sensation of his breath. "If we find any bugs, we could leave them to feed the spy false information. We've done that once before," he whispered. His lips had left feather-light touches against my ear, and it took me longer to comprehend his words than I was comfortable with admitting.

"Then do we have a way of discreetly checking?" I asked with a return whisper.

He nodded. "Let's go pay a visit to Guy."

The whole walk over there, I remembered what we did last night in my living room and then what we did upstairs. What if someone had been spying then? The thought of someone watching and listening disgusted me. It also worried me to no end. I could only imagine what kind of scandal that would cause if footage or audio was leaked. It would certainly be the end of my career and everything I'd worked for. I'd have no way of remaining in the country and searching for my father's killer. I wouldn't be able to look for dirt on President Faris, and I'd go back home a failure. That wasn't an option for me.

No, I was just going to have to hope for the best, like I'd been doing all along.

"Guy, we've got a question for you," Isaiah said as he barged into the guest house.

Guy looked up from his bowl of cereal. The spoon was halfway to his mouth, and he locked eyes with Isaiah before he lowered the spoon back into the bowl. An eye roll followed after.

"Do you remember back at Christine's when we went on a search and found a bunch of insects?"

"Uh, yeah?" Guy answered, but the response sounded more like a question.

"Take a walk with us. We might have some roaches over at Natalia's," Isaiah told him.

Guy's eyes widened briefly before he started quickly shoveling bites of cereal into his mouth. After thirty seconds, he looked like a chipmunk, with his cheeks full of cereal, but his bowl was empty, minus the leftover milk.

"You could have taken a few minutes to eat," I told him with a grin. I was thoroughly entertained.

"Well, you both had this look of urgency. I read between the lines," he said after he finished chewing. He pulled a shirt over his head, the hem falling over his muscular abdomen. I quickly looked away before he or Isaiah could notice me checking him out. All these guys were attractive, and I couldn't help but admire them.

He slipped into some shoes and grabbed a pistol off the table near the door, along with a small bag that rested at the foot of the stairs. I unlocked my front door and allowed Guy to enter first.

He reached into his bag and pulled out a small device. He turned it on and started slowly walking around. He made a pass through each room, including my bedroom. He didn't shoot either of us a knowing glance when he saw the rumbled sheets in my room and the untouched guest bedroom. I was grateful for that, because I was not as out and open about sex as Abby or Jasmine were.

When Guy was done, he simply shook his head. "There's nothing here. Why did you think you had bugs?"

"We found this," I said and passed him the note.

"And you've told no one else besides us?" he asked.

"Well, Kareem knows, too, but he wouldn't do something like this," I answered quickly. I was confident that Kareem would never try to pull a trick like this or betray me.

"Do you think he might have accidentally let your ulterior motives slip, or have you left your research laying around?" Guy asked.

"No, I'm super careful. So is he. He's got to keep state secrets, after all."

"Well, something isn't adding up. Maybe they used to have bugs here and removed them when they planted the note. Maybe they didn't like the fact that we showed up, knew our skillset, and didn't want to get caught. It's possible they cleared the place out."

None of this felt real. My biggest worries used to be getting enough supplies to take care of the embassy and help the community. Occasionally, I'd have to worry about some act of terrorism. But now, I had to worry about a spy in our midst and what their motive was, on top of trying to set up a trap for President Faris, and coax information about my father's death out of the secretary of state. On top of that giant pile of shit, I had to deal with growing feelings I had for the man who gave up everything to come help me and brought his friends along.

"You okay? You don't look so good," Guy said. His eyes were full of concern.

I felt Isaiah's hand grab my arm.

"Yeah, I'm just trying to process everything. I'm a planner, and I'm trying to figure out how I'm going to manage everything that's currently happening. Don't take this the wrong way, but my life was simpler before you all showed up."

"None taken. We solved some problems, but then other bigger problems popped up. That's how life goes sometimes. I'm going back to talk to the others. We will have to assume that this happened before the National Guard unit arrived. Whoever did this probably won't be ballsy enough to do something like this again. We know the house is clean, and we're the only ones here. Get a good night's sleep, we'll work through this tomorrow." With that, Guy left, and it was just Isaiah and me.

"That kind of killed the moment, didn't it?" he asked after a long, awkward pause.

I simply nodded.

"Then let's lock up and go to bed. Tomorrow will be here before you know it, and Abby has promised that your training is going to be rough," he said with a smirk.

He locked the front and back door, flicked off the lights, and then pulled me upstairs. Maybe I'd allow the mood to find us again.

natalia

"Think *Mr. and Mrs. Smith*. Angelina Jolie was a fucking badass. Channel her," Abby ordered me.

"Wasn't there a lot of violence in that movie?" I asked back. Didn't mean it wasn't a good one, but I'd rather get in and out of the mansion without a knife and gun fight, and preferably without an explosion or fire.

"So?"

"So I don't need to blow up the Syrian president's mansion to get what I need. I'm pretty sure that would be an act of war. Am I wrong?" I challenged. I guessed it depended if it was intentional and if I was caught.

"You're thinking too broad. Think narrower. Even when he should have wanted Jane dead, John couldn't pull the trigger. He knew just how lethal his wife was, but that didn't matter. He was way too attracted to her. She oozes sex appeal, confidence, and intelligence. That's who you need to be."

"But that's not me," I countered. And this was a dinner to negotiate a temporary lift of an embargo. Wouldn't I want to blend in with the other ambassadors?

"I beg to differ," Isaiah said from his perch on my staircase. We were in the living room where all the couches were pushed out of the way. Abby was introducing me into the world of espionage, and with that came hand-to-hand self-defense.

"He's right, Natalia. You have all the making of being one fine-ass spy. Now tell me, how well does the Syrian president actually know you?" Abby asked.

Abby and I circled the living room as I tried to come up with an answer to her question, an honest one. We didn't have much time for her to teach me about her years of exhaustive knowledge, so she was giving me the crash course for dummies. She called this "condensed training" because we were multitasking. "Thinking quickly on your feet while distracted" was apparently her favorite skill, and she wanted me to master it.

"I think we've had maybe ten conversations in the four years I've been ambassador," I answered. Half of them had been on the phone, and only one in-person meeting had been longer than fifteen minutes. Truth was he often had his own aides contact me if he needed something.

"Really?" Abby asked. Her footing changed, so I changed mine.

The man was a misogynist through and through. I was glad our interactions had been limited; it meant I wasn't on his radar. "Yeah, he's very anti-woman. I swear the main reason the president appointed me in my father's place was to piss the man off."

Those spectating my training chuckled at my joke. That was likely a half truth. I was sure there were other just as annoying reasons.

"You think so?" Abby asked and then rushed me. Her shoulder hit me in my stomach, knocking the wind out of me. My shoulder blades slammed into the ground, and the air left my body in a loud hiss. I groaned once I finally caught my breath. I was definitely going to feel that in the morning.

"Abby, don't you think that was a little too rough?" Isaiah asked from his place on the stairs. He looked concerned, and I didn't know if that was just because he cared about me or because Abby was lethal.

"Do you think that President Faris or his goonies will be any easier? What if she's caught and has to fight her way out? We can't all go busting into her rescue—not there—and you know it," she fired back at him. "Now, shut the fuck up and let me get her prepared." She shot me a grin that told me that the worst was still to come. I might learn a thing or two, but I was definitely going to collect injuries like trading cards.

"God damn if I don't love that mouth of yours," Strong said from his spot next to Isaiah.

She turned and shot him a wink with a seductive grin. "If you're lucky, it will do other things later." She turned back to face me. "You see, that kind of talk men find distracting. Use it. And while I was distracted by Strong, you should have come at me. That's called the window of opportunity. Now, tell me more about your previous inter-actions so we can figure out the best angle." She lightly placed her hand around my throat and showed me where to press and strike her to cause her to involuntarily lessen her hold.

"I've been to one other of his so-called dinner parties. The other interactions were over the phone, in passing, or at dinners hosted by other foreign affairs folks. Most of the time, we don't even make it at the same table. He's given a much more prominent seat. That used to piss me off, but now I'm guessing that's a good thing."

"And did you speak to him much?" Abby asked. This time she helped me to my feet and then spun around behind me. Her stomach was plastered to my back, and she held me in a choke hold. My chin was in the crook of her elbow. "You can headbutt and break their nose or stomp on their foot. If you can get a good footing, then kick them in the balls. It's one thing to break free, but your opponent will likely be faster than you, so you need to injure them, slow them down."

I went through the motion of stepping on her foot. I doubted that she wanted a broken nose. "Only at the dinner party, and a couple of brief calls. He asked me a few questions but seemed uninterested in my responses. During the calls, he basically barked orders at me as if I were on his staff, and then he ended the call. There's no such thing as polite chit-chat with him on the phone."

She stared at me briefly, her eyes narrowed. "Well, we could use this to our advantage then. Is there any room for him to consider you a shy person?" Abby asked. She put me in another chokehold, which I managed to escape.

"Yes…he could," I panted my answer. I could make shy work, a lot better than seductive. I was definitely not Abby, nor Angelina Jolie. I was just the ambassador looking to get answers for her father's death and help her country. I could play shy.

"Good, when you go into that dinner reception and negotiation, you are going to play that shy card, at first. But you need to slowly become bolder as the night progresses. You need to slowly attract him, so he doesn't even realize that you are suddenly of interest. He doesn't question his desire for you. It just…is," she shared.

"How do I do that?" I asked.

"Don't we want her to blend in with the others?" Isaiah asked. *Yeah, what he said!*

Abby shook her head. "In an ideal world, yes. But I'm working a second angle—the long con. What if she doesn't get what she needs on this visit? Suddenly she'll have an in for a return, a *private tour* of his residence."

I didn't even think of it like that. We were putting so much pressure on this one night, but if I could give myself a back door, a way to come back, I could be more thorough. "Go on, Abby. How do I make him interested without being obvious?"

Isaiah scoffed and mumbled something I couldn't make out. Abby ignored him entirely while Strong bumped his shoulder into his in a silent show of support.

"It starts subtly. Fluttering your eyelashes some. Prolonged eye contact with a small, sexy smirk. When the opportunity presents itself, slight touching when he speaks, and showing off your assets. You become the honey pot, and you subtly let him know you are interested in letting him have a taste."

"Babe, you are giving me a boner with all that euphemism," Strong said.

"Imagine what the real thing will do to a man who thinks women are only good for sex and making babies," Abby said with a wink to me.

She was absolutely right. I could do that. I could subtly flirt with the man. Would I be disgusted by it? For sure, but I could stomach it to get the answers that I need. Although I'd still have my limitations. This was a very conservative country in its customs, and he was a president. He wasn't some every day Joe Schmoe off the street.

"I can do it," I told her with a nod, watching her as she stalked me in a circle again.

"Show me." She turned her head to the stairs. "Yates, get your ass down here."

Isaiah looked very happy to comply.

"Yates, erase your current status with Natalia from your mind. She's an acquaintance you look down on. You think her place is as a homemaker, not in a political office. Now, Natalia, show me what you've got," Abby ordered.

I watched as Yates' soft eyes hardened, and his shoulders squared up. I didn't like this different version already.

"Mr. President, I was hoping that I might be able to pull you aside for a moment. I know it's not very polite, but I was hoping for a private tour of your mansion. It is quite…stately." I fluttered my eyes at the end and gently touched his elbow.

"And why would you think that I would give you a private tour?" Isaiah asked, mocking President Faris. His tone and accent were completely off, but I was able to look past that.

"Well, I was hoping we could discuss a couple of matters, some political and some…personal," I said and touched his hand again. I made a show of licking my lips.

"Well, she's got my attention," Yates commented with a goofy smile.

"I understand the premise here—get him to lower his guard enough to make him vulnerable—but do you think he's just going to tell me his plans? Do you think he's going to answer my questions truthfully when I ask him nicely?" I asked.

"Of course not," Abby answered quickly.

"Now you're losing me," Strong said.

Yates just simply shook his head. A slow smile creeped along his face.

"Okay, what am I missing here?" I asked, looking between the three of them.

"You're not going to ask him questions," Yates said to me. Then his gaze cut to Abby. "You and Guy decided on the bugs you want to use?"

"Are you just a know-it-all?" Abby asked.

"Absolutely when it comes to strategy and military history. I recognized the ulterior motive," he said.

"I'm still so lost," I commented.

"Yates is right. You won't be asking any questions or saying anything that hints to the fact you are asking questions about him. You just need to search for evidence and plant the bugs," Abby said and pinned him with a glare.

My mind was spinning because now I really understood what I was going to have to do. I was going to have to be ready to do anything to get away from the others and get unrestricted access to Faris' private residence. Then once there, I'd have to make sure I had plenty of time to search. If I got caught, I'd have two options: seduce or fight my way out.

Fuck me.

CHAPTER TWENTY-THREE

isaiah

"You good?" I asked Natalia. She looked a little spaced out. She put up more of a fight when Abby was the one running her drills.

"Yeah, just thinking," she said as she shook her head and we locked eyes. She put her fists up like she was ready to fight, but I could see that she wasn't.

"A penny for your thoughts?" I asked.

She let out a deflated sigh. "I'm still trying to figure out how I got myself in this mess. I'm about to walk into the lion's den. This man would rather see me dead than fork over even a penny of what the U.S. has given to the Syrians in aid. I'm going in with no help from my country, but a few friends. You have to understand how completely overwhelming this feels. I'm an ambassador, not CIA or FBI—and I have a sinking feeling that these sort of games are what got my father killed."

My insides knotted at the idea of Natalia following in her father's footsteps so completely that she got in over her head with the same mission. She previously had no idea why her father was targeted, but what if this new realization was right? What if he was given the same task, and he got caught? Of course, I couldn't agree or disagree with her suspicions without freaking her out or gaslighting her, so I diverted the conversation.

"You're a student of history, and politics, right?" I sure hoped so, because that was the butter to my bread, the Bailey's to my coffee.

"Yes, of course," she answered.

Thank God! "Did you ever go through your studies and wonder how those you read about—those you celebrated—had the guts to do what they did? Think about being a Tuskegee airman, or a Union general. Think about the amount of bravery someone like Harriett Tubman had to have. I'd argue her balls were bigger than mine—she risked certain death if she was caught, but look what she did anyways. She probably trembled in the face of the unknown, but she put one foot in front of the other. She changed the lives of so many, because she did what she felt was right." I paused, so the weight of the bravery could sink in. I needed Natalia to realize that those legends were human, with real emotions, long before we immortalized them in the pages of history.

"While I don't agree with your boss' methods, she is right. This is absolutely important to investigate. We could be funding the next big terrorist attack and not even know it. What you are doing could potentially save thousands of lives." I stopped the sparring we were doing to place my hands on her shoulders. She had every right to be nervous and in shock, but she needed to know how important this was.

"That's easy for you to say. You guys have already been on the winning side of history." Her sadness turned into slight defiance.

"And what you are about to do is going to one-up bringing down two trafficking rings and saving a rich heiress, don't you think?" I asked as I took a step closer to her.

She considered my words. "You think so?" she asked.

"Absolutely. Don't get me wrong, we saved lives, changed lives, and protected future ones that never knew they were in danger. I'm so proud of what we've done, maybe even more so than my time in the Army—but I see big things for your future, Natalia," I told her. It was absolutely the truth.

"Thank you," she said. The words were so soft I would have missed them if I weren't already staring at her face.

"What for?" I asked.

Her eyes held unshed tears, making them glossy—but perfect windows into her soul. "For believing in me. Not many people have. My dad did, but since he's been gone, my life has been full of naysayers. Then you came strolling in with your white box truck instead of a white stallion, aviators instead of armor, and your positive outlook as your sword." Her smile was soft and warm. *This woman will be the end of me.* She already had so much of my heart, and I hadn't truly realized it when we met years ago. How could I know just how badly she'd turn my world upside down or how much I'd enjoy the change of perspective? When her father pinned me with that look, could he see the possibilities between his daughter and me? Did he know then that fate would bring us together? Or did he just dislike me and my humor that much?

"Please, that's nothing. I've felt the desire to get to know you for five years, and it's really nice to know that my gut was right about you." Understatement of the year, I was a man obsessed. "You have this drive to do good, and that's something I've wanted for a long time. It's part of the reason I signed my life away in service to my country. I thought I was doing something good. While that was satisfying, I never felt like I fulfilled my purpose, but now I finally feel like I'm fulfilling it. Between rescuing a bunch of innocent people from trafficking, and now looking into your father's death and figuring out what President Faris is up to, I'm finding what I was meant to do," I told her. I had a whole second lease on life, regardless of the fact I no longer wore ACUs.

She reached out and touched my cheek.

"Maybe everything in life is about the long-term plan. Maybe my dad had to be kidnapped to bring you and your friends into my life. Maybe there's more to this than we will ever know," she whispered.

Fate, destiny, whatever you wanted to call it, I wasn't a believer. I still wasn't convinced, but if it really was real—this would be what made me believe in it. "Maybe," I said and leaned my head forward. I gently placed my lips on hers, testing the waters. When there was no resistance, I pulled her flush against me. It was quick and sudden, and she let out a surprised squeak. She smiled against my lips as I continued to kiss her.

Her arms slid behind my head, and I could feel a heat developing between us. It made me want to peel us out of our shirts.

There was a knock on the door, and it caused us to break apart quickly. Goddamn it!

Guy poked his head in. "I hate to interrupt, but can I talk to you for a second?" Garcia was right on his heels. "Alone."

"Yeah, sure." I looked back to Natalia. "You might want to use this time to do some work duties. Tomorrow is strictly for the mission," I told her.

"Got it," she said with a small smile. She was blushing at the fact we had been caught making out like teenagers.

I struggled to discreetly adjust my now-raging boner, then stepped out onto the front porch and followed them over to the guest house. "All right, what's going on and why can't Natalia know?" I asked. I wanted to add the fact that they were cockblocking, but I clamped my lips shut before the words could leave them.

"You're going to want to sit down for this," Garcia warned.

I rolled my eyes. "Get on with it." I didn't like drawn-out anticipation.

"It's a two-part whammy, so prepare yourself. The first is it's possible that Natalia's father might be alive," Guy said.

I blinked rapidly as if that would do anything to clear out my ears. It sounded like my friend had just shared that it was possible that the former ambassador was still alive. It was either that or the cruelest prank they or my mind could create.

"You need to explain, now," I growled. If it was a prank, I'd castrate them myself. I was the king of funny, and this was not it.

"So first there is this… It's the photos of the ambassador's body. It's very charred, but look where the burns are concentrated: the face and the hands. I was able to pull the autopsy report. The teeth had also been removed from the body," Guy explained.

"Those are the most common ways to ID someone. What about DNA testing? Was that not done?" I asked. That should have been done. It would have been easy to compare a sample between the corpse and Natalia or her brother.

"It doesn't appear so," Garcia answered.

"And why not?" I pressed.

"I don't know. The examiner didn't say. It was performed here and not in the States. Maybe that lab didn't have the capabilities, or maybe it wasn't requested by Natalia's family to confirm? Maybe the scraps of matching clothing and the positive ID of his wallet were enough for them? Either way, the death was already suspicious, but this upped the ante. Also the vehicle he was found in was missing for six months prior to his disappearance, but it was one that the ambassador personally used."

I tried to think about the implications of what that could mean. Was he hiding that vehicle from the embassy, or did someone else steal it, waiting for the opportunity to kill him and make it look like an accident?

Then a completely different thought hit me. *What if he did this?*

"Wait a second. If that's not his body, and it was planted inside his personal vehicle, do you think he staged his own death?" It was as if flashing carnival lights were going off behind my eyes. The bells were singing loudly in my head, and sirens were screaming. I hit it big.

Holy fuck balls.

"We were thinking along those lines. Although we have no idea what the motivation for something like that is. Why would he fake his own death, assuming that we are right?" Guy asked.

"Fuck if I know," I retorted. Now shit was really getting crazy.

"Wait a fucking second. The secretary had said that she had more info on what happened to Natalia's father. Dangled it in Natalia's face like a fucking carrot. Does that mean that she's lying about that, or did she know all along that he is alive?" I asked.

"Yo, this is way deeper than a superficial death of a public figure. Whatever happened has been covered up. Either the government is lying to Natalia, one of its own representatives, or it doesn't know what's going on. This is way bigger than we could have imagined," Guy said.

"Holy fuck..." I mumbled. Then I came to my senses about just how delicate this piece of information was. If the old ambassador faked his own death and was willing to suffer permanent separation from his family, there was a damned good reason why. It meant either he or his family were in danger.

"I bet he wouldn't have counted on Natalia filling his position, would he?" Garcia asked.

"No, probably not. Guy, are there enough cameras in the area for facial recognition software?" I asked.

"I have no idea. I haven't scoped that out. We need to think long and hard before seeking him out. That software can be hacked like anything else. We don't want to make it easier for any of his enemies to find him or for him to think of us as an enemy about to out him. Again, this is assuming that he's not a pile of ashes," Guy answered.

Gruesome imagery. But true nonetheless.

"We can't tell Natalia about this," Garcia said.

I instantly hated that decision. I knew he was right, but the idea of keeping something like this from her felt absolutely wrong. I could already see the look of utter despair this news would bring. Either we were right and she'd be upset that we kept it from her, or she'd be upset that it wasn't the truth and we kept the possibility hidden from her in the first place.

"This...this is a lot," I told them both.

"Yeah, we know. We're not telling the girls, because they will tell Natalia. What's Jones' line? He'd bet a testicle on it. Well, I'd bet mine on it. It's just going to be between us," Guy said.

"You don't think that Wells, Jones, and Strong won't tell their women?" I asked.

"Nope, not with something this life or death. It's not their secret to share. They know this. Christine still has no idea that we terminated that dictator years back. Wells is whipped, but he can still keep a secret," Garcia quipped.

"All right. What the hell am I supposed to tell Natalia? She's going to ask what this was about."

"Ah, that brings us to the second piece of the news. We found where President Faris probably disposed of his wife's body."

"What?" I asked, feeling shocked again.

"Yeah, it's amazing what satellite images can pick up. There is a patch of disturbed land, just big enough to be a grave, that's in the courtyard of his mansion. It's in the back of the garden," Guy shared.

"How do you know it's for her? It could be for their family dog. It's not like we can access that without getting caught. It's in his home," I countered.

"In satellite images taken two days before she was last seen, the soil is undisturbed. Two days after she was last seen, the hole was dug. If it looks like a duck, and quacks like a duck, it's probably a murder victim." Garcia was nonchalant about the whole thing, but I knew better. On the inside, he was brimming with intrigue; he liked a good mystery. Dude should have become a detective when he got out of the Army.

"How original," I countered sourly. Usually I could appreciate humor, but not today.

The only thing that news was going to do was freak Natalia out. Sure, we had our suspicions that the Syrian president killed his wife, but it was another thing to find evidence that supported the theory and then still willingly put yourself in his path.

"This is only going to make her scared to go to that negotiation."

"She's going to need to know. Knowledge is power. If she can get him to talk about his wife, he might let something slip. Again, we're assuming he killed her. If her death was an accident or was a hidden illness, then burying her there isn't illegal. It's just convenient." Guy pulled his phone out of his pocket, tapped away at the screen, and then pocketed it again.

There was no way we could let her bring up Faris' wife. No matter how it was asked, it would seem like an accusation to a man responsible for killing her.

"Now, I've got to try to dig into the archives to see what good old

Uncle Sam has on Natalia's father's supposed death," Guy said as he turned and walked away. *Wait, wouldn't that break the terms of his contract as a contractor?*

"Look, I know it's going to be hard to keep this from her, but it's for her own good right now," Garcia said, shooting me a sympathetic look as he placed his hand on my shoulder.

"No arguments there. I just hope she won't hate me for this."

The truth would come out eventually; it always did. The real question was what was the truth, and would it be something that Natalia and I could overcome?

CHAPTER TWENTY-FOUR

natalia

"**E**verything okay?" I asked as Isaiah walked back through the front door.

"Yeah, Guy and Garcia think they have a breakthrough in their investigation into President Faris," he answered.

"What is the development?" They were looking into my father's death, researching the three possible suspects, and President Faris and any ties he could have to funding extremism or controlled unrest in his country. If they were managing all of that and still finding developments, I'd have to trust that they knew what they were doing. They were highly trained and intelligent men. They brought my father home to me after springing him out of a terrorist controlled compound. That itself was extremely impressive. They might have a lot to do, but they seemed nothing but resourceful.

"They found an area of his private gardens where the soil is disturbed in the shape of a grave. It was untouched two days prior to her last public sighting and was then dug up two days after the last sighting," he explained.

My stomach dropped. Didn't that all but confirm what we thought we knew? He killed his wife, because she was nice to the poor, the same people who wanted to remove her husband from office.

My hands clammed up, and I swore I could feel my upset throbbing in my neck. What have I gotten myself into?

"Don't let that get to your head. We don't know for certain that he killed her. She really could have been ill. We don't know. If she did die from natural causes, it's not that odd that he'd want to keep her close, so that he could still visit with her," he tried to pacify me. Not that it was going to work. Deep down I knew Faris was a terrible man; there was no need to give him the benefit of the doubt. We weren't in the States. He wasn't innocent until proven guilty here.

"Yeah, but that is seeming less and less likely," I mumbled.

"Yeah." The one-word response showed me just how much he believed his own assurances. He hung around awkwardly for a minute, and it was just long enough to make me suspicious. Then, as if sensing I needed some space, or I was onto a secret he might be keeping, he left. He locked the front door behind him, and I was left alone in silence for the first time in days.

I sat on my couch with my laptop in my lap. I had so much to do and not enough time. Reports to generate, projects around the embassy to approve, the work was never ending—and that was just the shit that was in my job description. Espionage was conveniently left out when I stepped into this role.

I tried to accomplish what I could, but it felt like an uphill battle. If it wasn't all complete, it wasn't like it really mattered. If we caught President Faris in one of the largest embezzlement schemes and terror plots in our nation's history, I was as good as dead if I stayed in the country. If we succeeded, it certainly meant the end of my time as ambassador. Paperwork be damned.

Four years of hard work was going to conclude in a fiery explosion of accusations and treachery. I hoped that Isaiah's friends would keep trying to help me figure out what happened to my father, even when I had to return to the States. I had no expectation that we'd find the answers before the investigation into Faris came to a head.

The thought of Isaiah made my heart beat thump in my chest a little different. Something about the expression he wore when he entered the room caused me to feel uneasy. I only caught his face for the briefest of moments before it morphed into the concerned expression he had worn when he shared the news. But there was something else there, wasn't there? I felt it when he left the room, like maybe there was something else going on that I wasn't told about. Maybe I was just so used to being second guessed that the trait was starting to rub off on me. Maybe I was just looking for additional problems where there were none. The embassy was mine; there couldn't be anything going on that wouldn't be reported back to me.

I wondered what my father would have thought of Isaiah's help. I couldn't help but wonder if he would have given the man his approval, not that it mattered now. I still sometimes made my decisions based on what I thought he would have done. It wasn't healthy, I knew. I'd already spent hundreds of hours trying to get to the bottom of my own behavior. Part of me still felt like maybe my father was still alive out there somewhere, despite the knowledge that I stood over his casket. If I kept making decisions as if he was alive, that small, hopeful part of my heart could continue on in denial.

"He'd tell you to do what makes you happy," I muttered to myself. The words were absolutely true, even if they felt hollow. Even if I knew I was just telling myself what I wanted to hear.

What would make me happy was finding a way to help those who were being oppressed here and then heading back to the States with Isaiah and his friends. The realization startled me. Not the first part, but the second. Isaiah had only been in my life for a short time, but I didn't want him to leave it. I wasn't naive enough to think that he and his friends would stay here forever. I certainly wasn't stupid enough to think that I could stay here after I infiltrated Faris' home. If I had to make the trip back home, to never return here again, I'd rather do it with Isaiah and his friends by my side. They'd help me adjust to my new life, and maybe they'd help me find a way to continue my mission from the States. That was their thing, right? Making the best out of a shitty situation?

A deep, nagging feeling of guilt threatened to swallow me whole as I considered what would happen to those I left behind. They'd be in a war they didn't start, or they'd suffer in a power vacuum if Faris was removed from office, in whatever capacity that took.

But what if there doesn't have to be a vacuum?

I groaned. The thought was a prime example of why other countries disliked America's involvement in their affairs. However, if I could locate someone who would actually be a good leader to the country and take care of their people, then what was the harm? Hah, as if I'd be given that kind of privilege.

I stood up with another groan as I put my hands to my face in frustration. My father made this job and its responsibilities look easy. It was anything but easy. Difficult, frustrating, dangerous. It felt like playing chess, but never being able to get up and walk away from the board.

For the first time, I had something that made me want to stand up and walk away, and that itself felt terrifying. I hoped that one day, I'd stop feeling so scared.

CHAPTER TWENTY-FIVE

isaiah

I did not enjoy the fact that I had to keep a secret from Natalia. I wasn't sure if she and I were actually in a relationship or not, but if we were, this was not how I wanted to start it. But the idea of telling her that her father could be alive and out there but having no other answers felt cruel.

The thought of telling her the same and then being wrong felt even worse. There was a difference between giving someone hope because it gave them the strength they needed to get through challenging times and giving someone false hope just because. It was wrong. I was put between a rock and a hard place, and I needed to get out. Or at least a distraction that would make the discomfort a little better. I'd grit and bear just about anything for Nat, but it didn't make it any more enjoyable.

I spent the rest of the afternoon alternating between plotting with Abby for Nat's eventual infiltration of President Faris' mansion and helping the others look for anything we could on Nat's father. Syria wasn't like the United States. There wasn't a traffic camera on every corner or great paper trails. It felt a lot like casting out a line and waiting for something to bite, but the problem was the fish didn't want to be found.

So after a long afternoon of avoiding Nat, I quietly entered her home. The downstairs was dark, with only a small lamp that dimly lit the space. I quietly tip-toed up the stairs—if she was asleep, I didn't want to wake her.

When I entered her bedroom, her bedside lamp was on, and she was reading a book.

Naked.

My eyebrows shot up to my hairline. "This is a hell of a welcome back," I said as I entered the room and closed the door behind me.

"I hope so." Her tone was seductive as she closed the book, and I caught a glimpse of the cover. There was a half-naked man with a six-pack. A romance book. I'd heard stories about what those books did to women's sex drives, and I was all about it.

She sat up and slid off the edge of the bed and took a few steps toward me. She grabbed me by my shirt, the material fisted in her soft hands. "You were distracted earlier. Is everything okay?" I was unable to help myself; my eyes left hers and traveled down her body. How could anything not be okay when she stood in front of me naked like that?

I nodded. "It definitely is now." I pressed my lips to hers in a burst of passion and scooped her off her feet. Her legs found my waist and wrapped themselves around it. I took a few steps and deposited her on the bed and broke the kiss as she bounced on the mattress.

"So tell me what you were reading about in that romance book of yours." My words were a lust-filled order.

She reclined backward and arched her back, with her legs bent in the air, her feet resting on the edge of the bed. The view was sexy as fuck and had my cock fighting with the seam of my pants. Her hand slid from her chest down her abdomen to rest at her clit, touching but not toying.

"Well, I was just in the middle of a dirty scene." Her eyes were filled with lust and amusement. God, I wanted to grab her by the hair and shove my dick in her mouth. I wanted to watch her eyes close as she took all of me in her mouth.

"Oh really? Walk me through what happened," I ordered.

"He threw her on the bed, much like you did me. He played with her breasts and then sucked on her most sensitive areas until she came..." Before she could finish her sentence, I pulled her ass across the bed closer to me. I bent over her and roughly grabbed her right breast, pulling the hard nipple into my mouth. My tongue danced around the skin, and my other hand roughly grabbed the other breast. I alternated between kneading the soft flesh and pinching it between my fingers.

She let out a throaty moan as her back arched. I felt her hand move against my stomach as she played with her clit. I pulled back from her breasts, only for a second, to step out of my pants and boxers and pull my shirt over my head. Then I bent forward again and sucked her other breast into my mouth, giving it the attention it rightfully deserved. Her back arched again, and her finger picked up rhythm. I alternated between use of my tongue and teeth to switch between slightly painful nips and soothing motions. When she wouldn't stop withering beneath me, I pulled her hand away from her release button.

She cried out in rebellion as I gently blew across the skin but didn't touch her. "He sucked on her clit, huh?"

She moaned in response.

"Did reading about someone else coming turn you on?" I asked.

She nodded.

"Use your words, Natalia."

"Yes. Yes, it turned me on."

"Did you imagine that it was me sucking your clit as you turned the pages?" My voice was a deep growl, vibrating in my chest.

"Yes." The word was hardly a whisper. It was hidden inside of a breathy moan. I stuck my tongue out and ran it in one straight lick from opening to clit. Her body jerked off the bed before I quickly pinned her pelvis down with one hand on each hip. I sucked her clit into my mouth and clamped down with my lips, continuing the suction. Her hips jerked under my hold. She squirmed as much as she could under my grip, and I used my mouth and teeth to bring her to the edge of an orgasm, never quite letting her get there.

"Then what did he do?" I growled.

"He flipped her over and fucked her." Her tone echoed the passion I glimpsed in her eyes before they rolled back into her head. I'd inserted my finger deep into her, and I felt her stretch around my digit.

"Do you want me to flip you over and fuck you?" I asked.

"Yes." The word was barely audible as a cry followed it. I'd picked up my pace and inserted a second finger.

I pulled my fingers out before she could clench around them and reach a crescendo. I was going to drive her wild with desire before serving it to her on a silver platter. I sucked them into my mouth, savoring her taste. I'd never get enough.

I grabbed her hips and spun her so her tits and face pressed into the mattress. I pulled her legs up onto the edge of the mattress and ate her from behind, taking my time. It felt like it only took seconds for her back to arch further, her fingers to fist the sheets, and her legs to shake. I blew another breath against the sensitive area, pink from all the pleasure I caused.

"I'm going to fuck you so good. Do you want that?" I asked.

"So much." The words were a whine. A desperate plea for me to do just that. I grabbed her hips, and my hands squeezed hard as I brought them closer to me. I spit on my hand and roughly pumped it a few times over my straining cock. It wanted to join in on the fun, and it was about to get its wish.

I lined myself up, and in one swift thrust I was in her pussy, and I groaned in relief. Her muscles tightened beneath me as she worked to accommodate my size. "Good girl," I praised as she took all of me without so much as a whimper. She let out an audible sigh, and I slapped her ass. The sound of the smack echoed around the room as I lost myself in the motions of thrusting into Nat. Every time I went deeper, her knuckles got whiter against the sheets, and she slowly spread her legs further and further apart to take me deeper.

"Play with yourself," I ordered.

There was hesitation on her end, as if she wasn't sure she could handle the task.

I growled and laid my hand across her ass again. It took only seconds for a red handprint to form. Her hand snaked between her legs, and her ass jerked as she touched her clit.

"Good girl."

She clenched around me, and I damn near came then. I used her hips to push and pull her away from me, making my thrusts more intense. I wasn't sure how long I kept up the brutal pace, but Nat's cries got louder, and my balls got incredibly tight. Then a blinding sensation took over as I came. Nat clenched around me, taking everything I had while she tried to catch her breath. Her back was covered in a thin layer of sweat.

She turned her head and looked at me over her shoulder. The half-dazed expression only added to the lust, which still burned strong. Suddenly, I was ready for round two.

natalia

"Welcome," the president's butler said as he opened the front door to the mansion. I'd seen Faris' home a few times before, but up close it was impressive, no matter how many times I'd seen it.

"Thank you." He took my coat after I entered through the massive decorative doors. They looked like they weighed a hundred pounds each. Gold leaf adorned them in traditional patterns. The butler gave me a once-over—probably to figure out if he should let me step any further inside. His eyes raked over my brightly colored traditional dress and gave a slight nod of approval. I had a feeling that if I had worn anything western, I would have been denied entry.

"Right this way, Ambassador Ali," the older gentleman said. He slowly led me to a large sitting room, which was connected to the massive formal dining room. There were more people than I expected in attendance. They milled around the perimeter of the lavish room. More gold leaf adorned fixtures and frames. Dark and ornate wallpaper covered the walls, creating a stark contrast with the gold accents.

I scanned the faces of those in the room and only recognized a few people. The French ambassador, Jean-Luc, sat at the table swirling his drink around in his glass. He was in his late thirties and was by all means a good-looking man. His blond hair was slicked back, and his tux was perfection. He had just a hint of a five o'clock shadow, which gave him the slight edge of sex appeal he was probably looking to capture. He hadn't noticed me yet, but I was sure he would soon. I was one of the few friendly faces he'd come across tonight. Our countries were close allies, and that meant that we often corresponded or attended events together.

"Ambassador Natalia Ali of the United States," the butler said before he left me alone with the sharks. Not that the French ambassador was a shark, but he was certainly an opportunist. Even if we were friendly.

"Ambassador, welcome," President Faris greeted me. He placed a kiss on each cheek. While it wasn't his normal greeting, it was proper for most European countries—and while he had so many of them in the same place, he needed to play nice. He likely had no clue exactly how ten NATO countries decided to come to the table with temporary lifts in sanctions, and he was not stupid enough to look a gift horse in the mouth. He gave me a warm smile, one he'd never flashed my way before. It was meant to disarm me, to make me comfortable—and I felt anything but comfortable. I felt on edge and like an imposter. Like a child playing dress-up in a room full of adults.

Directly behind President Faris was a portrait of his wife. Her eyes were kind, and it only renewed my sense of purpose. I was here to expose the man for the devil he was. I put on my best poker face. I was going to manifest success if it was the last thing I did.

"Thank you, Mr. President. I'd like to take the opportunity to offer you condolences on the loss of your wife." I gestured to the portrait behind him, so my condolences wouldn't seem out of place. "I'm sure it's been very difficult for you. If there's anything I or my country can do, please let me know."

The French ambassador's eyes raised in curiosity, they met mine, and he sent me a knowing smirk before his attention went back to his drink. I wondered if he had the same suspicions about her death?

"Thank you, Ambassador. It has been a very difficult time for me and my family. Now I must look for another wife. Syria's president must have a beautiful and obedient bride by his side." The words were delivered with ease—it was hard to believe he was talking about the loss of his wife and his hunt to find a new one, all within the same breath. It hadn't been very long since she died, and he already wanted to find a new one.

Father had been gone for four years, and my mother still hadn't plunged into the dating pool. President Faris was absolutely heartless —but he was her likely killer. So why would I expect anything less?

"That's a shame," I said, trying to be polite.

"It is, but don't pity me. I know you lost your father quite suddenly as well. He and I didn't see eye to eye on many things, but I gathered that he was a good man and loved his family very deeply." His eyes didn't express the warmth that his tone was missing. It was as if he was a bad actor reading a script or saying words he didn't believe.

I did my best to show no emotion at his words. They seemed like a poison-dipped dagger, ready to end my night before it even started, but I held firm.

"You've got this," Isaiah whispered into my ear.

He was right, I did.

"Yes, he was a great man. He cared about his and your people greatly," I said to bridge the awkward silence I accidentally created by my delayed response.

He seemed to understand that we needed a subject change. "Come, let me introduce you to the others before we get started with dinner. He held his arm out for me to loop mine through. The gesture felt calculated on his part and cringeworthy on mine. I locked my arm in place so it wouldn't shake at the prolonged physical contact with President Faris. I couldn't imagine how I would get through a night of seducing him if I had to. The idea of him coming anywhere near me when no one else was around was enough to send me running for the hills.

I did my best to look like I wanted to be there as he escorted me over to some of the other guests who were chatting. The French ambassador's wife scurried over from where she was chatting with another attendee. Her curled dark hair contrasted with her bright yellow dress and her dark red lipstick. They both kissed my cheek in greeting. Faris had let go of my arm and distanced himself some, so she took advantage of the space to whisper in my ear. "This has been absolutely dreadful so far. You must simply take a walk with me later so that we can gossip." Her accent was beautiful, even when hushed.

I simply answered her with a small grin. She and I were by no means close, but she was very intelligent and powerful in her own right. She was one of the most brilliant minds in France and was even up for a Nobel Prize. If she wanted to talk to me about anything, it was certainly nothing trivial.

The British ambassador and his female companion also greeted me the same. I took a second to study her, because she was new to me. The British ambassador to Syria was not married and rarely brought a plus-one to any events. He was actually a very eligible bachelor, one I was sure my mother would love for me to introduce myself to formally.

"It's a pleasure to meet you," I said to her.

"It's all mine. I love your dress. It looks just like a dress that my friend Abbi wore once," she said with a wink.

I held back any sort of emotion besides a small smile as I thanked her. This woman was Abbi's asset who was going to make sure that I made it out of the mansion in one piece. She wasn't to be told anything about our mission, only that it was mutually beneficial for both of our countries. For MI6 to willingly spare an asset, it must mean that their official assets trusted Abbi. I instantly felt a little safer.

Other ambassadors came up to greet as well, including those to Luxembourg, Canada, and Belgium. Everyone was eager to take advantage of the situation. They all stared at Faris as if he was the key to recognition within their countries. I regretted the fact that this whole scenario benefited him, even for a minute.

Faris cleared his throat to gain everyone's attention. "Let's all make our way to the dining room. I'm sure the food is just about done." He led the way while we all followed behind, like sheep being led to slaughter.

I made eye contact with the British ambassador's date. She and the earpiece in my ear were my only lifelines to sanity.

Once in the grand dining room, the butler pulled out my chair for me and then pushed it in. My seat was right next to President Faris. The British ambassador and his date sat across from me, while the French ambassador sat to my left and his wife on his left. The German ambassador shot me an annoyed look, likely pissed off at my preferential seating arrangement.

"Please help yourself," the president says.

I politely declined, which was the custom in Syria. One always politely declined the food, and then once their host insisted, it was acceptable to take what was offered.

Once the president insisted, and I verbalized my agreement, a server loaded my plate for me. Everything was done with his right hand, which was a sign of being clean and respectful. When the server moved onto the French ambassador, I had a plate full of Dolma, my favorite food. The stuffed leaves were common here, but I didn't get to eat them nearly as often as I would like. We usually got most of our shipments of food straight from the U.S., and leaves weren't included in those boxes. On the edges of my plate were Kibbeh Bil Sanieh, a meat and onion dish, and Shish Barak.

I couldn't eat all of this or I was going to fall asleep before I ever had the chance to sneak away. I would savor as much of it as I could, especially the Dolma.

Faris led us in a traditional prayer before we were allowed to eat. The first thing that touched my lips was the Dolma, and I nearly moaned in delight. I'd made my way through three of them before Faris spoke. "So I hear that your countries have discussed the possibility of renegotiating trade agreements. Is there a reason that collectively half of NATO is suddenly interested in reversing years of damage done to my people and our economy?" The question was pointed, and his tone was hard and suspicious. If I didn't already know what he thought of the sanctions, his tone would have said it all. He was pissed they were placed in the first place.

The British ambassador piped up as I continued to chew. I wasn't sure if I'd be able to get a response out without my voice sounding squeaky. Isaiah's presence was quiet on the other end of my mic, and I had no idea if he could even hear what was going on around me or my chewing. "Yes, all the countries in attendance, and maybe some not here, are in agreement with renegotiating our trade agreements in a limited capacity for a limited time."

"For a limited time?" the president questioned. His tone portrayed his displeasure at the news of an expiration date.

The German ambassador's thick accent floated across the table. "Yes, Mr. President. Yes, we are here to negotiate limited deals. NATO has agreed that our deals can be extended up for ninety days."

"And why should I go to all the trouble for only such a small amount of time? It seems that these deals would benefit your countries, and at the end of the ninety days, Syria is left to rot like the filth under your shoes." Faris' tone had a hard and calculated edge. The hairs on my arms raised, and I was so glad that there was more than just a few people in the room. He couldn't kill us all, could he?

The British ambassador's date made eye contact with me and looked away. She could sense something was wrong here, too. I needed to do something to appease Faris before he got so angry he threw us all out or even worse. My opportunity to search the mansion could vanish before I could even start.

"If I may, Mr. President?" I said, jumping into the conversation. He nodded, but in a dismissive manner, as if he wasn't going to listen. "I think instead of looking at the end date of the opportunity, you should look at the opportunity itself and what it means for you and all of Syria. Syria has had over a decade of sanctions, and it's no secret the hardships your people face. Trust me, I've spent most of my tenure as ambassador trying to help your people survive, and I've climbed over hurdle after hurdle to help them."

"Yes, and you've given sanctuary to citizens who had no reason to seek refuge in America," he countered.

"Be that as it may, think about what ninety days of economic stimulus could do for your people, its economy, and its private organizations." I hoped he read between the lines and his mind jumped to how this could potentially fund his not-so-savory terror work. "You have ten countries here, all with needs to be filled, willing to work with you. Here's your chance to prove to the UN as a whole that Syria no longer deserves the sanctions. Prove that Syria is on the up-and-up, and you might look at this helping you ten-fold down the line." I cleared my throat, hoping to make one last pitch to his ego. "Think about what kind of hero you'd be to your people, injecting a healthy boost to their economy and lives. They'd worship you for the vast improvement, even if it's temporary. They'd remember who gave them that relief—and it would be more than I've ever been able to provide."

I felt breathless after my proposition. The room remained silent as we all awaited Faris' reaction to my reasoning, to my appeal to his pride.

"You care an awful lot about my people and how they view me, Ambassador." His intrigued tone matched his raised eyebrow. I was relieved that the cold, barely contained anger was replaced by something less terrifying.

"Good job, Nat," Isaiah whispered in my ear. We both knew I had Faris' attention now. The danger had passed, at least for the moment.

"I'm sure you can imagine that I don't have a particular interest in how your people view you, but that's a common worry for all leaders, even my own president. I'm merely pointing out your silver lining, where you stand to benefit, and that you certainly win in this scenario. I also hope it doesn't bother you that I care so much about your people? It's part of the reason the United States wishes to renegotiate the deal, and your tolerance of our work only benefits your people. It keeps them satisfied with your presidency, as you allow our work to continue," I retorted.

He rubbed his chin as he considered my point. "I'd like it better if you left my people here, to remain mine, but I'll concede to your evaluation. I can see where Syria might benefit from tonight's discussions." He turned away to look at the French ambassador. "What about you, what's France's motivation?"

"We are here to remain competitive on the world stage. The United States is one of our longest allies, but we can't roll over and let them make a deal that cuts us out," he said. He sent a competitive wink my way. Despite his thick French accent, his English was perfect.

Greed needed no further explanation. Faris nodded. "Who wishes to start?"

"Germany does. However, I do believe these conversations should be done individually," The ambassador said. His eyes traveled around the room, landing on each guest for only a second, but I couldn't help but feel the look he gave me like a physical touch.

"That is an interesting suggestion. I like it," the president said with a grin. He rubbed his palms together in excitement. My words must have been convincing because he grinned as if he won an international lottery. I hoped his desire to really bend the countries in their negotiations to his will would be enough to drag out the conversations. I was going to need a lot of time to search a mansion as large as this.

"May I suggest the garden? I've heard it's a delight," the British ambassador's date said.

"Of course, yes. The garden is a beautiful place to discuss business." Faris stood and folded his napkin onto the table. He picked up his crystal glass and then gestured toward the hallway, which would lead outside to the private gardens. Faris left the room with the German ambassador and his wife on his heels.

The room fell into an eerie silence as the tension was sucked out of the room. I took my first deep breath since entering the mansion, then got to work.

CHAPTER TWENTY-SEVEN

natalia

I wasn't even sure what my new partner in crime's name was, but I was positive she was MI6. She expertly drew attention to herself as she challenged several of the ambassadors to a game of darts, upping the stakes with crisp hundred-pound bills.

"I'm going to the bathroom," I mumbled as I stood up. No one paid me any attention as I quietly snuck into the hallway. My purse was draped over my shoulder; it was best not to leave a reminder of my absence. Hopefully with enough alcohol and a riveting game of darts, they'd forget about the American and concentrate on how they could best take advantage of ninety days with an economic reset in the region.

I followed a butler but kept my distance. A chill went up my spine as I felt a set of eyes on my back, watching me. The hairs on my arms stood on edge, and I picked up my pace just slightly. I stepped into the bathroom, hoping it seemed like my urge to disappear was related to releasing my bladder and not dodging my observer. I shut the door and flipped the lock. I held my breath and pressed my ear to the door. Foot-steps echoed down the hall as the person who'd been behind me walked past the door entirely. The steps continued until they reached what I imagined was the end of the hall. The sound of a door closing was a sweet relief.

I waited a moment, going through the motions of flushing the toilet and turning on the water so that if anyone was listening or waiting for me, everything would appear normal. I opened the door a crack and peeked out. Neither the butler nor the person who had been watching me was anywhere to be seen. I scanned my surroundings and couldn't spot one single camera nor a security guard. They were posted at the entrances and exits to the home, but not in the interior rooms, which was lucky for me.

I steeled myself for the task that was going to change the rest of my life. I'd either chicken out and be a coward, or I'd do what needed to be done and get what I needed. Either way, my next few steps decided my future. It was now or never.

I quietly pushed through the door and closed it behind me, leaving the light and fan on. If the person who had been watching me walked by again, hopefully they'd think I was still in there. I crept down the hallway as quickly as I dared. Heels weren't meant for stealth, but the cloth Abby glued to the bottom of my shoes certainly helped—they didn't clack against the floor. I moved silently through the hall. I wasn't certain where the president's office was, but I had a general idea.

My father had been to the mansion several times, and I'd pressed him for every detail he could share. I'd been interested in what the most lavish home in the country was like. The embassy certainly wasn't a ratty motel, but it certainly wasn't at the very top of the list for embassy remodels, that was for sure. Apparently, the office was on the second floor and decorated in gold and platinum. It overlooked the gardens with a large balcony that matched a second one on the same floor. With its proximity to the courtyard, and with the president within its sight, I'd have to search the room completely in the dark. Any light would risk drawing Faris' or his security's attention.

I slipped around the corner, finding the elaborate staircase. The wide staircase had a landing halfway up to the first floor, and from it the staircase split in two. After one more quick scan of my surroundings, I took my first step up. I didn't touch the railing, careful not to leave my fingerprints anywhere I wasn't supposed to be. By the time I made it to the top right side of the extravagant stairwell, I was panting.

I pushed past the discomfort and put my ear to the first door along the hallway to my right. It was the wall that I suspected faced the gardens. The room was silent, so I used the fabric of my dress to grab the doorknob. It turned easily, and I peeked my head inside. It was a bathroom. I silently pulled the door shut and moved onto the next door.

"You're doing great," Abby whispered into my ear. I was relieved to have her listening and watching through the tiny camera in my broach. I'd almost forgotten that she and Isaiah were both in my ear. My straight hair helped cover my small earpiece, and no one was aware that at any time they could turn on a recording device and record any conversation I was a part of.

I opened the next door, and it looked like an unused bedroom. The air felt stale and cool. Most of the room was blanketed by darkness, causing shadows from what I imagined would be large, grand furniture.

No need to linger here.

The next door squeaked as I opened it, and my heart nearly shot out of my chest. It too was an unused bedroom, with the same shadows and stale air. "I wish you could find floor plans for the house. It would be so much faster to look up the office," I whispered.

"To be fair, does the American embassy advertise its blueprints on the internet?" Isaiah asked with a chuckle.

"Okay, fair point. Still wishing, though..." I mumbled.

I silently bitched to myself as I wasted more time on two additional empty rooms. I knew the place was large and that Faris was a lonely individual, but this was almost pitiful. One of the richest men in the country was by himself in a home worth more than most people made in their entire lives. Granted, he did it to himself by murdering his wife, so my pity was very limited...

I moved onto the next door until only three were left. I'd made my way around the top of the stairs from the right to the left. I cursed myself for starting on the wrong side. I could have been done by now if

I'd made a better choice. I tried to turn the knob to the door in front of me; it was locked.

The first locked door I've found—that has to mean something.

"We might have something," I whispered.

"A locked door," Abby commented.

"Yeah, well, not for long."

I lifted my dress and pulled out the small lock-picking kit that Jones gifted me with. His training session was fun. It felt more like a mental exercise than a physical one, so it felt like an enjoyable break. In a short time I'd mastered opening most types of locks, and Isaiah gave me a very appreciative seductive smirk. Then he'd practiced unlocking me that night.

I pulled my mind from the gutter as I crouched in front of the door and got to work. It took only seconds, but they felt like hours. I was too vulnerable and exposed out in the hallway. I'd been here too long, and the chances of me being discovered were only escalating.

I instantly felt a very negative vibe, and I almost immediately backed out of the room. The room was dark, like all the others, but chills crept up my spine as I pushed the door open wider. The smell that hit me was unbearable, and I almost emptied my stomach right then and there. My eyes watered from the intrusive odor; it was worse than walking into a room of cut onions.

How did the smell not escape out into the hallway?

I looked up when I noticed the quiet noise of an exhaust fan. I could only imagine what the smell would be like if it weren't running.

In the moonlight that trickled in through the barred windows, the room looked like maybe it had once been a bathroom but was gutted. Only a cement floor and the barred windows remained. Shackles were mounted to the wall, and a sleeping man laid on the floor under the windows. He was curled up into the fetal position with not even a pillow or blanket to make him comfortable. The empty plate beside him didn't have a single crumb on it. His drinking glass was bone dry.

I let out a quiet gasp and quickly backed out of the doorway and closed the door—before he could see me.

There was a hiss in my ear. "Is that what I think it is?" Abby asked.

Her tone matched my plummeting mood. None of us had expected me to come across a prisoner, and now we all likely toiled with the resulting ethical dilemma.

I was having a hard time believing it, too, and I witnessed it first-hand. The scent was the most shocking part; it spoke of the neglect, and not even the dark shadows could hide it. "If you saw a bruised and bleeding man passed out on the floor, then yes, it is," I whispered back.

I didn't have time to debate with myself in front of a door in a very restricted part of the house. Instead, I wrestled with the guilt as I moved onto the next door. Leaving the man behind felt like a new character low for me; I didn't even check to see if he was alive. I could have at least checked his pulse before continuing on with the search.

It was as if Isaiah knew what I was feeling, because he said difficult words I needed to hear. "Nat, he's not part of the mission. The best way you can help him is getting the info we need. I don't know who he is, but I'm sure that he'd agree that justice served would be getting what we need on Faris and frying his ass. After we get what we need, he can be saved." *That was if he was still alive to be saved...*

I didn't vocalize an answer; the quieter I was, the better.

The next door was unlocked, and as I opened it, I realized it must have been the president's bedroom. Lovely, he had everything he needed on one side of the house...a prisoner, a bedroom, and hopefully his office.

Moonlight shone through the back glass balcony doors, creating enough light to see the decorative furniture and lavish fabrics. The room was beautiful, but it couldn't hide the ugliness in some of Faris' accessories. The cuffs attached to the oversize bed frame or the ones attached to the wall. There was a metal tray full of items I didn't want to look closely at.

Goosebumps formed on my arms and traveled down my back. Faris was a walking nightmare. I could only stare at the assaulting metal and feel wrecked for his poor wife.

My watch silently vibrated against my wrist. I'd set a timer hoping it would keep me on track, but all it did was let me know that I was going to run out of time. I wouldn't have enough time to search Faris' bedroom and the next room, which I still hoped was his office, before someone would come looking for me. I silently approached the balcony door and used my finger to move the edge of the sheer fabric just slightly. Through a small crack between the fabric and glass I saw President Faris there in the gardens, swirling the liquid in his cup. The French ambassador was speaking, and the president nodded along thoughtfully. The ambassador's wife walked along the flower beds, and Faris watched her like a hawk. Like he might just swipe her right out from under the ambassador's nose. I imagined her in Faris' room locked up in the cuffs and chains. I needed to get what I needed and then get my eyes back on that man. He was quietly unhinged.

I backpedaled and quickly left the room. It felt like the stakes were much higher. The French ambassador's wife might be Faris' next victim, and a man was dying in his own filth one door down. My hands shook under the pressure, making it difficult to pick the lock to the last door. When I felt the metal give, and the tiny unlatching sound, I nearly passed out from anticipation and nerves. If any room was bound to have security, or traps, it would be the office.

I entered the room and quietly shut the door behind me. The moonlight cast another white glow through the room, helping me see the over the top golden trinkets, the framed photographs of notorious extremists, and lots of ornate-looking jewels. Ancient-looking texts sat on a large, deep-colored wood that took up the whole wall, and a fine woven rug was laid on the ground delicately.

Jackpot.

The office didn't look like it belonged to an enforcer. It belonged to a rich mastermind, funneling money and aid from his people.

I moved to the desk in the far corner and started opening drawers. I started from the bottom making my way up. I ignored the gun, money, and drugs that I found in the largest drawer. It was like a free for all in there, and in the States, it would be enough to charge felonies. When I made my way to the top drawer, it was locked. I heard the sound of a door closing and nearly jumped out of my skin. It sounded like it was underneath my feet, but it was still much too close for my liking. I rushed to the door, and the president and ambassador were gone.

Time's up.

When Faris came back to the room, he was likely to notice my absence and send someone looking for me. If I got caught in here, there'd be no escaping this.

"Is something wrong?" Abby asked in my ear as my breath hitched.

"You could say that," I countered with a whisper.

"Is he done with the ambassador already?" Isaiah asked.

"Yeah," I breathed out.

"Shit," Abby mumbled. "I'll see if I can get my contact to create one more distraction." Her mic cut out, and I felt alone again in the room. I had to trust that I'd make it out of this, or I'd risked everything for nothing. The staggering amount of loss and suffering Faris was responsible for would certainly appall those mingling downstairs. The man in the other room was the tip of the iceberg.

I jimmied the delicate desk lock and rummaged through the last drawer. My fingers found something cold and hard, small enough to fit in the palm of my hands. I pulled the item out of the drawer where it was masked by the darkness. The moonlight reflected off the metal. A USB. It had to be important if it was tucked into the back of the drawer and locked away. Its outer layer was decorative, with the president's name carved into the copper.

I hurriedly shoved it into my bra as voices carried up to me from downstairs. A loud burst of laughter put me on edge but gave me enough sound cover to close all the drawers at once. I soundlessly tiptoed around the room. I had the feeling that there was more to be found. Leaving after securing one USB felt like a gamble, especially after making it this far. There could be safes hidden behind paintings or bookcases that protected hidden rooms. The possibilities were endless as a number of spy movie montages ran through my mind.

"I'm running out of time." My words were barely a whisper as panic crept up my spine. I needed hours to clear the room, not seconds. There had to be more than the USB. I didn't come all this way for one tiny piece of metal. There was no way he was dense enough to keep all his eggs in one non-fireproof basket...

I was a firm believer that nothing was ever that easy. "Abby, how's that distraction coming along?"

"It's in the works, but almost over. Instead, I've got another plan in place. When you're ready to leave that room, you're going to have to follow my instructions exactly," she answered. It sounded as if she was smirking, and I tried to bite back my own mischievous grin.

Maybe one day I'd look back on the moment and appreciate the adrenaline rush, but for now, I'd just have to appreciate my friends on the outside who had my back. They didn't want me to fail, so I wouldn't. I was going to make them, my country, and my father proud.

Faris, watch your back. I'm coming for your ass.

CHAPTER TWENTY-EIGHT

isaiah

I wished we didn't have to go with the contingency plan, but I had to say, Abby was worth her weight in gold and chocolate. Her undercover work was a little more catered to this situation than my combat experience. Sure, we could be stealthy, but we weren't delta. We had a healthy balance between tip-toe in with guns pointed and rush in and break shit. The latter was always my favorite, but I was thankful to have someone by my side who was the opposite. I was glad Strong's muscled ass didn't give up on her.

Abby had the good sense to buy an identical dress to the one that Natalia wore and made sure it was Jasmine's size. Jasmine's dark hair and similar frame and height made her the perfect body double for Natalia. The moment Natalia got to the president's compound, Abby directed Jasmine to get dressed and sat her down in a makeup chair. She and Christine applied so much makeup, but in the end, she looked so much like Natalia it was scary, and very confusing for my body… She wasn't Natalia but looked like Natalia. I was going to need therapy and to never bring this up in front of Jones—ever.

From a distance, no one would know that there was a fake ambassador in the house, allowing the real one to continue her search, out of sight.

The only real dilemma we ran into was how to sneak Jasmine into the house without her being noticed. With guards at all the exits, it appeared unlikely, even with Abby's contact's help. There was only so much she could do without arousing suspicion. So we were desperate to create a large enough distraction to get Jasmine in the same place as the ambassadors, and by default blend her into a crowd.

Abby mouthed to me, "Get her into position."

I quickly stepped out of the van, taking advantage of the darkness and shadows that the night and moon provided. I ushered Jasmine out, with Jones on our heels. The night was quiet, unfortunately for us. The only sounds I could hear from in the house came through Natalia's mic. With her location up in the office, the sounds were few and far between.

We moved across the front grounds of the compound and took cover behind a tree, barely slinking into the shadows before the guards shifted and faced our direction. Soon enough, the silence would be interrupted, chaos would reign, and Jasmine would slip right into a shaken-up crowd of politicians. Jones and I wore uniforms similar to the compound staff, which would help us blend in should Jasmine need our assistance.

Abby's voice cracked through my earpiece. "Nat, is there a lighter or some matches in the president's office?"

I heard fumbling and Natalia's combined mutters and heavy breaths through the earpiece. It felt like an eternity, but she finally released a self-satisfied, "Ah-hah!"

"Great." I could almost hear the smirk in Abby's voice. "You're going to sneak out of the room and start a fire, but you need to be very careful about where you start it. We want it to look like an accident, like something electrical, and it needs to be on the opposite end of the house from you."

"Are you serious?" Natalia hissed. I wasn't too keen on it, either. Natalia was already in enough danger. But she had a better chance of getting herself out of a house fire started on the other side of the mansion than she did away from a group of the president's men. The fire, while dangerous, was the most practical.

"Natalia, now's not the time to question me. You need a distraction, and a fire is perfect. No one will know that you are still inside. Jasmine's dressed like you and is going to be your body double for a while."

The seconds ticked by. It was so long I was worried that our mics stopped working.

"Are you..." Natalia paused, as if she had so many questions and was struggling to come up with the most important one first. "An evil genius?"

Abby cackled while Strong snorted in the background. The two of them were two peas in a pod, enjoying the compliment. I was sure that Abby considered that high praise.

It took her only a second to get her shit together. "Depends on who you ask, but it's quite possible. Now, get a move on. They are going to come looking for you soon. Better to have them not discover you setting the fire."

"Got it."

Another eternity passed while we waited, with nothing but the sound of Nat's heavy breathing. The camera that was inside of Nat's broach was hardly reliable. Between the darkness and being covered by her hair as it moved over her shoulder, it might as well not have been on.

Then through the camera I saw a small bright light. "Started it on the wall right below an outlet with a phone charger plugged in," she hissed. "This thing is going to spread quickly. It's like the paint has lighter fluid. Heading back to the office now."

Heavy breathing continued, and then a moment later the sound was drowned out by the blare of a fire alarm. It echoed through the night sky, interrupting the quiet Jasmine, Jones, and I had been hiding in. There was no turning back from this part of the plan now. We just had to hope that everyone got out okay and that it bought Nat the few extra minutes she'd need to search.

The shrieking of the alarm caught the attention of the guards who were stationed outside the front door. They rushed into the house, shouting commands at each other.

Nat muttered into her mic, "There's got to be something else here…" She wasn't as quiet, not that she needed to be. The piercing of the fire alarm now echoed strongly in my ear, threatening to blow up my eardrum.

"Check under rugs, push aside furniture, look under the table tops for documents taped underneath," I offered in a whisper. I didn't know when guests and staff might rush outside. If I had to guess, it would be any second, when they realized that they couldn't easily find the fire on the main level. It was tucked away in an unused bedroom. By the time it was found, it would be too late for them to put it out.

"On it."

A second fire alarm shrieked, adding further to the chaos. A few of the ambassadors funneled out, talking in hushed whispers. Some still carried their glass of wine. "Now's the time," I told Jasmine and gave her a gentle shove in the direction of the door.

Only a second after she joined the ambassadors, the staff began to exit the building. They barked orders at each other and left a wide berth around the ambassadors. And then a few more ambassadors and their dates funneled out, completing the crowd. But where was Faris?

My heart wanted to jump out of my chest. What if he tried to run for his office to retrieve documents or valuables before evacuating the house? What if instead of putting distance between them, we forced them together in a small space?

"Come on…come on…" Natalia sounded more impatient by the second, and my mood soured. All I could imagine was Faris bursting into the room and putting his hands on her, or worse.

"Is there a fireplace in the room?" Christine asked into Abby's mic.

There was a pause before Nat answered. "Yes."

"Check there," Christine encouraged. "That used to be my hiding spot. We never used the fireplace in my old house growing up. Check for loose bricks, a loose mantel, or papers shoved up into the chimney."

I heard Natalia fumbling, and then she let out a sharp breath. "Christine, I could kiss you!" Her whisper was loud in my ear, despite the two-alarm fire.

Screaming in the yard quickly stole the excitement from the moment of success. A large cloud of smoke plunged up and into the sky, and the low roar of a crackling fire grew in strength.

Panic spread through me like fog moving through a deep valley. I couldn't recall a time when I'd felt paralyzed by fear. Not in combat, not when I helped drag Wells out of a tank, or we were shit deep in a firefight that wasn't going our way. For the first time, I felt a panic that threatened to glue me to my place. "Not to be a buzzkill, but you need to move, Nat. That fire is sending large freaking smoke signals, and you might lose your chance of a safe escape soon," I warned. I didn't want my panic to seep into my voice, but I was always a shit actor. I was genuine, wore my heart or my dick on my sleeve—and if I was worried for Natalia, she was going to damn well know it.

"On my way." She coughed; the sound overpowered the sound of the alarm for a moment. "Shit! I've got to make a pitstop!"

What?

"Natalia, now's not the time for a bathroom break," Abby warned. This wasn't part of the plan, but my gut told me what Natalia was up to before my head could catch up. She was going to risk herself for a stranger, one who might already be dead.

"I've got to free the man I found." She coughed again, and I knew that the space she was in was starting to fill up with smoke.

She wasn't a firefighter; she couldn't drag the dead weight of a grown man through a burning house. I'd experienced firsthand what adrenaline could do for a person in a time of crisis, but that was beyond even adrenaline. "Nat, you don't have time. Listen to me: you need to get out," I whispered harshly. Something else began to churn in my gut, shoving some of the worry aside. Anger, frustration. If she made it through this, I was going to punish her. I wasn't one of those men who thought women should bow down to men, but would it kill her to listen to me when I was fucking right? Her life was on the line, and she was being absolutely careless with it.

It was all my fault.

The realization burned my throat like the cheapest vodka. I didn't think of a better distraction, so I went along with Abby's. I knew it was dangerous, but I went along with it anyway. I should have known Nat would go back for the prisoner, and I should have predicted it and found a way into the house to help her.

If she died, it would be because I failed to protect her, even from herself. I wouldn't let that happen. What kind of world would this place be without a kind soul like hers? What would I be if I lost her? Nothing. I'd be nothing. I could never live with the weight of that guilt.

I hoped that maybe I was being dramatic and she'd listen to me. She'd get out of the house, and we'd figure out another way to save the man. Maybe one of us could sneak into the courtyard and climb up to the window.

"Just give me one minute. I won't be able to live with myself if I don't try," she whispered.

I couldn't fault her, not one bit. She was just being Natalia. The need to beg her to stop and scream at her to listen to me alternated in the back of my head. The two needs only added to the overall chaos of the situation. When I needed to be calm, I was a fucking nightmare.

Shouting increased in volume as an external wall collapsed, sending up a shower of sparks into the night sky. The ground vibrated, and the roar of the fire grew.

There is no more time, Nat.

I sprang up from the bushes before Jones could get a good hold on me. The fabric of my uniform slipped through his fingers before he could put any strength into the hold. I bolted across the front of the compound like my life depended on it. In a way it did. Natalia was my life now, whether she knew it or not.

The shouting disappeared as I got closer to the building; the roar of the fire drowned it out. The heat radiating from the building was enough to steal my breath. The sound of support beams cracking and groaning were enough to push me even faster, despite my struggle to breathe. The flames were consuming the oxygen much faster than I could get it. There was not enough time to pull Nat from the building before the whole building would collapse, but damn if I wasn't going to die trying.

The nagging thought that I was going to die on foreign soil ate away at me as I leaped over a burning fallen beam. I thought I'd escaped that fate when I survived my trip back home. I was going to burden my dying father with the task of burying me when he had requested the same from me. Natalia's father burned to death, and she was going to do the same unless I could stop it. Fate was a cruel bitch.

"Holy shit," Natalia cried into her earpiece. I barely heard the words over the crackling wood around me.

My stomach dropped, as panic consumed me.

CHAPTER TWENTY-NINE

natalia

I couldn't stop sweating; the heat inside the house made everything slick, including my palms. I had to grab the doorknob with the bottom of my dress just to get a decent enough grip to turn the knob.

It was hot to the touch, even with fabric between the metal and my hand. I hissed, because my palm was already going to blister from my first attempt to turn the knob, without the barrier.

The door opened wide, and I spotted the man laying on the ground. The room was filled with smoke, and I couldn't tell if he was breathing or not. I wouldn't be able to live with myself if I didn't at least try to get him out. How would I ever be able to forgive myself for starting a fire that killed an innocent man? I had to assume he was innocent if he was the enemy of my enemy. Faris was a cold-hearted bastard, and this was only further proof. This man could be very valuable to the U.S.

I pressed the button on my earpiece, because I didn't need Abby or Isaiah to try to talk me out of what I was doing. I approached the man as slowly as I dared; after all, I was still in a hurry. "Can you hear me?"

There was no response. Only the sounds of the house falling apart around us.

I stepped closer. "Sir, I need you to wake up. I'm going to help you get out."

There was still nothing, and I had a really bad feeling in my gut. I pressed the mic button in my ear piece, just in case the man reached out to try to hurt me.

I got close enough and knelt down. His chest rose and fell slowly, in a labored fashion. I didn't have time to think about anything else. I slapped him hard across the face, and his eyes suddenly opened. I fell backward when I recognized the eyes and the face they belonged to.

Adil. My father's assistant. The same man who went missing three days after my father.

I saw the same recognition in his eyes. He knew who I was.

"Holy shit," I breathed. Then I remembered to hit the mute button on my earpiece again. So many thoughts went racing through my head, and I was so afraid that somehow they were going to escape through my lips, and all of my friends would hear them.

"Natalia?" Isaiah asked into the mic, his voice laced with desperation.

I held down the button again. "Upstairs, and I'm going to need some assistance."

"Natalia," the prisoner in front of me squeaked.

"Adil, it's good to see you, but we've got to get moving." My own voice sounded like a wheeze. The smoke was burning my throat.

He nodded and then tried to sit up, but he was still chained to the wall. I fisted the lock that secured the chains and then grabbed my lockpicking kit again from where I'd stashed it in my dress.

He watched as I picked the lock, with my brows sloped downward in concentration. "Where'd you learn to pick a lock?" A terrible cough followed his question, and it only served to increase my panic.

"A few friends. You'll love them." A small smile tugged up the corners of my mouth. Adil would like my friends, especially once he heard about how much they'd helped his own people recently.

The gravity of the situation hit me hard. It had been years since I'd last seen him, and the circumstances of his disappearance were very suspect. Who knew if he was the same person or if he was ever loyal to my father and the embassy in the first place?

The idea that the man I was risking my life to save could be a traitor was enough to make another strong round of nausea roll through me. I needed to get him out of here, because now more than ever, I needed answers. I was so close to learning the truth about the past, and yet I was still so far from the reveal.

"Adil, do you know what happened to my father?" I asked as the lock was released. I pulled the chains free from the wall.

Tears formed in the corner of his eyes as he rubbed his raw wrists. I wasn't sure if the tears were confirmation to my question or from the relief of being free.

He tried to sit up but couldn't get his feet beneath him. "I need an answer, Adil."

My warning tone surprised me, but I'd waited years to get a nugget of truth, and I wasn't going to take a chance of dying without knowing it. I'd get the answers I needed, even if it killed me.

He nodded.

I crouched closer to him and shoved my arm around his back. "When we get out of here, you are going to tell me everything. You owe me that, Adil."

He silently nodded. Even the smoke-filled room couldn't hide the tears in his eyes.

I leaned my shoulder under his armpit and attempted to lift him. I grunted as I tried to support his weight. He leaned over too far and nearly fell on his face. Only my sheer effort kept him upright.

"How long has it been since you've stood?" I asked. I was going to ask about a shower, too, but that would be rude. We both knew it had been a long time since the dirt and stench had been cleansed from his skin.

"I don't know."

I felt so sad and angry for him. Clearly Faris kept him here for a slow and painful death. He was skin and bones, his hair long and greasy. If Faris went to all the trouble to keep him chained up and alive for years, he wouldn't willingly let him go. I hadn't even thought about what Faris would do when I walked through the front doors with his prisoner. I was going to have to trust that Isaiah and the team would have my back. It would have been great to have the National Guard unit come to our aid, but getting their aid on a covert operation was going to be impossible. Technically, this was spy-level shit, and the government didn't need to know until the job was done.

I shuffled Adil to the door, and a figure came to a screeching halt in front of us, startling me. Through the thick smoke, I recognized the hazy figure.

Isaiah.

He didn't say a word; he immediately put his shoulder under Adil's other arm, and lifted him up. He immediately took most of Adil's weight, and I was able to stand taller. We'd move much faster.

"We've got to go. This building is coming down in seconds." Isaiah's voice didn't seem to hold the same panic I felt. He appeared cool, calm, and collected, aside from his heavy breaths. Once again the man came to my aid, no questions asked, and I couldn't help but love him for it.

We put one foot in front of another out into the hallway, and it looked like we'd stepped through the gates of Hell. Fire seemed to coat almost every surface, and ash floated through the air. The air was stifling hot—it felt like we were walking toward the sun. I was going to need buckets of aloe if we made it out of here. The overwhelming smell of burned wood gagged me; the smoke in the air took over most of my senses. It was like walking through a living nightmare, the real-life version of Hell.

The sound of a loud snap sent my heart through my stomach and to my feet. Whatever that was, I knew it was going to be trouble.

isaiah

The support beam that slammed to the ground behind us threw burning-hot air our way. It was like trying to cross through a windstorm in Hell, complete with sparks, ash, smoke, and the smell of destruction. I did my best to get a lungful of air, but all I tasted was ash, and I tried not to choke on it. This was going to take ten years off my life and give me emphysema; I was sure of it. Assuming we didn't burn to a crisp before we made it through the front doors. I could already feel blisters forming from the extreme heat. I wasn't a firefighter, and I certainly didn't have a single piece of their equipment.

The situation put things into perspective for me. I tucked my head lower, keeping my eyes down. I could be a firefighter; I had what it took with the right training and the right equipment. I guess I could thank Abby and Natalia for helping me get my shit together. It just took a massive house fire to figure it out.

All around us, there was nothing but red. Through the exploded-out glass of the front door I made out spotlights. Like shining through the open portal to Hell. That was what it had to look like. Steam came up from the floor, and the ground turned slick. I couldn't see the water being sprayed, but I felt the boiling steam that was being doused on the flames to try to tame them. They were going to boil us alive like a fucking Louisiana boil.

The man Natalia rescued was unable to support his weight. His feet left a line in the slushy soot as we made it through the foyer. We struggled to take the last few steps through the doorway; Nat growled as she pushed herself further. She was one tough woman. My woman. There was no doubt she was mine, mind, body, and soul. I was going to show her exactly what that meant when we made it out of here. There was nothing like almost dying to make you feel alive. Or to make you want to fuck the one person you'd ever truly loved.

God, I'm such a sappy fuck. They might as well start calling me Strong now.

When my face hit the cooler night air, my lungs screamed in relief, and then I burst into a coughing fit. I was left with a new appreciation for the equipment the Army did outfit us with. Sometimes it was old and worn, but it would have made rushing into a fire a lot easier.

Nat and the man we rescued coughed up a lung beside me, but she still held the man's weight as we dragged him off to the left and out of view. Miraculously they were distracted by someone laying on the grass near the opposite end of the house.

My friends, all dressed in the staff's uniform, rushed to form a circle around us. "The president's looking for you," Abby said to Natalia. They took the man from our arms and then began dragging him back toward our vehicle. Whoever he was, he was safe for now.

"You need to go. The president can't see the dirty, grungy version of you here," Abby warned.

"But what about the talks? Surely I can't propose this whole meeting and not negotiate a deal for the United States?" Her voice sounded raw and strained. She did her best to clear her throat.

"What are you going to say to him when he sees you covered in soot, and ash, looking like you started a fire?" I asked. I pinned her with a concerned look as she swallowed hard. She was just going to have to accept that ship sailed, and other countries likely missed out, too. "What if he blames this on you or asks why you ran back in?"

He'd have seen Jasmine masquerading as Natalia; that was the whole purpose.

"Let's get this guy out of sight, yeah?" Jones said as he and Abby took hold of the man under his arms and hauled him in the direction of the van.

We were alone for a moment, so I grabbed Nat by the waist and pulled her to my chest. I spun her around so we were face to face, and I tangled my fingers in her hair. I pulled her lips to mine and let them tell her everything that I wouldn't be able to put in words. How scared I was at the possibility of losing her, how angry I was that she put herself in such a dangerous situation, and how proud I was of her for continuing to push on, even when the task was too much.

I felt her body relax against mine, and her arms moved up my chest to rest comfortably there. Her hands tangled in the fabric at the collar of my shirt. Despite how hot I'd been in the fire, I relished in the warmth of her body. It meant we were both alive, and our mission had been a success—even if she threw the plans into the wind.

I gently untangled my fingers from her silky hair and ran them down her back and underneath her ass. I gripped the back of her thighs tightly and then lifted her so that she could wrap her legs around my waist.

"That was so stupid." My words were half mumbled from my lips pressed on hers.

"I know," she breathed out. Her lips never stopped their assault of mine.

"You could have been hurt." Now that I was talking, I didn't think that I'd be able to stop.

"I knew the risks. I accepted them." She pulled back, her hot breath tickling my chin and neck.

"Never again, do you understand me?" I looked down in her eyes to make sure she could see how deadly serious I was.

"Does that mean you're sticking around to enforce that?" she asked. Her eyes were full of hope. She knew that deep down I wasn't a man who settled down. I was lost, despite the purpose my friends had given me. I was still alone in a crowded room, but that was until she saw me. I'd settle wherever she wanted me to.

I nod with a small chuckle. "It means that you're stuck with me, Ambassador." I said her title like I was mocking it, and she merely smiled up at me like I was her whole world.

"Then I can agree to those terms." She smiled even wider. "Never again."

I kissed her again, the passion between us threatening to burn hotter than the compound somewhere behind us. I wanted to snake my hands under her dress and show her just how much I needed her, although I was sure she could tell by how hard I was. Her center was resting against my hard shaft, after all, with only our clothes as a cruel barrier.

Someone cleared their throats to announce their presence. "I hate to break up this make-out session, but the man is asking for you, Natalia." Strong sounded like he wasn't sorry at all to break up our reunion. The giant bastard was all too happy to tease me the way I had the rest of the group when they'd found their women.

Natalia's body tensed around mine briefly before she loosened her hold and slid down my front, like a fireman's pole. I reached forward and grabbed her chin, forcing her to look at me. "What was that reaction for?"

She stared up at me with a sad smile. "Because this conversation's about to hurt. A lot. You'll see." Her tone was full of a wispy sadness that she normally reserved for her father.

She grabbed my hand and softly tugged me toward the vehicle. Once again, she was heading straight into the emotional deep end.

natalia

My thoughts spun around in my head like moons spinning around planets in a diorama—play the footage on a times sixteen fast forward function. That was what it felt like to be stuck with my own thoughts. I could barely focus on one before another caught my attention, taking me in another direction—another mood.

I took a deep breath before Strong opened the van door, and I jumped in with Isaiah on my heels. The inside was gutted. Only the driver and passenger seats remained. The carpet on the floor looked worn and in dire need of a good clean. Or better yet, it needed to be ripped out and torched. Chucked into the house fire, never to be seen again.

All around the perimeter of the large van were my friends. They stared at me with mixed emotions. There was a mixture of relief, pity, and pride. I didn't have time to read into each one and who it belonged to. Instead, my attention snapped to the person sitting in the center, Adil. He was the one person alive who could answer my questions. While my boss might have answers on paper files, Adil was infinitely more knowledgeable; I was sure of it.

I climbed further into the van and sat on my knees in front of Adil.

He looked up at me with a soft smile. The urge to throw myself at him and squeeze him tight in a hug was strong, but I wrestled with my self-control. I barely won. I thought I knew the old Adil, but I didn't know who he was as he sat in front of me, and until I did, I couldn't let him see my kindness as weakness.

"Adil." My tone was a mixture of polite firmness and an uneasy hesitancy.

"Natty," he returned. It was my nickname, referencing a beer popular back in the States. It drove my father insane, one of the many reasons the name stuck.

We stared at each other. If he felt anything that I did, he was at a loss for what to say.

Isaiah took advantage of the silence that developed between me and Adil as we took the sight of the other in. "Adil, who are you?"

Adil's eyes shifted to my boyfriend and sized him up. He must have seen the protective way in which Isaiah was glued to my back or something in his eyes, because he gave him a warm smile in response to the question.

"A man very happy to see that Natalia Ali found a man worthy of her." He reached out to shake Isaiah's hand. Isaiah hesitantly returned the gesture. He looked down at me in what I could tell was an unsure gesture. He trusted I wouldn't let him shake hands with someone he shouldn't.

"He was my father's assistant," I blurted out. I felt everyone's eyes on my face as I struggled to put our history into words. "He went missing a few days after my father did. We assumed he was dead, murdered by whoever killed my father." I winced because my tone almost became accusatory. I wanted to regret the insinuation, but I didn't. I saved Adil's life, and I'd be damned if I hadn't earned the right to pin a little blame. "What happened, Adil?" My voice hitched at the end, unable to hide the pain that I felt.

He took a deep breath, resigned to his fate. Like whatever he was going to tell me was going to make me hate him. Tears filled his eyes, and I took my own breath to steel myself against what was to come. "I've been keeping a terrible secret, Natty. One I promised your father

I'd keep. It nearly cost me my life—it's ironic that his daughter was the one to save it."

Jasmine cleared her throat. "I don't mean to be a bitch, but can we stop with the theatrics and get on with the truth? Nat's been waiting years for answers." Her arms were crossed, and her face was not amused by the scene as it played out in front of her. She was right, though; I'd waited years, and it'd been long enough.

Adil nodded. "Yes, sorry." His eyes never left mine as he muttered the words that would forever change my whole world. They shattered everything I thought I knew. Sliced me up, and healed me, all at the same time. It was the end of an era and the start of a new one.

"Your father didn't die. He was alive when I was captured a year ago."

My ears began to ring and my breath came out in what sounded like a hiss, but I barely registered that it belonged to me. My vision started to blur, my head started to spin, and every bit of strength I thought I had just slipped right out through my spine. Isaiah put a steadying hand on me, as if he knew I was about to fall to pieces.

"I'm so sorry that we lied to you," Adil added. I heard the regret in his voice, but he had to know just how much those words didn't matter. It was too late to be sorry that he hurt me. The damage was done, the emotional scars long ago carved.

My father was alive. *Alive.*

I let out a sob that shook my whole body. Isaiah pulled me back into his chest and kept his arms locked tight around me, as if brute strength would help hold me together.

"How?" My question was barely understandable beneath the accompanying sob that escaped my chest. I was going to slip into a full-scale hyperventilation, but I was going to push through. What was one more *be strong* moment when I'd already been through so many? It was practically muscle memory to ignore my own limits.

"He faked his death. He was certain that President Faris was organizing, or at least heavily backing, a series of terrorism groups, determined to take war to the West. He heard a lot while he was held captive in that damn compound. He couldn't just sit by and pretend he didn't hear their plans. He couldn't look the other way and let the experience be in vain."

I'm sorry, I grieved the loss of my father because he couldn't just report what he heard to the authorities? It was a different environment. The U.S. was war hungry; the government would have believed him. I wanted to scream in frustration. My father faked his own death, left his family behind to grieve, so what? He could do a job that he had no business attempting? Pure hurt and anger pumped through my veins, stronger than any energy drink–fueled rampage. I was deceived by the very man I spent years quietly crying for. I dedicated years of my life trying to find justice for him, only to find out that he betrayed his family.

What kind of bullshit is that?

"Did anyone else know?" I could barely see him, my eyes were so full of tears. I needed to know how deep this betrayal went. If there was anyone else deserving of my wrath. Did my mother know?

He shook his head softly. "No. Just me." His voice was solemn and full of remorse.

I hiccupped, and exhaustion took over. I remained silent, unable to make myself speak another thought. I was numb. How else could I express that besides silence?

Garcia jumped in to end the growing silence. "How did you end up here? What happened to you right after the ambassador went missing?"

"I couldn't stay and look into the faces of his family who loved him so much. I couldn't bear to lie to them every day. I left with a small bag in the middle of the night. I did what I could to get a new identity and stayed nearby in case he needed me."

"And you ended up here, how?" Guy asked, leading him through the questions we all needed to know.

"Unfortunately, President Faris had an associate that found me out, recognized me, and dragged me right back here. He assumed that if I was alive, the former ambassador was, too. He's been torturing me ever since, trying to get me to crack." His own voice hitched with emotion. The truth of his words was blatantly obvious. He was covered in dirt that predated the fire, his hair was disgusting, but it had nothing on the smell of his body odor or soiled clothes. If Faris knew that my father was trying to expose him, he'd probably stop at nothing to find and give him a real death.

"Do you know where he is now?" I piped up. Despite everything, I didn't dare hope that he was alive and well wandering the streets, just waiting for me to find him. It couldn't be that easy, not after all this time, and he went to all this trouble.

"No, but I have a way to contact him—if he's still alive. I'm going to need a phone that can't be traced," he answered.

Despite my better judgment, a little spark of hope lit somewhere in my chest, and I was determined to keep it burning. I had absolutely no idea what I'd say to my father if I found him, but I knew one thing was for certain: my efforts weren't in vain, and I wasn't going to stop until I could look him in the eyes.

He owed me so many answers. I was going to get them, come hell or high water.

CHAPTER THIRTY-TWO

natalia

The ride back to the embassy was quiet. I struggled to keep a hold on my sanity as my thoughts threw me through whiplash. My back rested against Isaiah's warm chest as he held me close. He was my life raft in a storm so strong I was sure I was going to drown.

No one said anything as the gate was opened and we drove back onto the embassy grounds. *Home for now.*

Guy, Mendez, and Garcia offered to take Adil and get him cleaned up and find him some clean clothes to wear. As Mendez and Guy led an exhausted and regretful Adil away, Garcia leaned in and whispered, "We'll find out everything he knows, don't worry. Just go get some rest. It's been a long day, and I don't know if anyone's told you yet— but you did great." He gave me a pat on the back of my neck and flashed me a small, reassuring smile.

His words did something to soothe some of the rigid cracks that defaced my heart. Isaiah's friends had my back, whether it be from loyalty to their friend or they actually liked me, I wasn't sure. Either way, I wouldn't look a gift horse in the mouth.

After all these years, I finally got some of the answers I had been wishing for. I spent too much time trying to convince myself that I wasn't stupid for wishful thinking, and it was worth it…at least I think?

Adil said that my father didn't die in the car, but who knew where he was now? How long was Adil held captive, and what did that mean for my father? Was it possible that he survived all this time, and then something snuffed him out from the world right when he was within my reach?

I prayed not.

The world is cruel, I've seen it first hand, but even it couldn't be that demented, could it?

My body shifted as Isaiah crawled out from behind me. He grabbed my ankles and gently dragged me across the floor of the van. He scooped me up into his arms and pulled me close. His body heat helped thaw the ice-cold doubt that threatened to consume me.

"Nat, let us know if you need anything," Christine said from nearby. Her words were filled with so much warmth and empathy, I wanted to burst out into tears again. I shook my head quickly, unable to form any words. I was absolutely overwhelmed, my head threatening to short circuit. It was all too much. Relief, anger, doubt, betrayal, excitement, the emotions came and went before I could process them.

My body shifted again; my nose was pressed to Isaiah's shoulder as he carried me into my house. I smell his scent, hidden under the layers of ash and sweat. It brought me peace. I could count on him, always.

As soon as we were in the front door to my home, I kicked off my heels. The sound of them bouncing off the floor echoed through the whole house. I half expected my father to come running down the stairs and lecture me about taking care of the house. I shook my head to clear the image, like my mind was an Etch-a-Sketch, and it was that simple to erase a memory.

"As much as I know you want to sleep right now, we've got to get clean first. The only good way to mess up those nice sheets is sex, not soot." He winked and gave me a small grin that forced the tiniest of giggles out of me. He was right. I'd be pissed if I woke up in the morning and my expensive linens were ruined from soot. Despite the seriousness of the past couple of days, I appreciated the humor. It was a small light to focus on, pulling me out of a dark tunnel of spiraling thoughts.

Isaiah placed me on the bathroom vanity, turned on the water, and grabbed us towels. I watched his face closely as he stripped out of his clothes. My eyes couldn't help themselves and eagerly traced a path down to where his hands worked quickly. Like an addict who couldn't get enough, my eyes roamed his whole body. They stopped on his prosthetic, and panic flared in me. I searched for any visible signs of damage. The bottom was completely black, and I prayed it was just dirt and smoke. If there was permanent damage, I'd be wracked with guilt. Those prosthetics were very expensive, and he wasn't working. His pride would never allow me to purchase a replacement. Men and their pride were responsible for so much destruction and devastation…and yet, Isaiah's was like a laser sight, keeping him focused on what was important.

"Relax." His voice startled me from my thoughts. My eyes popped up to meet his. "It's all good. Just dirty. There's no warps, no cracks, and no pain." I must have laser focused on the metal as I spaced out.

I let out a sigh of relief.

He approached me with a boyish grin, and my attention suddenly fixed to his naked form. Even covered in blisters, dirt, and grime, he was a work of art. He could have been carved from the most perfect stone—even Michelangelo would have been jealous of him. I knew I was. For anyone to look as good as he did, it would create insecurities for those they kept close. How would I compete with women who were just as beautiful as he was?

"What do you say I peel you out of these clothes and rub you down with the finest of body washes?" His playful tone, suggestive eyebrow raise, and soft touches were enough to distract me from my insecurities. It didn't matter if other women flocked to him. As long as I was the only back he was washing and the only ass he was grabbing, then I'd work through the rest. He was worth it.

It was hard to pinpoint my favorite thing about him; what drew me to him so that I could never turn away? Like a moth flying toward a flame? The man ran into a raging fire for me, and he didn't even try to convince me to leave the prisoner behind. He trusted my judgment, just like that. I might not be a big, bad ex-soldier, and we didn't serve together in all kinds of shitstorms, but he still saw me as an equal, someone he was never going to leave behind. Right then and there, as he stripped me out of the last of my clothing and guided me across the bathroom floor, I knew I was so head over heels in love, I'd never come up for air. I almost died in a fire, and that was terrifying, but I'd happily drown from the feeling of loving him so deeply.

Who would have known that our service to our country, no matter how different the service was, would have brought us to our soulmate? Years ago I had no idea that the man who saved my father and dared to joke with him would be the one who would come to my aid, over and over again. If I'd known, I would have been flabbergasted at the news —but would have fantasized about him every night until we were reunited.

The spray of the shower was warm. I didn't dare look down at what it washed from my body. I didn't need to see the proof to feel the relief. Isaiah's hands massaged my whole body as he worked my cheap body wash into my skin. I let out a little moan of satisfaction before I spun around in his arms and made a show of washing him. He wasn't just cleaning my body, but my soul, too. I could only wonder what I did right to earn the affection of someone as good as him. I'd do it the rest of my life if it meant I got to keep him.

What happened when this was all over, when I had my answers and I had to leave the country? I knew I wouldn't be able to stay. It was only a matter of time before Faris figured out what happened. When he figured out that I set the fire, or when the U.S. was breathing down his neck with the evidence of his traitorism, he'd be out for blood. He'd put a bounty on my head, and the lives of Isaiah and his friends, along with all the other staff and military personnel, would hang in the balance. Would Isaiah go back to the States and try to live a normal life, and would he bring me along? I was destined to go back to D.C., to a life of politics and negotiations, but would he be content with following me?

It seemed to go unspoken that what we had between us was real.

We were so focused on surviving the present that everything about our future seemed so unknown.

Isaiah's hands gently squeezed my biceps to bring me back to him. "You know, what you did was very stupid…but I've never been so proud of someone. You were so brave, so strong, and very determined." His lips turned up in the corner; his small, encouraging smile was warm and sincere. His eyes turned intense as I stared up into them. The windows to his soul told me what his words couldn't. He'd been the one who was scared, as if I'd fall to pieces right in his arms.

I shivered at his intensity. "So you aren't mad?"

His expression changed, and his eyes pinned me with a glare that had me wishing I could take back my question. His brows furrowed, his eyes hardened, and his jaw tensed. His Adam's apple bobbed as he swallowed.

I rambled, afraid of what he was about to say to me. The urge to fill the uneasy silence was too much to ignore. "All I can think of is what would have happened if he burned to death in that house. I would have never been able to live with that guilt, and I never would have gotten any answers."

His eyes softened just a smidge, but his jaw remained tense, his brows still sloped to meet. "I'm angry, but not completely with you, Nat. I'm angry that you ignored me. You could have died. Died. I don't know if that's sunken in for you. You're so much like my brothers and I, act first and deal with the consequences later. For fuck's sake, the day I arrived here, you shot back at the attackers instead of taking cover in the building." He was silent and shook his head, as if what he was going to say next didn't matter. "Point is, you scare me. I've never wanted to control someone before, not until I met you. I want to protect you from everything that wishes to harm you, and I can't."

He wasn't just talking about the fire now.

"I'm angry you've been put in this position and that I can't solve all your problems for you. Your boss, she put you in way over your head, and you almost lost your life tonight because of it. And your father…you won't like what I have to say, so I'll shut the fuck up about him. I'm furious you've spent all of your adult years doing nothing but searching for answers and helping those who can't help themselves, and now you'll have to leave it behind. Your purpose, your aspirations will be ripped away from you because you aren't safe here anymore. And I can't make that better. I can't protect you from that. Even with the help of my brothers, we can't take on an entire corrupt foreign government and the groups that Faris has rallied behind him."

He let out a sigh, and his spine slackened, his jaw loosened, and his brows relaxed. The angry edge he held inside slipped from his grasp, and instead the soul I fell for appeared before me. He looked torn by his own words.

"I'm angry that I can't do more to help you. I'm angry for you, but not at you." His voice was low, its rumble soothing. His touch was a gentle wave washing across the shore. He was exactly what I needed.

I snaked my arms around his neck and pulled his face down to mine. There weren't any words that I could formulate that would explain how much his words, his support, meant to me. I felt seen and heard. Despite being in a public office for years, I'd never truly felt like anyone really got me or my mission until now. Isaiah Yates saw me, and I burned for him.

My lips pressed against his, and he opened his mouth to accept my greedy tongue. I needed to steal his breath like I needed his hands all over my body; I might die without it. His tongue tangled with mine, and it was a battle of wills to show who needed the other more. I might not be a soldier, but this was going to be a battle I'd win. I backed him up into the shower wall, feeling every bit a predator, and he let me. My fingertips left red scratches down his neck and pecs as they made their way south.

I was going to show him just how bad I burned for him.

isaiah

Natalia was like a woman possessed. Her eyes burned with a passion that rivaled the fire she escaped from an hour ago. Her passion was focused solely on me, and it was like standing directly in the path of the sun, but I loved it. I'd been missing something for years, and it wasn't just my leg. It was a purpose greater than myself; it was her. The work I'd been doing with my brothers and their women had been meaningful, but it was nothing compared to finding that someone who saw past my charm and my disability. She looked at me like I was her savior and her sun.

Her fingertips raked over my skin as she sank down to her knees in front of me. Her eyes snapped up to mine. I saw an inferno of need, and the sight alone was enough to make a lesser man cum. Her long lashes held drops of water, and her hair was soaking wet and plastered to her neck and chest. She wrapped her fingers around my shaft as the skin on my abdomen still tingled from her nails. She gave a sexy smirk before her lips wrapped around the head. I groaned as my head dropped backward and rested against the hard tile. I blindly reached forward, collecting her hair in my hand. I gave it a hard tug. She moaned around my dick, the vibrations went straight through me, and I knew that I wasn't going to be able to hold out for long. She was a vision of seduction at my feet, worshiping me, when it should have been me at hers.

I gave another hard tug on her hair, pulling my cock out of her mouth. She stared up at me with a mischievous yet sexy grin. She knew exactly what she was doing to me, how badly I wanted her, and how little patience I had to wait for her. She was going to be my torturous but sweet end.

I grabbed her arms and pulled her up to her feet. I quickly spun her around and pressed her against the shower wall. Her body jerked when her chest hit the cold tiles, and then she quickly relaxed, trusting my hold.

I bent her forward and rubbed my hand against her ass, giving it a hard smack. "You make me feel alive," I admitted as I slipped a finger into her wet pussy. She moaned, and I felt her clench around me.

"You make me..." She let out a gasp as I stuck in a second finger.

"Want to come?" I asked, my voice deep and lust filled.

"Yes..." she panted. "You also make me feel so much more than alive. You make me feel wanted, and I don't know that I've ever felt that way until you." Her breathing picked up, and I wasn't sure if it was because of my talented fingers or this emotional connection that we'd supercharged.

I pulled out abruptly and spun her back around, slamming her shoulder blades into the tile. I grabbed her face with one hand, tilting it toward mine. I wanted to see her eyes for what was next. With my other hand, I grabbed her leg and hitched it up to my hip to give me better access. I slid into her, and her eyes rolled back in her head.

"Look at me," I commanded.

Her eyes closed for a second before she re-opened them. They were hazy but focused on me. "I've wanted you since the moment I met you. Every second I spent in firefights, crawling through sand..." I slowly pumped into her, and she whimpered at the tortured, slow place. "Wading through swamps and freezing my balls off with my brothers, it was all worth it. It brought me here to the most incredible woman I've ever met. I don't have one single regret."

I brought my lips down on hers hungrily, and it was like she sucked my soul inside her body. I pulled away so I could say one last thing. "Now lift your leg up higher and you come when I say so. Understood?"

She nodded her head, her eyes half closed.

"Good girl." She whimpered and brought her lip between her teeth, but there was no disguising the smirk she was too slow to hide. She enjoyed it when I took control, when I praised her. There was so much more where that came from. I'd say anything to please her if it meant feeling her beneath me. If it brought her even a drop of ecstasy, I would say it.

She lifted her leg, and I picked up my pace. I pumped into her hard and fast. Her warm breath surrounded me as she panted. Her leg began to quiver, so I placed both hands under her ass to support her weight.

She whimpered, her fingers digging into my shoulders. The nails left little crescent moons that I wanted to tattoo there, so they'd stay forever.

Too soon I felt the tingle in my balls that told me I wasn't going to last. It was time to give her the release she pulled back from. It was time for her reward. I removed a hand from her ass and tweaked her right nipple. "Come." My voice was a growl, and I instantly felt her respond. Her back arched, her stomach pressed into mine, and her pussy clenched around me. She let out a loud cry as she came on my dick, and I roared with my release.

She turned to Jell-O in my arms, but I'd anticipated that. I caught her and quickly washed our bodies again before I turned off the water.

"Did you really mean what you said?" she asked quietly as I set her feet on the bathmat.

I looked down at the beautiful siren in my arms. "Every word."

"Good." Her smile was soft but happy. Dreamy almost.

She dried herself and padded into the bedroom. I followed. I'd follow her anywhere. As if running into a burning building for her wasn't the perfect example of the lengths I'd go to for her.

She crawled into bed, and within minutes, she was softly snoring against my side. Her stomach grumbled, and I quietly smirked. I was hungry, too, but not just for food. I wanted answers and to finally bring Nat some peace.

I laid wide awake thinking of what fresh horror Adil's words would bring her tomorrow.

natalia

Adil looked much better after a shower and a change of clothes. He sipped on a warm tea, and the only thing left on his plate was crumbs. "Are you sure I can't have more?" he asked.

"No." Garcia shook his head. "He's been starving you for a long time. If you eat too much, you're going to be sick. You'll have to eat small meals and eat them slowly for a while."

Adil looked a little dejected, but when he saw me, he sat straighter and set his cup down in front of him.

"Natty."

I kept my back ramrod straight. I wanted to wrap him in a hug, because I was relieved that he was safe, but I couldn't get past what he had done. He helped my father fake his death and lie to his family. Then he looked us in the eye and told how sorry he was for our loss before he disappeared on us, too. The level of hurt and pain I felt was hard to erase, and even relief for his well-being wasn't going to soften me now. Not until I had answers from him and my father. Not until they begged for my forgiveness and I could somehow move on. Would I hate him forever? Probably not. Could I hate him now? Absolutely.

I woke up this morning after the best sex of my life with nothing but resolve and a backbone of steel. I'd invested years of my life into getting the answers that would bring me closure, and no one was going to stand in my way, not even my father himself. I was a woman on a mission, determined to make sure that everyone answered for their sins. Faris, Adil, my father. They were all liars, and I was done being played the fool.

I pulled out the chair in front of Adil and plopped down in a seat in front of him. "He wouldn't talk to us but told us he'd tell you everything you needed to know. Wanted to do it himself, and I didn't think you'd want us to torture it out of him." Strong stood next to me with his arms crossed as he stared down at Adil.

"You're right, no torture should be necessary. I'm sure Adil is wracked with guilt and he's going to tell me everything—and I mean everything." My words were as pointed as a knife. He wasn't going to leave anything out, even if I had to pry the words from him. What he did was a crime, and if I wanted to, I could sell him out to my pick of law enforcement agencies, or I could send him right back to Faris himself. Would I really? Probably not, but maybe he didn't know that.

"You're different," Adil commented as his eyes narrowed. He leaned back in his chair as if he had to see more of me to determine just how different I was.

"And whose fault is that?" I fired back coolly.

He nodded his head. "I guess that's a fair accusation. Your father and I have a lot to atone for, but you must understand. We thought this was for the greater good."

I sat forward, slamming my hands on the table. What the fuck was there to gain? "The greater good? What the hell is that supposed to mean? Why couldn't he just share the information he had with the U.S. government, you know…who he worked for? Why did he have to fake his death and go undercover himself?" I took a deep breath to try to calm the anger that was flickering up my spine. "Why lie?"

I saw the looks of pity from my friends as they stood on the perimeter of the room. I did my best to ignore it, because their faces didn't matter right now; Adil's did. I needed to see every emotion flicker across his face.

"He did tell the U.S. government. At the time, they were searching for several operatives to implant into President Faris' ranks. They were one short, and he volunteered."

"That doesn't make sense. They won't just let an untrained ambassador fill in for a FBI or CIA asset," Abby quipped.

"She's right, that's not how they operate," Wells commented as he crossed his arms in annoyance. The rest of the group shook their heads in agreement. They'd worked pretty closely with the FBI over the past couple of years, so I trusted their judgment. Something wasn't right.

Adil coughed and began looking a little uncomfortable. Like he had another secret that he really didn't want to share but knew he had no choice. It was as if we were pulling out his fingernails. "How much of your father's past did you look into when you were searching for him?"

"As much as I could. I have his old yearbooks, his employment records from his time working on the Hill. I have *all* of it. What aren't you saying?" I pinned him with a glare that I hoped spoke volumes about my limited patience.

I knew it was impossible to have every document related to my father, but I thought I had most of it. At least enough to be able to use that word without sounding like a dumbass.

He shook his head gently. "No. You have what they wanted you to have, Natty."

Those in the room began to speak in hushed whispers; it created a low buzz in the room. "What are you implying, some kind of government cover-up? What does that have to do with the FBI allowing the ambassador to go undercover when he was completely unqualified?" Mendez asked.

"Because he wasn't," Abby said at the same time as Adil. Her eyes held a spark of recognition that had the hairs on my arms standing on end. Why did I have a bad feeling about this?

"Was he a prior asset?" Guy asked.

The nod caused me to break out into a cold sweat. "That's what he told me, although I was in the dark for most of the time I knew him. He told me the night he asked me to help him fake his death. I never worked for the agency, so he couldn't tell me everything. He shared what he could, which wasn't much. His time on the Hill was a cover. He spent fifteen years as an asset for the FBI as an investigator for money laundering."

The spinning sensation from last night was back in full force. I gripped the edge of the table to keep myself upright. *Another lie my father told us*. Did I even know who the man was? Did I dedicate the last few years of my life chasing after someone I never actually knew? Did he ever even love us, or was our family just a cover for him, too?

The hurt that threatened to sear through me was suffocating. It felt like I might choke on nothing but my own tongue.

"Did my mother know?" I asked. If she lied to me this whole time, I wasn't sure if I'd be able to forgive her. It would explain the distance she put between us after I told her I was going to step into my father's role. She didn't understand my need to stay here, to continue with his work.

Adil shook his head. "No, she had no idea."

I felt my spine sag in relief. Even though she was emotionally distant, she hadn't played a part in this grand lie...or mission. Whatever the hell it was. At least she'd been honest.

"Tell us more about the mission," Isaiah ordered. Like Wells, his arms were crossed in front of him, and he looked as angry as I felt. Despite that, I could feel his silent support from here. After last night, I was only more afraid of what the future held, because I wasn't sure if I'd survive it if we didn't end up together. We hadn't talked about what would happen after we were done here, but it was a conversation that loomed over my head, just like this conversation with Adil did. I had to have faith that I'd feel much better after he and I finally had that conversation.

"I don't know much about it myself. He said he was protecting me by keeping me in the dark. He mentioned something about a compound. He was going to infiltrate the ranks and feed information back to his handler. He was hoping to find enough information to prevent the next large-grade terrorist attack."

"Do you know who his handler is? Did he have an exit plan?" Abby pressed.

Adil shook his head, and disappointment sunk into my bones. "None of that. I simply have a memorized phone number for absolute emergencies. He told me to only use it if his life or his family's lives were in danger."

Silence hung in the air for a few minutes as we processed the news. My father was an operative. He volunteered for this. The very government I worked for covered this up, let me believe my father was dead.

The two sides of my brain were at war with each other. Logically, I knew that the intelligence agencies had to keep these secrets and I simply wasn't cleared to know this information. My father's life and his cover were far too important to risk. Yet the emotional part of me was absolutely destroyed by what felt like betrayal from my country and my father.

"The secretary, she said she had information on what happened to my father. She dangled the information like a carrot to convince me to help her get information from President Faris. Does she know how truly deep this goes, and was she going to tell me the truth?" The question was more of a spoken thought then a legitimate question they could answer. As I looked around, I saw my friends trying to put together the pieces, too.

Adil gave me a quizzical look. "Who is the current secretary of state?"

"Antoinette Walton."

His eyebrows nearly met. "Wasn't she previously the secretary of defense?"

I thought back through what I knew of the woman. She was a dinosaur in D.C. holding many roles under different administrations. Adil was right, she was the secretary of defense for four years, and she very likely knew her successor. It wouldn't be hard for her to look into what actually happened to my father if she wasn't somehow involved in the execution of the plan herself. So she really knew this whole time that my father was alive. She let me believe he was dead, pretended to give a damn about how my family and I felt. Then she had the audacity to dangle the truth in my face, knowing that giving me that info, if she ever planned to, would put my father's life in danger. It would put me in further danger.

It was as if red colored my vision and thunder filled my ears. My fist hit the table hard enough to send a shooting pain up my arm. My hand immediately throbbed, but I couldn't bring myself to care. What did a broken hand matter when everyone had been lying to me?

"This was so much deeper than we thought," Jones mumbled.

His words echoed in my mind for a moment. It was as if they caused an itch that I couldn't scratch. "We thought?" His words continued to bounce around in my subconscious for a moment, just waiting for me to fully grasp them. "We didn't know anything about this, about my father being alive. Did we?"

Jones looked like a deer lost in the headlights for a moment before he looked to Isaiah for help.

My stomach dropped through my ass and out onto the ground. I was going to lose it.

"What exactly did you know?"

natalia

"What exactly did you know?" My words hung in the air; the accusation tasted bitter.

The room was so silent, I'd be able to hear a soldier fart outside. My heart pounded in my chest, because the silence was an admission of guilt. *They knew.*

Wells took a soft step forward with his hands positioned in front of him, as if he were talking down an angry bear. "We suspected that maybe your father was alive. We didn't have definitive proof, just a hunch based on the reports you had on his death. We didn't want to get your hopes up in case we were wrong."

I was disappointed that the words didn't come from Isaiah. I was destroyed by the fact that he kept this secret from me. After the risk I took by letting him in, by letting him help me.

"All of you suspected?" I gave them one more chance to explain themselves, to try to make this right. The hurt welled up inside of me like water against the wall of a dam.

"Not the women," Wells replied instantly.

I let out a shaky breath and then a pissed-off snort. My anger flared in full force. "Good, at least there's someone in this room who hasn't been lying to me." I stood quickly. The chair made a loud screeching noise as the feet dragged across the concrete floor. "I need a moment to digest this…" There was nothing else to say, really.

I turned my back on them and stomped out of the room, determined to make sure no one saw my tears. As soon as the door slammed behind me, I broke out into an undignified run. My sneakers made echoing footsteps as I blindly navigated the halls. I was trapped in the embassy compound, so eventually someone would find me. I couldn't leave unless I wanted to risk being snatched up by any number of people who wanted me dead. It'd been, what, days since the hit was put out on me? On top of that, I was sure Faris had a guess at what really happened to his home and who did it. Especially after he hadn't located Adil's charred remains, and he'd likely make a connection between us.

I'd have to hope that maybe he suspected that a mole leaked Adil's location to me and that it was a direct rescue mission. Maybe weeding out a nonexistent mole would keep him busy for a while.

My feet carried me through the halls and to the janitor's closet next to the stairs to the roof. I grabbed a broom and dragged it up the stairs to the roof with me. I jammed it in the handle of the rooftop door once it closed behind me, locking myself away. I didn't want anyone's company. I needed only me and my thoughts.

Once I was hidden away, my energy left me in one fell swoop. Tears spilled down my face as I stumbled over to my lawn chair. I plopped down into it and closed my eyes against the bright sun. It was such a stark contrast to the despair I felt inside.

Betrayal was such an ugly word. Yet it summarized the past few years of my life perfectly. No one was perfect, and I was generally able to look past the flaws of most people, but lying felt unforgivable. It wasn't an accidental mistake or a character flaw. It was an intentional action meant to deceive, no matter how you sugarcoated it or what your intentions were. It was that tall wall I couldn't scale over or that one bridge I refused to drive over. Yet it'd invaded my life in such an ugly way so quickly. My father, Adil, my friends, *Isaiah.* The last one hurt the most.

I let out a sob. My chest threatened to cave in, as the trust I had in him collapsed. Why couldn't he be bothered to share his suspicions with me? It was my father we were investigating. It was my life, and yet he didn't think I could handle something as big as this? I'd rather him have been upfront with me and wrong. I was capable of managing my expectations, and even if I couldn't, that was my problem. Not his. Who gave him the right to decide what I could and couldn't handle?

I was a fucking ambassador. I dealt with high-stakes situations all the time. I could have handled this, even if it was news about my father. Sure, the news shook me to my core, but who wouldn't have been? To find out my father could still be alive, I'd have to be a mannequin to not have feelings about that fact. No, I could handle that news, but it was the lying from my friends and Isaiah that did me in. That was what completely wrecked me.

I could handle anything, and they should have trusted me with this like I trusted them.

My spine straightened as a feeling cold as ice washed over me. I could handle their lies. If they didn't think I could handle the news, I was going to prove to them just how wrong they were. No one broke Natalia Ali. *No one.*

The only thing I couldn't handle was looking Isaiah in the eye. He made me feel like a fool for trusting him. What he said to me last night was meaningless now. If this was what it felt like to make him feel alive, I wanted no part in it. He could find someone else to light up his world, a new damsel to save. I would not be anyone's fool, and that was exactly what he made me when he decided to leave me in the dark. I was blindsided with Adil's admission when the guys weren't.

God, how stupid did I look to them when they'd already known?

Doesn't matter, Nat. Pull yourself together and show them just how wrong they were to underestimate you. Take this pity party and save it for when you're left jobless and homeless back in the States.

I had a job to do, and first thing's first. I had a secretary to confront.

✦

"Ambassador Ali, to what do I owe the pleasure of being woken up to a call in the middle of the night for?" The secretary was annoyed; her tone made it abundantly clear. All it did was make me grin. Good, I hope she was a lot worse than annoyed, because that was the least of her worries.

"It's okay, Madam Secretary. You can say what you really meant, displeasure. You see, I have a plan for this conversation. Neither of us is going to lie to each other. I'm going to tell you what I know, and then you are going to tell me what you know. No bullshit, no lies." My tone was flat with an edge of contempt. I hoped it was as icy and sharp as I wanted it to be. I hoped she felt my burning hatred.

There was a moment of silence on the other end of the line and then the sound of quiet shuffling. I heard a door close softly, and then she finally spoke.

"Someone has finally grown a spine," she tsked. "Fine, I'll play ball. No lies, no bullshit. Get on with it, Ambassador."

"I know my father's not dead. He was on an assignment with the FBI or CIA, but you already knew that, didn't you?"

There was silence for a moment. "Come on, Madam Secretary, you promised you wouldn't lie." The venom in my tone was scary, even to myself.

"Yes, it's true. Now you know why I was so against your appointment as ambassador. I knew you weren't going to rest until you figured out what happened to him, and ultimately you'd risk the whole mission."

"So instead of just letting me blindly stumble for answers on my own, you what, used me the same way the country used my father? Pump me for information after sending me in blind, way over my head? You used the promise of information to make me bend to your will, but were you ever going to tell me the truth?"

My heart raced in my chest as I waited for her answer.

Her breath hitched just slightly. The ice queen wasn't as in control as she would have liked me to believe. "I would have told you that he's alive, but the rest was highly classified."

"So you would have given me just enough to fulfill your promise, but not enough to satisfy me in any way?" My tone was bitter. I choked back a hate-filled chuckle. I felt like a villain in the moment, even though I was far from the villain in my own story.

"Yes. The truth hurts, Natalia. Politics, whether it be life on the Hill, or life abroad, it's all ruthless. The sooner you toughen up and realize everyone is out for themselves, the better off you'll be. Do your father a favor and drop this for now."

"I can't," I countered quickly.

She sighed in annoyance. "You must. Do you think he faked his death because he wanted to?" She scoffed. "Natalia, any association with him puts you both in worlds of danger. It's bad enough that you burned down Faris' home last night. He's already going to want to put your head on a spike and wave it through the poorest of villages in victory. If you risk finding your father before he's ready to be extracted, well, you might as well sign his actual death certificate yourself." She spat the words as if they were venom. I flinched at her implication.

The words wrapped themselves around my throat like a noose. She was right, even if I didn't want her to be. Instead of commenting on the danger, I circled back to the events of last night. "Word gets out fast, huh?" Somehow that felt like the safer subject. *How ironic.*

"Like an STD in a nursing home." She chuckled, but it sounded bitter and forced. She was laughing at me, not with me. "I hope it was worth it."

I bit my lip to keep from snorting, because despite her tone, the words were still funny. Who knew the bitch would be the first to lift my spirits after the past two days I'd had? "It was. I managed to steal a hidden USB that looked pretty important. I also found several rings carved with the symbols of different terrorism groups. It's as if he changes his jewelry each time he meets with a different group."

"And you didn't lead with this?" the secretary asked with annoyance dipped in sarcasm. There was no mistaking the edge of excitement she was desperately trying to cover.

I rolled my eyes. "I've been waiting longer for answers than you have. You could wait five minutes and answer for your dishonesty before I gave you the keys to your kingdom."

She scoffed but continued on. "I'm going to send you the link to a secure server. Upload the entire contents of the USB in the drop box, and do not show anyone else. They aren't cleared for this information, and if they see it, it could honestly put their lives in danger, no bullshit."

It was my turn to scoff. "My safety's already forfeit, so it doesn't matter if I see it, huh?" I couldn't help but let my snarkiness out. She and I were past the niceties of our positions now.

"Your words. As long as you don't tell a soul, you're safe on home soil. Get the files uploaded, and I'll get working on finding your replacement and getting you out of there."

I could tell she was about to hang up, but I couldn't let her. "Wait!"

She let out an irritated sigh. "What?"

"I can't leave yet. I can't just leave him behind." As hurt as I was by my father, I couldn't leave him behind. I logically knew that I couldn't contact him, not if I wanted him to stay safe, but I couldn't leave him here knowing I could never come back for him.

"You can and you will. Depending on what's on that thumb drive of yours, it might be all the information we need to pull him and the other assets out. Your soldier friends know what it means to follow orders, and you will take a page from their book, Ambassador. Two days and you're out of there. Make your arrangements."

The line clicked, and I slammed my screen shut. I leaned back against the back of my chair, and for what felt like the first time in days, I allowed myself to enjoy the sunshine. I finally had some answers, even if I had to wreck my whole life to get them.

CHAPTER THIRTY-SIX

isaiah

"I fucked up by not telling her, didn't I?" My words sounded hollow and full of regret. They echoed through the emptiness, the way I felt inside.

"I think we all did," Jones answered. His green eyes, normally full of mockery, seemed full of regret.

"Correction, you all did," Jasmine said as she crossed her arms in front of her. Her eyes shot daggers at each one of us. Nat wasn't the only one left in the dark, and now all the coupled-up dudes were about to feel some feminine wrath.

"I can't believe you didn't even tell me," Abby scoffed. She looked hurt by our decision to keep her in the dark. Out of all the women, I had to admit, she would be the one we could trust with the information the most. She could be objective. But she was still a woman, and I didn't know if she'd stick with the *"hoes before bros"* thing.

"Look, we weren't sure, okay?" Wells let out an annoyed sigh. "We didn't want to get Natalia's hopes up if we were wrong. There was no need for her to lose him twice if we had our info wrong. Would you want to do that to her?" he asked as he pinned the ladies with a challenging glare.

"If it meant not lying to her or keeping secrets, yeah. I would have told her my suspicions. What she does or doesn't feel related to that information is on her, not you. The betrayal and hurt she feels right now…that's on you guys." Christine spun as her words sliced through me like a knife. She was right. Why were the women always right?

"You better fix this, funny man. There are powerful people who want Natalia dead, and now she's probably questioning who she can trust. I wouldn't blame her one bit for running from us…you. Let's hope this is where the regret stops, and not at her funeral." Jasmine followed Christine out, and I wasn't surprised at the ruthless nature of her blame. Abby didn't even spare a glance in Strong's direction as she left in Jasmine's wake. They were one for all. *Hoes before bros.*

"Well, that went well," Mendez commented once the door slammed shut behind Abby.

"As well as JRTC during that hurricane, remember?" Garcia asked.

I knew what he was doing, trying to cheer us up, but it wasn't going to work. "Yeah, whose bright idea was it not to secure the tent down? To make us more mobile," Guy teased.

"That was Isaiah," Mendez quipped, biting back a smile.

I brought my hands up to my face and rubbed my eyes in frustration. "I'm sorry, guys. Not only is Natalia mad at me, but your women are pissed at you, too. I made a bad call, and you guys are suffering."

The guilt threatened to eat me alive, and for the first time in a long time, I felt helpless.

"Dude, none of that pity-party shit. Abby and I will duke it out, and I'll admit that I was wrong to listen to you boneheads. Then Abby and I will have hot make-up sex that will make the minor inconvenience of the argument very worth it. No harm, no foul. Although I don't think Natalia would say the same." Strong's smirk was enough to lessen some of the guilt. Jones and Wells didn't look too worried, either.

"Do you feel the same?" I asked them.

"I mean, I wasn't going to be so crude about it, but yeah, bro. Our women are hurt that they weren't in on the secret and that their friend is hurting. They probably feel like had they known, they would have been able to prevent this, and they would probably be right. We'll grovel and then kiss and make up. Deep down, it takes more than one bad judgment call to destroy something that's meant to be. If you and Natalia are the real deal, she'll see that, too," Jones explained.

"You should really perfect the art of groveling and be absolutely sincere. If she loves you, she will eventually see that you made this decision with the best of intentions, and she will forgive you."

I rubbed my hands across my face again and wished that the consuming black sludge inside my chest would ease its hold. "I hope you guys are right."

"Us too."

✦

It was hours later when I ran into my friends again. All of them seemingly had made up with their better halves. Only I was left without any sort of resolution. Nat wouldn't even open the door of her office so that I could talk to her. She wouldn't respond any time I tried to talk to her through the door, nor did she answer any of my texts or calls. I was completely iced out.

"You need a grand gesture." Christine sat down on the floor beside me, in front of Nat's door.

"No, I just need her to give me five minutes. I know I can convince her that I meant well, that I was just trying to protect her."

She looked at me like I was dumb; the expression was eerily close to Jasmine's. "Hence the need for the grand gesture. I know you're used to smooth-talking women into your bed, but this is completely different. A wink and a one-liner isn't going to fix this, Yates."

I didn't want to admit it, but maybe she was right. I was so out of my element—but one thing's for sure, my pride was not nearly as important as Nat. Last night was earth-shattering, and I wanted that every night.

"What do you think I should do?" I asked with my hands on my face.

I peeked through my fingers, and she rolled her eyes like I was hopeless. "Now I can't tell you that. But what would make Natalia happy?"

I didn't hesitate. "Having her father back."

"Well, we can't pull him from his mission, so roll again."

I thought about Natalia's heart and what would mean the world to her. It was as if a lightbulb lit above me. "The people here mean a lot to her. What if we make sure that all those supplies we brought don't go to waste when she leaves?"

"You might just be worthy of that second chance after all," she praised. She stood up, took a few steps away, and then turned around to look at me. "What are you waiting for? You've got an event to plan."

CHAPTER THIRTY-SEVEN

natalia

Isaiah kept his distance last night, opting to stay in the guesthouse with his friends. Smart move. I was ready to prove to him and his friends that I was tough, but I wasn't tough enough to share space with him right now. The house felt lonely, and my bed felt cold, but the feeling wasn't enough to make me forgive and forget. I had too much self-respect to let him back in just to warm my bed.

I scrolled through the secured folder that housed a copy of the USB's contents. The cold metal sported a gold chain, and it hung around my neck. I'd still need to keep the original safe until it could be brought back to the States and vetted. They had all kinds of computer analysts and cyber experts who would be pawing for a chance to work on this for their country.

Holy shit.

If this wasn't enough to bring my father off mission, I didn't know what would. Most of it I wasn't able to open or I wasn't able to fully understand. But what I could make sense of made my head spin. Some of the photos of the destruction he had a hand in made me understand the meaning of *"the end justifies the means."* Invading Faris' home and the high possibility of getting caught now felt worth it, except to my tired lungs and raw throat. The documents that I stared at would save thousands.

The electronic money transfer statements I studied would be crucial in identifying Faris' secret inner circle. They'd also help trace some of the money all the way back to the foreign aid payments that the U.S. was sending Syria.

I rested my forehead on my desk in exhaustion. I closed my eyes, which felt scratchy and raw from staring at the screen for so long. They still hadn't recovered from the smoke and flames.

When the secure server beeped that the last document was saved and secured, I let out a sigh of relief, closing the laptop without even looking at it. I just wanted a moment of blessed silence before I figured out what I was going to do about Isaiah and my father. I only had a day and a half left, and I still needed to figure out how I was going to leave this all behind. I'd given up completely about doing anything else that was going to make a difference. There were so many that I'd never get to say goodbye to, and I felt wracked with guilt that I was leaving them to suffer alone.

The silence was interrupted by the sound of voices outside my window. Down below the gate was open, and women and children flooded through.

What was going on?

I hurried through the halls; my flats were almost silent against the tile. My breathing was loud enough to announce where I was for anyone paying attention. I stepped outside, the sun felt warm against my skin, but it wasn't what thawed my iced-over heart.

I was blown away by the tables stacked high with supplies and my friends nearby distributing them. A white tent stood tall over to the right, with a red cross sign taped onto the canvas. A medical tent.

Tears flooded my eyes, and I quickly blinked them away. This was grander than any clinics I'd managed to throw together, and I'd been doing them since I started as ambassador. This was their first.

Christine hurried by with a box that overflowed with vitamin bottles.

"Christine...how?" I was too blown away to string together a full question. She turned and smiled at me. "I think you know the answer… Consider it *the* grand gesture." She shifted the box in her hands so it rested comfortably against her hip.

Of course it was. I wanted to stay mad for a little bit longer, because his mistake was really shitty. He was going to make that impossible, though this was a great start to an apology. "Isaiah did this?"

It was a massive grand gesture.

"He sure did. He knows he fucked up, and he just wants a chance to explain himself. Do you think you can hear him out?"

I looked all around me. "I don't think I have a choice," I mumbled, more to myself than her. "Where is he?"

She turned to look around before her lips curved upward into a smile. "If you were Isaiah, where would you be?" she asked.

If I were making a grand gesture to ask for forgiveness, I'd make sure I'd have a visual on the person I wanted to ask forgiveness from from the moment they entered the area. I looked to my right and saw him propped up against the wall. His prosthetic rested over his other leg, with his arms bent in front of him. His eyes were intense, as if he was just waiting for me to turn my back on him and what he did. Like he was used to those he cared for hurting him.

He certainly knew how to ensure I wouldn't walk away before he had the chance to apologize. I took a deep breath and casually strolled over to him, trying to portray a cool confidence I didn't feel. Inside I was a wreck, torn between forgiving him already and wanting to hear the apology paired with this clinic before I decided. Was I cruel for making him want to sweat it out a little more?

"I hear this was some sort of grand gesture," I started at the same time he said, "Nat, I'm so sorry."

He chuckled after he registered my words. "Yeah, I had to draw you out of your office somehow. I need you to know how sorry I am. I was trying to protect you. I wanted my suspicions to be right, but I was afraid we were wrong. I didn't want you to lose your father all over again. I couldn't be the one to do that to you, Nat." A little boy ran by us, screeching even as his mother chased him, shouting for him to behave. That didn't faze Isaiah; his eyes never left my face. "My only regret is that my decision caused you pain and broke your trust in me. But I will do whatever I have to to protect your heart, even if it upsets you."

"Is that your best apology?" I asked. He stared into my eyes searching for any signs of what I was thinking. His guess was as good as mine, because I was full of thoughts and emotions.

Deep down, I knew he didn't keep his suspicions to himself to be spiteful or to make a fool of me. The way he looked at me now, I knew that every word of his apology was true. He looked like he'd tear himself apart limb from limb if it would make me happy.

That fact didn't change how much hurt his decision caused me, but just maybe I overreacted a bit. Maybe I placed a bit of the hurt and frustration I felt for my father at Isaiah's feet. Deep down, that wasn't right, even if at the time it felt good to have someone I could physically give the cold shoulder. It was hard to ice someone out who has no idea that they'd been found out in the first place.

I'd been in survival mode ever since I thought my father died, and part of that meant keeping the circle of people I trusted small. I wasn't used to others making decisions for me, because no one had cared about how I felt in a long time. Yet Isaiah and his friends did. They'd made a bad decision, but at least they were here for me. At least they made their mistake with the best of intentions. My father had to have known he was leaving with more than five minutes of notice; he could have at least bothered to make sure we had a meaningful goodbye. His mistake was leaving things where he left them before he faked his death.

I swallowed, because that guilt I'd been saddled with since my father went missing felt just a little bit lighter. I might just get the opportunity to tell him I was sorry. Once he groveled for leaving us and for keeping so many secrets.

I looked all around the clinic again. The locals seemed just a little more spirited—carefree even. Children were smiling over bowls of mac and cheese, and some of the mothers wiped their tear-streaked faces as they took in the joy their children were experiencing between the food options, the small toybox someone had stocked, the larger hygiene kits and upgraded first aid kit. This was much more impressive than anything they'd seen thrown at the embassy before.

I spotted the rest of Isaiah's friends—my friends, throughout the crowd. They wore smiles and did their best to interact with those they were helping, despite the language barrier. Christine's smile didn't need a translation, nor did the hug that Jasmine gave to a mom holding two small babies. They did this for me—for Isaiah.

"I mean, I've got a much better apology, but I don't think you're into public sex... Are you?" His grin was devilish, and he was forgiven, right then and there—not that I'd let him know that.

"You're impossible! I accept your apology, only if you promise not to do this again. I know you said you'd do it again if you had to, but don't."

His smirk grew serious. "You drive a hard bargain, Ambassador." He held his hand out for a handshake, as if this was a business deal.

"Shut up and kiss me." I snagged his hand and pulled him to me. I wrapped my arms around the back of his neck and my lips found his.

"With pleasure," he said with a smile against my lips. The kiss was sweet and slow, barely appropriate for the audience we had around us.

"Finally! Now break it up and help us give away all this shit before we leave." Jones' green eyes were sparkling with mischief. I imagined if we had an older crowd around us, he would have made some sexual innuendos and teased us, just as Isaiah would do to him.

I looked up at Isaiah, and all those butterflies threatened to explode from me like a Disney Princess in a musical number. No one had ever made me feel the way he did, and I didn't ever want to let it go.

"I love you." I smiled at him.

His eyes went wide before he broke out into a stupidly cute grin. "I love you more. I think it was love from the first time I laid eyes on you."

"Really?" I grinned so hard that my cheeks hurt. Happy laughter filled my voice.

"Yeah." I leaned forward and kissed him again. I turned away before I could let my feelings take over. I wanted nothing more than to take him back to my room and repeat our steamy shower sex.

I grabbed a box of dried food from the stack next to us and left Isaiah behind so that I could properly say goodbye to the people I spent so much time and energy to help.

natalia

It had been a long day, and I was exhausted, but none of that mattered as Isaiah tossed me onto the bed and I let out an excited squeal. I bounced and landed flat on my back. I blinked, and the next second Isaiah was on top of me. His legs pinned me down at my hips, and his hands grabbed my wrists and pinned them above my head. He stared down at me as if he were starving, and I was the only thing that would ever satisfy him.

Lust clouded his eyes as they traveled down my body, stopping at my breasts. "There are too many layers on," he commented as he transferred one of my wrists to his other hand. With a hand now freed, he pulled the hem of my shirt over my head. With it gone, my flesh broke out into goosebumps. He gently traced a finger over my cleavage, and I shivered.

He leaned forward, and his lips crushed mine with a force that was breathtaking. His tongue tangled with mine, alternating between soft and desperate. When I thought I was going to pass out from lack of oxygen, he pulled back. I let out a gasp as air flooded my lungs, and his lips danced across my throat.

He nipped the skin there, and my fingernails sunk into the back of his hand.

"Do you like that?" he asked. I felt the vibrations of his voice against my throat.

I nodded, unable to form any words.

"Let me hear you say it, Natalia." His voice was deep with just an edge of dominance. If I wasn't already sopping wet, that moment would have done it for me.

"Yes." The word was a breathy moan.

"Good." His lips met my neck again, and his teeth dragged across the skin. His free hand turned my face away from him, giving him more room to play with. I closed my eyes as the heat of his lips took over my thoughts.

His hand on my jaw slid down and lightly gripped my throat. I gasped in pleasure and surprise. I had no idea that I liked to be dominated this much, but I had a feeling I'd like just about anything Isaiah did to me in bed. He'd make sure I enjoyed it.

His lips traveled down my chest and gently nipped at my cleavage. He used his teeth to grab the edge of my bra and pull it away from my skin, freeing a nipple. I flinched at the cold air for only a second before he wrapped his lips around it, eliciting a moan from me. He quickly switched to the other, and I became a squirming mess in his hands.

"Please," I begged.

"Please, what?" I could just hear the smugness in his tone. He was pleased by what he was doing to me.

"Please, I want to come." My voice was barely a whimper, but I knew he heard me.

He chuckled a throaty laugh that made my stomach clench in anticipation. "And you will...in due time. I need to make sure you know just how sorry I am."

He rolled his hips against mine, and the friction instantly started building in my core. If he kept that up, he was going to make me cum before he ever took my pants off.

As if the motions reminded him of the fact I was still half clothed, he released my wrists with one hand and kept hold of my throat with the other. His free hand quickly freed me of my pants; the denim tickled as the fabric slid down my legs. He sniffed the air. "I can see you might be starting to understand the lesson." He hooked his finger into the delicate lace and pulled it off of me. Then he stared down at my near-naked body beneath him. "Beautiful. I don't know what I would have done if you didn't forgive me." He palmed my left breast with his right hand as he began to roll his hips from where he straddled mine. The friction of bare skin against the denim drove me wild and left a stain on his pants.

He raised his hips and quickly slid his pants and boxers down his body, then placed himself back down on top of me and pulled his shirt over his head. I eyed his naked body like it was a work of art on display at a museum. I'd buy every ticket to the place to enjoy the show.

He spread my legs slightly beneath him, opening me to the gentle touches he left with his fingers. His fingers found just the right spot, and my fingers fisted the sheets. It felt like only seconds before he brought me to the brink of destruction and let me shatter around him. My release hit me hard, like a freight train. My eyes rolled into the back of my head, my back arched, and my toes curled.

Before I had time to catch my breath, he dragged the length of his dick through my arousal. That was all the preparation he needed. My breath caught in my throat as he entered me quickly and forcefully, with the desperation we both felt.

I had only a few seconds to adjust before he began to thrust in and out of me. He readjusted his grip on my throat, and with his other hand he used his thumb to play with my clit.

"Is this a good apology, Natalia?" he asked. The words penetrated the quiet rhythm of our bodies slapping and panted breaths.

I nodded my head.

"I can't hear you," he warned.

"Yes, it's a great apology." My answer sounded desperate. I wanted more.

"Hm, I don't know. I don't quite believe you. Maybe I should be doing more." The words were a lustful tease that shot up my spine like a firework. More? How could he possibly do more when it was already phenomenal? What was better than an A++?

He applied more pressure to my clit as he bent forward and sucked my nipple into his mouth. He rolled the sensitive skin between his teeth. The suction, the stimulation, and the thrusts were all too much. I let out a scream as my body locked up, and a tidal wave of euphoria flooded through my body. I damn near forgot my own name as I came back down from the high.

My body went slack under Isaiah's, but he didn't move.

"Don't think I'm done with you yet, Ambassador." The words were a lust-filled promise. He pulled back, and his dick stood at full mast, covered in my cum. "Flip over, ass up and in the air." The words were an order, as if I were a private he were instructing. I'd show him privates.

I did what he said and pressed my face into the sheets as I got on my knees. He slapped my ass, and the sound rang through the now-quiet room. I flinched, and then he did it again.

I felt him slide two fingers into me, and then they curled and uncurled in a fast rhythm. He placed his other hand in the center of my back, keeping me down as he coaxed another orgasm from me. The skin on my knuckles threatened to split from gripping the sheets so hard.

I was mid pant when he pulled his fingers from me and then slid his cock back inside. I moaned at the sensation of feeling full, and he wasted no time. I felt him slam against my inner walls; if I weren't so incredibly turned on, it might have hurt. He leaned over me as his pelvis slammed into my ass over and over. His hands found my nipples and gave them a gentle tug. I bit my lip as I swallowed down the sensation to cry out. I couldn't let him make me cum again so quickly, not without him finding his release.

I reached between my legs, and my fingers cupped his balls, massaging them.

"You naughty girl, taking control over your own apology. Are you ready to come together, Ambassador?" he whispered into my ear.

I shivered again. My answer was to apply more pressure to his balls. His pelvis slammed even harder into my ass, his hips making an upward motion.

"Come," he growled.

My toes curled, my eyes slammed shut, and my back arched. I let loose a pleasure-filled cry, and his growl filled my ears.

In the quiet of the night, I whispered, "Apology. Fucking. Accepted."

isaiah

"Wait, what?"

My breath caught in my throat. There was absolutely no way that my eyes weren't deceiving me. There was no way that an entire arsenal was hidden inside of the embassy, and no one had any idea.

Scratch that, Nat's father knew—and possibly his boss.

"This is magnificent," Jones said as he dragged his palm across the surface of a sleek table in the middle of the room. The air was stale, and the dust that collected on some of the surfaces was thick. There must have been fifty different guns, all behind a plexiglass case. They were various sizes and different manufacturers. On another wall was a display of knives and other equipment. It felt like walking onto the set of a spy movie.

"You had no idea this was here?" Garcia asked, and his eyes met Nat's. His eyebrow was pitched awfully high on his forehead.

"That's cute," Jasmine countered. She raised her eyebrow to mock Garcia. I couldn't contain my snicker. "She clearly had no idea. I mean, look at the place. We've left footprints in the dust. No one's been in here for years."

She was right, there wasn't a single footprint left on the dusty floor when we entered, and now we left evidence of our entry all around.

"Abby, why wouldn't an agency come back and take these?" Christine asked.

"If they thought he might need them on his current mission, they'd leave this. He's an American citizen. This would still be a safe fallback area where he'd be offered protection, if he could make it here."

"So who owns these, the FBI?" Wells asked.

"Do I look like a database?" Abby snorted. "No clue. I'm guessing since they are in a foreign country any serial numbers have been scrubbed and their ghost weapons."

"I want to take these out to play," Mendez commented, and I could see the same urge in Jones and Wells' eyes. Hell, even Abby looked like she was considering it.

Natalia shook her head. "Nope." She popped the *P* at the end. "These stay right where he left them. If we have to leave him here, I don't want to screw him over by messing with his shit."

"So we're just going to leave it all?" Christine asked as she looked around.

Nat nodded. "My marching orders were clear. Get everything ready for my replacement, and don't fuck anything up. I'm sure discharging hundreds of rounds and testing weapons on an embassy compound would certainly cause a conflict with the second."

She was right, as much as it pained me. I'd love to get my hands on some of those rifles gleaming behind their protective cases. But I could see the chaos and questions that would create. The National Guard and embassy security forces probably had no idea that a weapons cache sat under their feet. The entrance to the hidden room was disguised as a mirror. Once we realized that Natalia's father had connections to an agency, Abby started combing the building with a fine-tooth comb, looking for any of the tricks she knew they liked to play. It took a while, but when she figured out the mirror in Natalia's office wasn't a standard one, we all crammed into the room and found the secret latch. The door swung open on a hinge, and we discovered the mirror was actually a two-way mirror.

"We can't even shoot one?" Strong complained.

"No." A smile tugged on Nat's lips as she delivered the final word. I thought she might enjoy messing with my friends as much as I did.

"Then what are we supposed to do?" I asked.

She shrugged her shoulders and looked at me thoughtfully for a moment. "Stay out of trouble."

As if her words had cued pandemonium, a siren began to blare. The dark room lit up red, and a high pitch assaulted our ears.

"What the fuck is that?" I growled.

"It means we're under attack!" Nat had to scream the words to be heard, but they still felt hollow, like they were disconnected from the urgency the light and sound created.

Just then Nat's phone rang. She pulled it from her pocket; her eyes were wide as they stared up at me. Her expression was full of fear, and her lip trembled.

She put the phone to her ear anyways. "Hello?"

She was quiet as she listened to whoever was on the other end. By the fear in her eyes, I suspected it was Faris. Her eyes only got wider as the seconds ticked by, and I couldn't help but feel like shit was about to hit the fan.

natalia

"Ambassador Ali, I must say—I'm disappointed we didn't get to speak much at dinner the other night. I apologize that the night…and my home went up in flames."

I swallowed down the lump of fear that formed in my throat, threatening to choke me. "There's no need to apologize, President Faris. I'm disappointed as well." Lie. In hindsight, I was actually relieved. "Was anyone hurt?"

He paused for a moment. "There are a few people still unaccounted for."

I gasped in what I hoped was believable horror. "I hope they come up alive and well." Except Adil, he was going to stay free.

"Me too. But I didn't call to discuss other people." He paused again. "Pardon me, it sounds like I caught you at a bad time. Is everything okay over there?" he asked.

It was hard to pin what exactly it was about his tone, but it sent off my internal alarms like it was a nuclear warning. If I could see his face through the phone, he'd probably look smug as could be.

"I'm afraid so. Do you think we could schedule a call for another time?" I tried to be polite despite the fact that the embassy was falling into chaos around me. I might be underground, but I could still hear the footsteps of those on top of us. Not to mention the sounds of panic echoed through my office and down the stairs to us. I wasn't even near the staff, and I could still hear them through the alarm.

That was really fucking bad.

"We've got to go, Nat." Isaiah's eyes held the calm determination I needed to get my feet moving. All around me his friends had picked up the weapons that just minutes ago I told them they couldn't play with. Some of them were even grinning at the fact.

Isaiah took my hand and tugged me up the stairs. "No, that won't be necessary, Ms. Ali. I just wanted to say I know you are responsible for my home burning. Imagine my surprise that not even a few full days after the burning of my home, the presidential mansion, I'm being summoned to testify in front of the UN." He paused for a moment, and I held my breath. I was waiting for his proverbial kill shot.

Isaiah slid my rifle over my back, its strap resting over my shoulder. He continued to tug me out of the office, and I was surrounded by his circle of friends. Christine and Jasmine's shoulders were shoved up against mine; our feet kept stepping on each other. No one dared to hiss or complain. The men and Abby formed a circle around us with their weapons drawn.

"Hang up," Isaiah mouthed to me. I held up a finger. I just needed one minute to figure out the warning.

"That's terrible." My tone was full of forced sympathy I didn't feel.

"Indeed, it is. So naturally I had to get to the bottom of this. Turns out espionage runs in your family, Ms. Ali. I'm not sure how I didn't see that one coming."

It was becoming hard to hear even with my finger pressed against my other ear.

"Kudos to you, Ms. Ali. You've succeeded where your father could not. Let's just hope you live long enough to enjoy the fruits of your labor. Tell Adil I said hello."

The phone disconnected and with it took the only measure of calm I felt.

"Faris knows everything. He knows it was me who set the fire, knows I freed Adil, and he knows my father was an operative. This attack is all his doing. We've got to go!"

"Do you think Tom finished setting up the transport out?" Strong asked Isaiah.

"He was supposed to. Let's hope the man sets the same standard for himself as he does others or we are fucked up the ass." Isaiah's brow was set in determination.

The men rushed us through the hallway as the sound of gunfire outside echoed down the corridor. "Go, go, go!" Wells shouted at us as he hustled us out the back door near the kitchen.

"Tom, are you ready for an emergency evacuation?" Strong asked as we made a mad dash across the compound grounds to the security building.

"Got the choppers ready thirty minutes before the alarm went off, fuel, safety checks, and all."

"Where's Kareem?" I asked Tom.

"Right here, did you think you were leaving without me?" Kareem asked from one of the seats in the Blackhawk next to us.

"Not a chance." I smiled back. "And Adil?"

"Waiting for your father, apparently," Tom commented.

"Wait, what?" all of us asked at the same time.

"Oh please, I know you know. I've gotten strict orders to get you the hell out of here, and those come from two different people, one of them being your father himself."

I took an accusatory step toward him as Abby and Strong started grabbing gear for us from the security building. It didn't matter that bullets ricocheted off various surfaces. Had even Tom been lying to me?

"No, calm down and put that on." I accepted the gear that was shoved into my hands. "Adil brought me up to speed when I told him I had orders to get you out, Ambassador. He told me he's been in contact with your father, who wasn't dead, and he wants you safely evacuated at all costs." He shot me an accusatory look of his own. "You aren't going to make that difficult for me, are you, Ambassador?" His raised eyebrow contradicted his words.

I was so torn in two. My father and I were about to cross paths, but I had to run when I wanted to stay and fight. To see him.

"If you stay you are defying a presidential order, ma'am. The other order for evacuation came from the big man himself. He needs you alive to give you some ribbon. He's sending in a whole other security team to support the embassy and evacuate nonessential personnel."

Fuck the ribbon. I cared about those who worked for me and for my father and Adil.

"Will you make me the same promise? Will you get them on a bird and get Father and Adil the fuck out as soon as the opportunity arises? And anyone else who wants out?" My glare was intense, I was sure. But I needed Tom to see just how serious I was. I wasn't going to fight him if he could make and keep that one promise.

"I promise if you get that butt of yours on that bird right now. You and your friends are out of here. Say goodbye to Syria, Ms. Ali." Tom reached out his hand, and I put my palm in his to shake.

"Come visit me in the States sometime?" I asked.

"Only if you're cooking," he said with a wink, and then he turned to shake the hands of my friends before he turned his back on us. He took up a position at the perimeter of the wall that surrounded the embassy.

"Let's go!" Abby ordered as she shoved us all into the Blackhawks.

Wells, Christine, Jones, Jasmine, and Guy got into the first Blackhawk with Kareem. Their soldier escorts eyed the weapons they were strapped with but didn't say a word. Instead, Jones showed them some tattoo on his arm, likely a unit patch of some sort. He pointed at the other guys, too. The soldiers nodded, and that was all she wrote. They slipped on their headsets as Isaiah, Strong, Abby, Garcia, Mendez, and I slipped on our headsets.

"Do you know how to work those things?" The co-pilot asked as he took in the weapons we carried.

Strong turned to look at the man. "Likely better than you. Green Berets, a FBI agent, and a highly trained ambassador. Think we passed the safety course, bud."

The co-pilot barely refrained from rolling his eyes, but he turned to face forward, and seconds later our Blackhawk left the ground.

I took in the chaos that had developed as we got a little higher. There were numerous vehicles parked all around the perimeter of the embassy. It was hard to see from an aerial point of view, but bodies poured out and ran toward the walls.

"Ground intel says no launchers have been observed. We're going to do a low flyover and give ground some additional cover. You itching to show me how much better you are at shooting than we are?" the co-pilot asked.

"You bet!" Abby said as she pivoted toward the door and flicked her safety off.

The guys just grinned, and Abby looked like she was legitimately having the time of her life as the sound of gunfire filled the sky. Luckily the headsets helped mute the sound.

I watched from the window. I had no desire to add to the chaos. I'd leave that to those better suited for it. I only fired my weapon in self-defense, and this no longer felt like that kind of situation. We were in the sky and had the advantage. The assailants on the ground took fire from in front and above.

After two quick circles, the attackers were thinned out, so we left so that the soldiers on the ground in the embassy could clear the sky and launch missiles to disable the vehicles for those who remained behind. We did not want them to regroup.

Of course, this narration didn't come from the pilots themselves, but Isaiah who gave me the play by play as he watched.

I took one long last look at my home as we flew out of view. Everything I owned was in my home, my pictures of my family, my memories, everything.

"Goodbye, Syria."

CHAPTER FORTY-ONE

isaiah

After we left Syrian airspace, the ride was a lot less eventful. Our Blackhawks landed in Israel, where we then got on a commercial flight for the rest of the journey. The weapons we carried were left in the U.S. embassy for safekeeping in case Nat's father wanted them back.

Our stay in Israel was very brief, but the ambassador himself came by to congratulate Natalia on a job well done. Apparently the embassy's in the area had been briefed by the president's staff on just what Natalia uncovered. I wasn't exactly sure of the contents myself. The opportunity to discuss the USB hadn't come up. I knew she had it with her but didn't realize she'd already looked through it.

Our flight from Israel felt long, but most of us slept a good portion of the flight. With no luggage to haul, most of us had nothing to do but sleep or play on our phones. I had to hope that whoever stayed behind to ship back our belongings would send my laptop timely.

I took in Natalia's sleeping form. She was slumped over, her head rested on my shoulder, and she softly snored. "Hey, Nat," I whispered.

She woke up with a gentle start. She turned her head to look at me, and her face was creased with lines from my shirt. I simply smiled at her; she was still beautiful.

"Do you know what you are going to do when you get back to the States?" I asked.

She shook her head. "No, I haven't thought that far ahead. I imagine I'll have to appear before the president and Congress. But I don't know after that."

"Might I make a suggestion?"

"I don't see why not," she retorted with an eyebrow raised in interest.

"Come live with me. Or hell, if you have to stay in Washington, I'll come live with you." My heart hammered hard in my chest. I was really going all the way here. On my flight to Syria, I thought maybe my feelings about Nat were something I'd be able to work out of my system. It was on the return flight that I realized just how delusional I was. There was no working a woman like Nat out of your head or your heart. I just hoped she'd still want me around.

"You'd move to Washington for me?" she asked. She had unshed tears in her eyes that I saw her try to blink away.

"Nat, there is literally nothing on this planet that I wouldn't do for you. Yes, moving to the nation's capital is not very high up there on difficult tasks. If that's what you want, we can make the arrangements."

She nodded her head eagerly. "If I still have some sort of job in Washington, yes!"

I twined my fingers with hers, and she snuggled closer to me. "What's next for you, though, besides a new roommate? What are you going to do for work? I can't believe you're going to give up every-thing for me." Her smile was blinding. I'd beg on the streets everyday if it meant causing her that kind of happiness.

"There's lots of rich types in D.C., right? I'm sure someone needs some private security."

"They always do," she added with a smaller smile.

Her face turned to look out the window, and over what seemed like minutes, she seemed to deflate.

"Hey, what's wrong?" I asked and turned her chin toward me.

"I just feel bad. I'm jetting back home to happiness while my staff is back at the embassy, and my father and Adil are still in Syria. I guess I'm feeling guilty…"

"Don't." I stopped her. "Don't think for even a moment you had a choice about getting on that Blackhawk. So many of us were prepared to toss you over our shoulder if you refused. Then you'd feel guilty for slowing us down." I gently kissed her nose. "Feel happy that such a large group of people respected you enough that they want you out of harm's way first."

"How do you do that?" she asked. Her eyes twinkled, and I wasn't sure if it was a trick from the setting sun that shined through the windows or just amusement.

"What?"

"Know just what to say?"

"I don't. Most of the time I don't know what I'm saying until the words leave my mouth. That shows you my jokes are actually funny. They aren't pre-written, waiting for the perfect opportunity. They come to me straight at the moment. You know what else I'd like to come in at this moment?" I sent her the most non-subtle wink I could.

Her eyes heated, as if she could pull the thoughts from my mind.

"Get a room, assholes!" Mendez called from behind us somewhere, and the whole plane chuckled. I didn't realize we had a whole audience.

Nat turned around in her seat. "Are you guys looking forward to going home?"

"I'm looking forward to seeing my hot tub, but that's about it. It's not like I've stopped working, even from Syria." Christine was a workhorse; she seemed to never stop going. Her dream to help lead her father's company into the future was realized only a few short years ago. She wasn't going to give it up for anything, not when she could make it fit into her life.

"Yeah, I do miss that hot tub and a solid internet connection for gaming." Wells would be there to make sure that Christine found her balance, that she'd remember she was a valuable part of her company, and she needed to take care of herself, too.

"I do miss football," Jones joked as he reclined in his chair. He missed playing professional football more than he enjoyed watching it.

"No, you miss that luxury bathroom you remodeled for me…and your sister," Jasmine called him out.

"Okay, but what's not to miss about that shower, Jasmine? You praise it and me all the time when I—"

"Nope!!" Garcia cut Jones off. "Don't want to hear it." He shook his head with one of his goofy smiles he didn't wear enough.

"You ready to get back to the grind?" Abby asked Strong with a soft, playful shove to his arm. He nodded and turned to face us. "Abby and I are opening our own MMA gym. We've got a few investors, and a professional fighter that wants to make it his exclusive club."

"Congratulations!" the cabin chorused.

"No more tracking down missing people?" Guy asked as he plugged away on his phone.

"Of course we are. I could never stop doing that, but the MMA gym is more like a passion project that will give us passive income as we jet all over the country looking for those who need us." Abby almost looked hurt at the insinuation that she gave up her life's mission, even for a moment.

"Good, because you're damn good at it," Guy said with a wink.

"Now, now, Guy. No need to remind you who'd win in a fight," Strong teased.

"Yeah, and there's no need to remind you who could hack your bank accounts and steal everything you own in a snap of a finger." He winked for good measure.

"What about you three?" Nat asked Mendez, Garcia, and Guy.

"Not sure," Mendez said as he shook his head. "Might jump back into private security, might try out something new."

"Yeah, same here. I've got some time to figure it out," Garcia added.

We all turned to look at Guy. "Hey, I've already told you. I've got my private contracting gigs. I'm in the middle of one right now. They're going to be pissed that my laptop is in the middle of Syria."

"What about you two?" Christine asked. "What are your big plans, besides getting an award from the president?"

"I don't know. I guess I'll figure that out once we're in D.C." Nat wore a dreamy smile as she squeezed my hand a little tighter.

Finally it was my turn. "Maybe private security. I'd given some thought to being a firefighter before I left for Syria. Maybe I'll give that a go. You know, since I've already tested the waters?"

The cabin groaned. They could play all they wanted. I was funny, and they knew it.

Now I knew why people went to go see psychologists, and I was able to feel what it was that everyone was after. Peace. Peace with their choices, their relationships, and the trauma that happened to them.

At that moment, with my friends surrounding me, the girl I love in my arms, a reunion to look forward to with my dad, and a whole future to write, I felt at peace. This was what people dreamed of, and now I was living it. If those nightmares ever plagued me again, I had no doubt that Nat would sooth them away. She was the only one allowed in my dreams.

epilogue

Natalia

Weeks flew by after we landed back in the States. The whole gang went their separate ways, and Isaiah and I stayed in a hotel as we searched for apartments in D.C. It took two weeks, but we found a charming apartment that was only a short walk from Capitol Hill. I was offered a position in the president's cabinet as the Ambassador to the United Nations. Honestly, it was a huge deal, and my name was on the political map.

But with the good came the bad. Isaiah's father passed away right before Isaiah started the fire academy. I'd only met him once briefly. When Isaiah called to tell him that he'd returned to the States and was in D.C., he was on the first plane out he could get. Isaiah had been shocked and anxious, because the behavior was a polar opposite of the man who was in and out of his life.

"I know I could never say this to you enough to make up for the past, but I'm so proud of you son." His hand had clasped Isaiah's shoulder, and it was the first time I'd ever seen the man I loved in tears. The second time was at his funeral. We flew back to Isaiah's hometown in the middle of nowhere Kansas. It poured during the whole service, and we were the traditional scene of grief as we stood dressed in black with black umbrellas, staring at the ground in respect. Isaiah's shoulders shook as those who he once thought judged him based on his father and family paid their respects and shared stories about all the good things his father had done since he'd been released from prison. After the funeral, I'd learned Isaiah inherited a house, which was a silver lining. It was proof of just how hard his father had worked.

That night we sat in the house and tried to figure out what to do with it.

"Our life is in D.C. now. We can't move here, not now." Isaiah swirled the scotch in his glass. He occupied the armchair in front of the fireplace. The rainy, cold fall weather gave us the perfect reason to start a fire in the fireplace.

"You're right, but I've been thinking..." I looked down at his face from where I perched on the chair's armrest. He looked up at me. "Uh oh, that's never a good thing."

I playfully slapped him. "Everyone's always asking what's next in politics. Sure, I'm the Ambassador to the United Nations now, but what in a few years from now? What if I decided to run for the Senate? We could declare Kansas our home, this our home, and when the time's right, we make your dad proud. We use this home he built to be our home when we aren't in Washington."

"You'd move to Kansas?" he asked me. He didn't sound convinced.

"Well, we'd be back and forth between here and D.C., but I don't see why not." I looked around the room. It was warm and cozy, and despite this being Isaiah's first time in this house, too, it felt like home. I could see pieces of him here. There were a few photos of him as a kid, even a photo of him and his mom. This was something that Isaiah needed, even if he didn't know it yet.

"What about your family?" he asked. He shifted in his seat, so I knew he was at least considering my proposal.

"They're a hell of a lot closer here than they were when I was in Syria, are they not?"

"But what about your father?" he pressed.

"He will come see me when he's ready. Until then, I have to be happy that at least one of us got a special reunion. I'm glad it's you."

"And I'm glad it's you that I have by my side in all of this. I don't want to freak you out, but one day I'm going to marry you and we are going to raise a child or two in this house. You're going to be crazy successful, and I'll always be there to sweep you off your feet when things become too much. Natalia Ali, you were the light I didn't know I needed in my life."

I shook my head with tears in my eyes. "That doesn't freak me out at all. In fact, I look forward to it." I leaned forward and kissed him soft and sweet, but soon it was nothing but burning passion.

"Are we about to do this in your father's house?" I asked with a tease.

"You mean our house?" he questioned with a raised eyebrow.

"Mine?" I asked.

"What's mine is yours, Nat. Now come here so I can carry you over the doorstep and we can go practice making those kids." He scooped me up as I giggled in his ear. He was something else, but as promised, he scooped me into his arms like I weighed nothing. He carried me to the spare bedroom when he pinned me against the door, lifted my leg, and plunged two fingers into me. I grabbed the doorknob and his shoulder, just to have something to hold onto. Otherwise my back was going to slide up the wall.

My nails dug into his skin as his lips met my neck, sucking the skin there as he removed his fingers and unzipped his dress pants. They dropped to the floor, and in seconds, Isaiah slid my black dress off my shoulders. It landed on the floor next to his clothes.

"Turn around and put your hands against the door," he demanded.

"I think you're practicing for the wrong job. You're a firefighter, not a cop," I breathed out as I did what he said.

"Ass facing out to me, spread your legs." I did what he commanded, because why the fuck would I care what order he gave? I knew he was going to make me feel good; that was a given with Isaiah Yates.

He slapped my ass, once, twice, three times. Then he soothed it and plunged right into me. I stretched around him, and my head dropped low as I enjoyed the feeling of him bottoming out. I moaned as he grabbed my hair and pulled my head backward.

He was a savage with his pace, but it left me feeling very satisfied when my legs turned to jelly after I came, and he caught me around my waist.

I was on cloud nine, and for the first time in weeks Syria was far, far from my mind.

bonus epilogue

Natalia

"Nat, were you expecting a visitor?" Isaiah asked. He went to check the doorbell as I was in the middle of brushing my teeth. I was cutting it close to being late for work.

My eyebrows pinched together in confusion. I was not expecting anyone, although Christine kept mentioning that she wanted to come see our new place. I mentioned I was having a hard time picking out our style, and I swore it was as if the clouds opened a ray of sunshine on her and the angels sang. She made me promise that I'd let her come decorate the apartment. It was an easy promise to make. She showed me her and Wells' place. It was a vision of a modern farmhouse in whites and grays.

"No?" I answered. I set down my makeup brush on the bathroom counter and pulled my sweater closer to my body as I made my way through the narrow hallway. When I made it to the living room, I stopped dead in my tracks. Past Isaiah's shoulder I saw a familiar hairline, one I hadn't seen except in photographs for a long time.

"Dad?" My voice cracked.

"Natty?"

I let out a sob as Isaiah took a step out of the way. I didn't remember telling myself to run, so my feet must have instinctively known what to do. I made a dash to my father, and he extended his arms out. He caught me in a hug to keep me from knocking him into the common area hallway behind him.

"Natty," he cooed softly as I sobbed into his chest. I felt his cheek on the top of my head. In that moment, I felt a massive weight fall from my shoulders, my lungs deflated, and the tension in my spine released.

I heard my mom let out a soft sob from next to us, and my brother had the audacity to laugh. I ignored him for the moment as I took in the moment I'd barely dared to dream about. There was a real heartbeat beneath my cheek, and he was warm, breathing. Alive.

I could feel Isaiah's quiet presence from behind me, and I wondered if he felt all the things I did when I watched him reunite with his father.

I took a step back and pulled my father into the apartment and then grabbed my mom and brother and wrapped them in a quick hug before shutting the door behind them. We all shuffled into our eleven-hundred-square-foot apartment.

"Natty, I don't even know where to start…" my father started.

I slapped his arm and fixed him with a stern expression. "You could start with, 'I'm sorry'!"

"We both know that's not good enough." At least he was honest about that.

"You're right, it's not, but I'll accept it." I sniffled at the end, and Isaiah placed a comforting hand on my shoulder. It was warm and all the strength I needed. He was my rock, my comfort in the harsh world of D.C.

"Well, I'm sorry. I wish I could have sat you all down and explained what was going on and what I needed to do. I felt the call to help my country after my kidnapping. I knew that they were planning something truly destructive, and with my training, my past, there was no ignoring that call. I can imagine that Sergeant Yates would understand that call."

"I would, sir," Isaiah answered.

"Please, none of that." My father extended his hand, and Isaiah shook it. "I've got a couple of things to thank you for, but most importantly, thank you for taking care of my daughter and keeping her safe."

"It's been my pleasure. She's special. I knew it that day I met her in front of the Israeli Embassy, when all she could do was worry about picking our brains on how she could best help you adjust."

I scoffed. "Yeah, if only I'd known that you were already well versed in that kind of stuff."

"I was debriefed by my handler and okay within the first twenty-four hours." My father chuckled. Then he turned serious again. "I know I've got a lot of lost time to make up for, but I wanted to let you know that I've hung my hat up with the agency. I'm retired now and looking forward to a quiet life getting to know my family again."

"Yeah, and you still have a lot to apologize for. A lot to explain," I added.

He nodded. "I do. But I see you are on your way to the office, and I don't want to keep you. We are at the hotel down the street. We will catch dinner tonight and every night until you're satisfied that you know everything. Sound good?"

I gave him a tight-lipped smile. "Only if you're buying."

"I'm a former dead man. What makes you think I have any money?" he asked playfully.

"Oh, I know you do. I saw all the nice shiny toys in your bunker. You've got money."

He just shot me a noncommittal grin and a wink.

I grinned, because after all this time, it was possible to have everything I ever wanted. I'd have my answers, my family, and the man of my dreams.

Isaiah's hand grasped mine and gave my fingers a gentle squeeze. With him by my side, I could conquer anything.

afterword

Readers!

I hope you enjoyed Isaiah and Natalia's story. I know Yates is a fan favorite and I hope I've done his story justice. If you want to read about his and Natalia's first meet then check out the prequel short story, *Torn.*

Book five is already in the works. Find out what happens when Garcia gets a job offer he can't refuse—bodyguard to the President's daughter.

* * *

In the meant time, if you want more updates on upcoming releases, you can catch me at the following:

Interested in joining my ARC readers team? Sign up here.

Interested in joining my mailing list? Click here.

Find me on Facebook. Click here.

I'm on TikTok and Instagram too.

* * *

Thank you to my Beta readers!
Alyssa Nagel
Natalie C

also by k.w. coleson

HEROES FOR HIRE SERIES

Torn: A Prequel Short Story

Buried

Missing

Liar

Deceived

Hidden

STAND ALONES:

Dive

* 9 7 9 8 9 8 7 7 6 7 5 3 5 *